Tex Monroe was a throwback to another time, Kimberly thought.

The men she was used to wore suits, and battled with words and money and power. But *this* man was a *warrior*....

A thrill of purely female appreciation swept through her. She traced his rib cage, counting the bones beneath slabs of heavy, hard muscle.

A low warning growl rumbled in his chest, but she ignored it.

She moved against him, lifted her mouth to his neck, tasting the salt on his skin, smelling the lightly musky scent of him.

She couldn't get enough of it. She pressed even closer to him, dying for more.

Then, suddenly, she was on her back with him looming above her, his hands pinning her arms to the jungle floor. "Enough," he growled. "No more games...."

Dear Reader,

This is a month full of greats: great authors, great miniseries…great books. Start off with award-winning Marie Ferrarella's *Racing Against Time,* the first in a new miniseries called CAVANAUGH JUSTICE. This family fights for what's right—and their reward is lasting love.

The miniseries excitement continues with the second of Carla Cassidy's CHEROKEE CORNERS trilogy. *Dead Certain* brings the hero and heroine together to solve a terrible crime, but it keeps them together with love. Candace Irvin's latest features *A Dangerous Engagement,* and it's also the first SISTERS IN ARMS title, introducing a group of military women bonded through friendship and destined to find men worthy of their hearts.

Of course, you won't want to miss our stand-alone books, either. Marilyn Tracy's *A Warrior's Vow* is built around a suspenseful search for a missing child, and it's there, in the rugged Southwest, that her hero and heroine find each other. Cindy Dees has an irresistible Special Forces officer for a hero in *Line of Fire*—and he takes aim right at the heroine's heart. Finally, welcome new author Loreth Anne White, who came to us via our eHarlequin.com Web site. *Melting the Ice* is her first book—and we're all eagerly awaiting her next.

Enjoy—and come back next month for more exciting romantic reading, only from Silhouette Intimate Moments.

Leslie J. Wainger
Executive Editor

Please address questions and book requests to:
Silhouette Reader Service
U.S.: 3010 Walden Ave., P.O. Box 1325, Buffalo, NY 14269
Canadian: P.O. Box 609, Fort Erie, Ont. L2A 5X3

Line of Fire
CINDY DEES

Silhouette®

INTIMATE MOMENTS™

Published by Silhouette Books

America's Publisher of Contemporary Romance

SILHOUETTE BOOKS

ISBN 0-373-27323-1

LINE OF FIRE

Visit Silhouette at www.eHarlequin.com

Printed in U.S.A.

Books by Cindy Dees

Silhouette Intimate Moments

Behind Enemy Lines #1176
Line of Fire #1253

CINDY DEES

started flying airplanes, sitting in her dad's lap, when she was three, and she was the only kid in the neighborhood who got a pilot's license before she got a driver's license. After college, she fulfilled a lifelong dream and became a U.S. Air Force pilot. She flew everything from supersonic jets to C-5's, the world's largest cargo airplane. During her career, she got shot at, met her husband, flew in the Gulf War and amassed a lifetime supply of war stories. After she left flying to have a family, she was lucky enough to fulfill another lifelong dream—writing a book. Little did she imagine that it would win the RWA Golden Heart Contest and sell to Silhouette! She's thrilled to be able to share her dream with you. She'd love to hear what you think of her books. Write to her at www.cindydees.com or P.O. Box 210, Azle, TX 76098.

My sincerest thanks to all of my incredibly knowledgeable instructors at the Air Force Aircrew SERE (Survival, Evasion, Resistance and Escape) School at Fairchild AFB, Washington. Thank goodness I never had to use my training for anything except writing this book!

Chapter 1

"Pick a target," the man beside her ordered quietly.

There was no mistaking it. The man lying on the ground, cradling his rifle like a lover, had just shifted into killing mode. Instinctive fear of him, of his innate violence, broke over her, drenching her in her own nervous perspiration.

Tex Monroe, she'd been told his name was. He was supposedly some sort of genius at murdering people and blowing stuff up. Frankly she'd been expecting an intimidating, vicious-looking, commando type. She hadn't been prepared for a lazy smile, dashing good looks and engaging charm from this killer.

He could have jumped straight out of the pages of *Soldier of Fortune* magazine. He had the determined jaw, chiseled cheekbones and intense blue eyes of a cover-model mercenary, and his outdoorsman's tan emphasized the white flash of his smile. Broad-shouldered, narrow-hipped and oozing muscle, the guy wore green camouflage fatigues with the panache of a tailored tuxedo.

As if that wasn't enough, he had a lazy, graceful way

of moving and an easy Southern accent that screamed of Rhett Butler and old school Southern charm. It wasn't the fake, plastic friendliness of so many of the politicians she worked around. He had genuine charisma. Flesh impact. Whatever the label, the whole gentleman-soldier package was devastating.

He was a huge monkey wrench in her plan. But it wasn't like she was about to turn back. She'd see this thing through. No sweet talking assassin was going to derail her now.

Kimberly Stanton lifted the bulky binoculars to her eyes, adjusting their focus with her fingertips. Two black blobs converged into a single sharp image of the back of a man's head. Even with the powerful Zeiss binoculars, he was little more than a pea-size dot in her vision, over a mile away.

"The guy in the black turtleneck with the black hair," she said. Darn it. She sounded all breathless, like some teenage groupie in the presence of her idol.

In Tex Monroe's world, life and death were held cheaply. Say a few words and a human being was snuffed out. No fuss, no muss. A shudder of revulsion whisked down her spine, but her determination to see justice prevail stiffened it again.

Tex lowered his face to the high-tech, computer-targeted rifle. Almost tenderly, his arm settled over the weapon. He caressed a knob on the side of his scope, teasing it to a peak of perfection. His cheek rested against the sleek shape of the weapon, his eyes heavy-lidded as he became one with it.

Voyeuristic discomfort blossomed inside her as she watched him make love to his rifle. And then he settled into a stillness that enveloped not only him and the cumbersome sniper rifle but also reached out to stifle her breath into complete suspension.

The sheer presence of the man was overwhelming. How could an act of such cold brutality generate such shocking heat in her? She was supposed to be appalled by men like him. Her life's work was devoted to stopping this sort of killing.

Pull yourself together! No questions. No doubts. If this gorgeous commando had to be the sacrificial lamb to her cause, so be it.

She made herself look through the binoculars at the dark-haired head she'd just targeted for execution. Any second now.

Bang!

The shot rang out, kick-starting her breathing with an involuntary burst of adrenaline. She jumped hard, even though she'd expected the explosion of sound.

She registered in a strange sort of slow motion the way the tiny head in the distance exploded into a million pieces.

Good Lord.

Shaken, her breath rattled tremulously. She took a deep breath, forcibly calming herself. This was part of the plan. She could do it. Her need to stop men like Tex coalesced into a hard knot of resolve deep in her stomach.

"Again," she commanded.

The dazzling sniper beside her nodded and shifted position, pivoting the rifle gently on its low tripod stand, tugging it close to his chest.

She choked out, "Let's see you take out a moving target, hotshot."

He flashed her a slow, intimate grin that slammed into her gut like one of his well-aimed bullets. "Yes, ma'am," he drawled. "Pick me another victim."

Victim. The casually uttered word made her shudder. Heck, the whole man made her shudder. But with horror or fascination, she wasn't sure. It ought to be the former. She feared it was the latter.

In the distance a series of caricatured human figures moved across her field of vision, scurrying back and forth like mice trapped in a corner by a cat. "The blond man in the red shirt," she announced. He was moving quickly in and out among other targets and would be extremely difficult to hit.

"Done," was the sniper's confident reply.

Bang!

The blond head exploded effortlessly.

Her hands shaking, Kimberly lowered the binoculars and stared down at the man beside her, overwhelmed in spite of her resolve not to be. Even if those annihilated heads were only clay targets on a firing range, they just as easily could have been real people getting their heads blown off.

Problem was, no matter how dangerous he was with that gun in the killing fields, Tex Monroe was potentially even more lethal to her project here today.

"That's an impressive toy you've got, soldier," she managed to say lightly.

He grinned up at her. "If you're nice to me, I'll let you play with it."

A thrill of sexual awareness raced down her spine. Drat. Why couldn't her hormones get with the program and be revolted by this guy?

The group of journalists behind her chuckled. Double drat. The last thing she needed was this cocky Special Forces type charming the press into doing favorable pieces on the new sniper rifle. Of course, the real purpose of today's demonstration at Quantico's firing range wasn't the gun at all. It was to paint soldiers like Tex Monroe as the cold, calculating killers they were.

It had taken some fancy maneuvering to set up this outing. She was a known antimilitary lobbyist, and the Air Force hadn't been enthusiastic about giving her this demonstration. They suspected, rightly, that she'd turn the whole thing against them somehow in a splashy media blitz. Of course, she hadn't anticipated that the Air Force would sabotage her campaign with a P.R. savvy poster boy like Tex Monroe.

She tossed back her tawny locks and flashed her million-dollar smile at the press corps. "As you can see, gentlemen, with one of these new generation rifles, a single soldier like this one can become a nearly unstoppable killing machine."

The killing machine in question scowled up at her. Good. The meaner he looked, the more impact her remarks would have.

An audio circuit on one of the video cameras screeched abruptly, and the soldier jumped, his hands flying up into a defensive position.

"See? That's what I'm talking about," she said smoothly. "Observe the reflexes of the trained killer."

"Miss Stanton," Tex drawled with a lazy smile, "jumping at a squealing speaker is hardly a demonstration of my propensity to kill people."

The reporters chuckled again. She had to get these guys away from him and his slick Southern charm before he ruined this day's work entirely.

Thankfully the sound of a thwocking helicopter became audible in the distance. She announced pleasantly, "That will be our ride, gentlemen. Shall we go? I made reservations at the Watergate Club for us. We can finish our discussion over lunch."

She'd learned at her father's knee that there was nothing quite like prime rib and a few beers for getting reporters to see things exactly her way. Nobody worked the press better than Senator William Stanton, except maybe his only daughter.

A sleek, black helicopter settled in the middle of the firing range. She mentally flinched at its sharklike profile. How appropriate to her calculated manipulation of the press. Sharklike, indeed. Like father, like daughter.

Tex Monroe popped up to his feet, rising to his full six-foot-two height. He shouldered the heavy sniper rifle with a quick bunching of impressive muscles. She gulped. None of the men she knew had the time or inclination to work out in a gym. Those who exercised at all talked on the cell phone while they put in a couple of miles on a treadmill.

Tex's long legs lengthened into an easy, ground-eating jog that bespoke many miles of carrying heavy rifles like the one slung over his shoulder. She pulled out the fuzzy collar of her pink angora sweater and blew surreptitiously down her front, cooling her abruptly overheated system.

His shoulders were so broad they blocked the entire helicopter door as he approached it. She couldn't help but notice his panther-like grace as he pivoted smoothly to a stop to wait for her.

She scowled at the picture he made, poised and alert beside the sleek chopper. The last thing she needed in the newspapers were photos of a killer who came across like a knight in shining armor. She made a mental note to discourage the reporters from printing any pictures with this particular story.

A couple of military police held everyone back while the helicopter finished its landing procedures, but she adroitly slipped past the outstretched arm of the nearest cop.

She strode after the annoying commando, leaving the surprised reporters to hurry after her once the police let them pass. Rule number three on her father's list of how to manage the press. Always keep them off balance and one step behind you. That way they were much more likely to go in the direction you wanted them to. Rules one and two dealt with never showing fear and never answering the entire question.

She ducked beneath the spinning rotor blade and moved toward Tex where he waited beside the helicopter door. Her knees threatened to buckle when he flashed her another one of those drop-dead smiles of his.

''Y'all come back and see us sometime,'' he shouted over the helicopter noise.

She scowled into his laughing blue gaze. He knew exactly what she'd been up to today. He also knew he'd thrown her a serious curve ball. The rat.

"Maybe I will at that, Mr. Monroe," she shouted back.

He grinned at the threat implied in her words, his eyes glinting in all-male challenge.

In another place, another time, she might have considered taking up the sexually charged gauntlet he'd just tossed at her feet. But not with a half-dozen nosy, camera-toting reporters straggling across the field to join them. Rule number four: never, ever, make a spectacle of oneself in public, especially if there are cameras nearby.

She stepped forward in a subtle power play, waiting expectantly for him to get the door for her. But he anticipated her ploy and had already leaned forward, reaching for the black door. The movement brought him close enough for her to see him look down at her mouth in sensual speculation.

To her utter shock, she found herself leaning toward him in return. His head angled down slightly and she felt her chin tilt up in response.

Oh, God. Rule number four!

Reporters. With cameras. Closing in on them. No public spectacles!

She jerked back, breathing hard.

She looked up at him, expecting derision in his azure gaze. But what she saw was sex. Pure and simple.

"Anytime, darlin'," he murmured. "Call me and I'll be there."

No words would form in her throat. She stared, momentarily dazed. And then the cheek of what he'd just said hit her. "I'll see you in front of Congress," she hissed.

His eyebrows went up innocently. "It takes an act of Congress to date you?"

Her gaze narrowed. "Charlie Squad and the other Special Forces teams like yours are done, soldier. I'm the final nail in your coffin."

She watched with satisfaction as his smirk faded into

uncertainty. "What are you talking about?" he asked, his voice soft and dangerous.

"I've proposed a reform bill to do away with government funding for all trained hit squads. The American taxpayers are done supporting killers like you," she snapped.

He stared narrowly at her, absorbing her declaration. Hard knowledge filled his gaze. Finally he drawled, "Darlin', I hope you never find out why the taxpayers *need* killers like me."

His eyes glittered like diamonds, determined and intelligent. He reached out with one hand for the helicopter door and with the other for her elbow to help her inside.

Without warning, the door flew open. Four black-clad figures burst out.

Kimberly jumped, violently startled by the unexpected explosion of motion. Out of the corner of her eye, she registered ski masks and weapons slung from men's shoulders. A quick frown flashed across Tex's face. Her mind vaguely processed that this was bad.

But then someone shoved her between the shoulder blades, throwing her forward into the helicopter in a stumbling half-fall.

What in the world…

Someone pushed her down roughly. Her forehead hit the metal floor and stars burst forth behind her eyelids. She distantly heard her own voice cry out in pain. The dreamlike unreality of whatever farce was abruptly playing out around her refused to compute in her brain.

Something, someone, thudded to the floor beside her, landing with a grunt. A warm, hard body sprawled half across hers. A shock of recognition shot through her as her gaze met Tex Monroe's Caribbean blue one.

"You okay?" he bit out.

She was now. His presence eased her terror. Instinctively she knew he would take control of whatever bizarre situation was unfolding here. "Yes," she gasped.

Then his gaze darted away in all directions, quickly assessing the situation. "I'll take care of you," he murmured. "Stay down."

Unexpected warmth flowed through her at his muttered reassurance. Somehow she believed him. She watched in awe as he rolled away from her and exploded into action. He threw his fists and feet with lethal precision. Grunts and cursing erupted from behind the black-masked men who surrounded them as Tex fought back with grim determination.

Hands grabbed her shoulders and a slender, silver aerosol canister descended toward her. Cool white spray misted into her face. The last thing she remembered before she spun away into oblivion was Tex's voice expressing his disgust in a single succinct curse.

Then everything went dark.

A sleek female body rubbed up against Tex, bringing feeling roaring back into every portion of his body. She stretched against him languorously, her silken hair teasing his ear and making his body throb with life, after what seemed like a long, cloudy slumber.

The round softness of her breast caressed his arm, its weight tempting him to cup it. Its resilience begged him to test it, the hard bud of her nipple demanded that he taste and tease it. He turned toward her, reaching for her.

His hands wouldn't cooperate.

What the hell was going on?

His shoulders hurt, too. And his feet were acting the same uncooperative way as his hands.

Tex kept his eyes closed as full awareness gradually seeped back into his fuzzy brain. The dream of the gorgeous blonde seducing him faded in part. But the soft curves pressed against him remained. Something important had happened, something he needed to remember…

He'd been standing on the firing range at Quantico beside a late-model Sikorsky helicopter. An image of a stunning young woman with green cat eyes and legs a mile long floated, disembodied, in his mind. He'd wanted to kiss her so badly he could barely stand up.

There was something else...

Bits and pieces of memory returned and he attached a name to the woman. Kimberly Stanton. Senator Stanton's militantly liberal daughter. She'd been with a bevy of reporters watching him fire a new sniper rifle equipped with the Roving Instant Target Acquisition system, also known as RITA.

And then something happened...

He struggled for memory.

It all rushed back at once. Armed men had jumped out of the helicopter and caught him as flat-footed as his grandmother. There hadn't been a damned thing to do but roll with the blow to his head and fall inside the bird.

He'd counted six men. Heavily armed, wearing headsets and body armor, moving swiftly and in well-coordinated fashion. They'd kidnapped the influential senator's daughter. For ransom? Blackmail on a political decision? Publicity, maybe? Kimberly Stanton was nearly as famous as her father. And her father was a national hero.

Tex frowned. How long he and Kimberly had been unconscious was anybody's guess. You could keep a guy out cold for days on a good knockout spray. Awareness of his immediate surroundings began to register. He wasn't in a helicopter anymore—the rumbling noise under his ear was a diesel engine. The hard floor he laid on bounced like a truck hitting a rut.

His right side was warm. The kind of warm that comes from having a naked woman plastered to you after sweaty sex. How real *was* that dream? He cracked open his eyes for a look.

She wasn't naked, but Kimberly Stanton was definitely plastered against him. In fact, her leg was lying on top of his thigh and her knee was rubbing against his...

Damn! He finally had a gorgeous blonde tied up and draped all over him, and she had to be unconscious. Yeah, well, this wasn't the time to be thinking about that. He noticed curved metal ribs covered in canvas overhead. Yup, a truck.

He waited until the next good bump in the road and turned his head to the left under cover of the jostling. He slitted his eyes open again. The sight that greeted him caused his eyes to pop fully open in surprise. One man in military fatigues with an AK-47 rifle propped across his lap leaned against the far wall of the truck, fast asleep.

Either the guy was a complete moron, or else their captors expected Tex to be unconscious for a good while longer. They probably hadn't accounted for the fact that he could hold his breath for nearly three minutes. Most of the knockout gas they'd sprayed at him in the helicopter had dissipated before he'd been forced to inhale it.

He noticed something else lying tossed in the corner behind the soldier. The bulky sniper rifle he'd been carrying when he approached the helicopter. He smiled briefly at that bit of good luck. It was a hell of a weapon and would come in handy if he and the senator's daughter managed to escape.

He tested the bonds holding his hands behind his back. Big mistake by his captors. The rope had some give in it. He worked on it for no more than a minute before his right hand slid free of the restraint.

Urgency rode him hard. He didn't have the foggiest idea what he'd gotten tangled up in, but it couldn't be good. The initial attack bore all the signs of a professional job— the yahoo snoring across the truck bed aside, of course. Tex disentangled himself from the girl and sat up cautiously. Still the guard didn't move. Quickly, Tex reached down and untied his feet.

This was almost too easy. He eased himself high enough to peer over the tailgate and out the back of the truck. No other vehicles were following them.

Sonofagun. The kidnappers, who'd been so organized up till now, had actually left open a window of opportunity for him and the girl to escape. Hell, a big, gaping door of opportunity. He briefly weighed the risk to her life of attempting to escape versus staying. The odds of her living on the run were slim, but her chances with the kidnappers were zero.

He went to work.

As silent and deadly as a snake, he struck, leaping across the width of the truck. He brought down the edge of his hand in a quick, rigid chop to the guard's left temple. The guy crumpled over to the floor. Tex paused for a moment to blink away the dizziness that hit him after moving fast. They'd gotten some of that gas into him and he was still suffering the effects.

Pushing himself to concentrate, Tex stole the guy's watch, then tied the guard's hands tightly using the same ropes that had bound him. He tore off a piece of the guy's shirt and stuffed it into the fool's mouth. The guy's belt secured the gag tightly in place.

After a glance at Ms. Stanton's short skirt, which was riding perilously high on her hips, he stripped the guard of his pants. Quickly, he searched the guy and grabbed a cigarette lighter, tobacco, and the fellow's red beret. He finished immobilizing the guy by trussing his feet to the side of the truck.

Then Tex turned his attention to the woman. Even unconscious, she radiated class. From her smooth golden hair and sculpted cheekbones to the chic elegance of her conservative skirt and sweater, to her perfectly buffed fingernails. Kimberly Stanton was upper crust all the way.

She also was dead to the world.

He slapped her cheeks a few times and lifted her eyelids, but she was out cold. He dared not wait around for her to revive. He fought off a wave of nausea and kept moving.

After he untied her, he stuffed the rope into a deep pocket on the thigh of his fatigue pants. Then he shouldered both the RITA rifle and the guard's AK-47. Leaning down, he lifted her over his other shoulder with a grunt.

Thank goodness she was slender. He nearly passed out as it was from the exertion of lifting even her slight weight. He silently blessed the years of rigorous training that kept him functioning reasonably efficiently, even though his brain felt like mush.

He eased the tailgate down and sat in the middle of it, out of sight of any rearview mirrors the truck might have. He dangled his legs over the edge, cradling the girl's limp form in his arms, waiting for his chance to jump. God, she even smelled rich. Her sophisticated perfume made him want to sink into it and into her and lose himself in both.

The truck was going maybe thirty miles an hour over a dirt surface. Thick jungle lined the edges of the road. His vision blurred and a shapeless sea of green swam all around him. He shook it off as the truck's brakes squeaked. The vehicle slowed and started around a bend in the road. He tightened his arms around the woman, crushing her against his chest and tucking her head against his shoulder. He didn't need to rescue her just to turn around and break her neck. He took a deep breath and jumped to the outside of the curve.

Twisting in midair to absorb most of the impact on his left shoulder, he cushioned the woman's fall. Unfortunately he wore the weapons on that side. The metal slammed into his flesh, numbing his left arm completely.

They rolled over and over down an embankment, coming to a jarring stop in a grassy ditch.

It took several seconds for him to register cold water soaking through his clothes. He rolled over in alarm, dragging the woman's unconscious face out of the shallow water. In her state, a few tablespoons of inhaled water would be enough to kill her.

He ran his hands quickly over her arms and legs, quietly checking for injuries from the jump out of the truck. Medically speaking, he ought to check her more thoroughly. But he had to get her out of here right away. He scrambled onto his hands and knees. Shooting pain radiated outward

from his left shoulder. He tested it gingerly. Good news—
it was functional. Bad news—it hurt like hell.

He hoisted her across his back and crawled up the far
side of the embankment. There was no help for the deep,
black gouges he left in the dirt as he dragged himself, two
rifles, and the dead weight of Kimberly Stanton out of the
ditch.

When he'd gained the cover of the underbrush, he rose
to his feet, steadying himself against a rough tree. He'd be
glad when this damned woozy feeling passed.

He ignored the weakness in his knees, draped her arms
over his shoulders and stood upright. Her breasts pressed
against his back and he groaned under his breath at the
sensation. *Concentrate, pal.* Save the woman's life first.
Then he could move on to more…interesting prospects.

Time was against him. He had to get her as far from the
road as possible before her captors realized they'd bailed
out of the truck. Anyone who'd gone to the trouble of
landing a helicopter in the middle of a military base to
kidnap a senator's daughter wasn't about to let her escape
without a chase.

They—whoever *they* were—would be coming after him
and Miss Kimberly Stanton, antimilitary lobbyist extraordinaire. Soon.

The irony of the situation struck him. If he managed to
return her safely to Washington, D.C., she'd launch a campaign to destroy him for having the very skills he'd used
to save her life.

Go figure.

He took quick stock of the situation. He was loaded
down with eighty pounds of weapons, plus a hundred and
twenty or so more of unconscious female. His head spun,
his shoulder hurt like hell and his legs weren't cooperating
properly. Nonetheless he had to hump it out of here pronto.
No doubt about it, the next few hours were going to purely
suck.

And when Kimberly Stanton woke up, he had faith this
day would go from bad to worse.

Chapter 2

Kimberly opened her eyes and was assailed by a series of strange impressions. A veritable ocean of green all around her. The pungent smell of rotting grass clippings. Dappled sunlight overhead. It felt almost as if she were lying on cold, damp ground.

The vision had no basis in any reality she'd ever experienced. It had to be a dream. A *really* vivid one.

She closed her eyes and willed that briefly glimpsed alternate reality back into the oblivion it had come from.

A hand shook her shoulder.

Part of the dream. She ignored it.

It shook her harder.

She opened her eyes again. "Stop that!" she ordered the pesky dream, which was quickly escalating to the status of an hallucination.

A male voice, right beside her, said, "I know you can hear me. Wake up, Miss Stanton."

She blinked up at the man. Short, light brown hair with

touches of red and gold. Bright blue eyes. Nice tan. Heck, nice everything.

Wait a minute. She knew that face from somewhere. Finally something in this bizarre dream that she recognized. She experimented with talking to the apparition. "Where have I met you before?"

"The Quantico firing range."

Images of this man blowing people's brains out flashed into her mind's eye. She recoiled violently from the hand on her upper arm.

"Easy, darlin'," he murmured.

She looked around. For all the world, it looked like she was sitting on her derriere in the middle of a jungle. The National Botanical Garden, maybe? But how did she get from a military base in suburban Virginia to downtown Washington, D.C.?

Nothing about this dream made sense. Freud would've had a field day with it. "Where am I?" she asked disjointedly.

The man answered with a straight face. "I don't know for sure, but I think we're in Gavarone."

She laughed in disbelief. "Gavarone? As in South America?"

"Yup. Nasty little place. In the middle of a civil war."

Absurd. Her subconscious had really cooked up a whopper this time. "Next you're going to tell me we're lost in the jungle and your name's Tarzan."

"Actually," the cover model hunk said gravely, "we are lost in the jungle. But the name's Tex. Tex Monroe."

She frowned. Tex Monroe. A snippet of memory popped into her head. He was a Special Forces soldier on loan to give her and a bunch of reporters a demonstration with some sort of new gun. She remembered standing beside him while he shot it.

She looked around again. The birds sounded all wrong. Where were the traffic noises always faintly audible at the National Botanical Gardens? It smelled funny, too. Earthy and green. This lush tropic was definitely not Washington, D.C.

A seed of doubt took root in her mind. Surely this wasn't real. "If you and I met at Quantico, then how did we end up in Gavarone?"

"I don't know, ma'am."

"Any guesses?" she challenged.

He shrugged. "After you and I got tossed in the helicopter, your captors hit us with knockout spray. They probably transferred us to an airplane and flew us down here."

She frowned. His words made sense, but the scenario he described was ludicrous.

His voice cut across her confusion. "How do you feel? Any pain? Swelling? Numbness?"

Why, yes. Her whole brain was numb. "What time is it?" If anything, her disorientation was deepening, not fading.

"It was about noon when they grabbed us. The watch I lifted says it's ten o'clock. From the light and temperature conditions, I'd assume it's morning."

She frowned. "Tossed in a helicopter?"

He nodded and, as if willing her to remember, looked deeply into her eyes. *Eyes.* Turquoise blue. Staring at her in surprise. Widened in concern. Then narrowed with lethal intent.

An abrupt image of a sleek black chopper came to her. Men in black clothes and masks bursting out of it. Being shoved inside. Combat boots. Guns. Tex landing beside her. And then a silver aerosol can. Good grief! That couldn't be real. This was all a figment of her imagination run amuck.

Wasn't it?

She asked slowly, "Am I awake?"

He grinned and her heart tripped at the masculine flash of white against tanned skin. He leaned close to her, his gaze fixed on her mouth like he was contemplating kissing her. A sense of déjà vu flashed in her brain.

Riding the wave of the pseudo memory, she lifted her chin like she had before to kiss him back. Their breaths mingled, the humid heat caressing her lips. She knew him. Knew the taste of him. But how? One thing she was certain of— If she'd ever kissed this man before, she'd definitely remember it.

He pulled back abruptly, far enough for her to see his turbulent gaze. "Oh, yeah. This is for real, darlin'."

She shivered appreciatively at the honey-sweet drawl in his words. Then the import of what he'd said slammed into her.

This was *real*. All of it! Horror started low in her belly and bubbled upward, expanding and growing until it nearly choked her.

She scrabbled backward, away from the man seated beside her. "No! It can't be!" she exclaimed in dismay.

He looked around sharply and snapped, "Keep your voice down. Whoever tried to kidnap you is still out there somewhere. We don't need to scare up a bunch of wildlife with your screeching and give away our position."

"By all means," she snapped back. "Let's not upset the baboons!"

"Especially not the ones with AK-47s who kidnapped you," he bit out.

"Kidnapped…" Her? Ridiculous. "How did we end up in a jungle in Gavarone if someone actually tried to kidnap me?" she demanded skeptically.

"Because Maui was booked?" he suggested casually.

She scowled. "I'm serious. Someone really tried to kidnap me?"

His voice went grim. "They more than tried, darlin'. They succeeded. But I managed to break us out."

She stared at him, dumbfounded. "How?"

He merely shrugged in response.

"How did we end up out here?" She swept a hand around at the lush greenery crowding in on them.

"I carried you. Look, eventually the bad guys will realize we jumped out of their truck, and they'll be back. We need to get going."

She simply stared. Ample evidence that he was telling the truth crowded in on her from all sides, but her brain refused to accept it.

"Now that you're awake, Princess, we need to get moving again. We should put as much distance behind us as we can while we're still in fairly good shape."

She felt in anything but good shape at the moment. Complete, paralyzing shock was a more accurate description of her state. Furthermore, the idea of traipsing around a jungle held no appeal whatsoever. "Which way's the road?" she asked reasonably.

"If, in fact, we're in Gavarone, most of the countryside is controlled by the rebels. The guard in the truck with us was wearing a red beret," he answered obliquely.

She could ferret information out of the most close-mouthed politicians or the slimiest reporters, but this man's logic completely escaped her. "And your point?" she challenged.

"The Gavronese rebels wear red berets."

She spoke slowly, working her way through what he'd said. "So Gavronese rebels kidnapped me—although I can't imagine why—and we're in their territory. Hence, any car that drives by is probably friendly to the people who tried to nab me."

"Exactly!" He seemed inordinately pleased that she'd grasped the scenario.

"Okay, so we avoid the road." She scowled at Tex. "And no road means no ride. So what exactly do you propose we do to get out of here? Hijack a flying carpet?"

"We avoid all contact with people and walk to the nearest big city where we can get help from government or antirebel forces."

He made it all sound so easy. "And just how far away is this big city?" she asked suspiciously.

He shrugged. "Hey, I'm not even sure we're in Gavarone, let alone where the nearest city is."

She threw up her hands. "So you want us to wander around aimlessly in a jungle until we either starve to death or get rescued?"

"There's plenty of food out here," he answered casually. *Too casually.* "We won't starve. Getting shot, however... Or bit by a snake... Or eaten by a wild animal..."

Her eyes widened in alarm. "I'm sorry. I don't recall putting jaguar repellent in my purse this morning. I don't think so, G.I. Joe."

"Look, it's not that bad," he cajoled her. "There's a road just over that way. If we parallel it, it'll eventually lead to civilization. Since the truck went south, we head north. Hopefully to St. George and the Atlantic Ocean."

St. George, she vaguely recollected, was the capital of Gavarone and was situated on the northern coast of that tiny nation. God bless her private education for supplying that wonderful bit of trivia, she thought sardonically.

She planted her hands on her hips. "Let me get this straight. You're going to walk the length of a country, through a jungle, avoiding God knows who or what. At the ocean, you'll flag down...what? The nearest aircraft carrier to take us home?"

"You're going to walk the length of the country with me, Princess."

She stared in disbelief. "That's insane!"

His only response was to shrug.

She spoke with forced calm through the creeping panic that was wrapping itself slowly around her chest and beginning to squeeze. "It's impossible. You're not Superman, and Lord knows I'm not. You're going to get us both killed."

His gaze went a stormy, sea-tossed shade of blue. "Got

any better ideas?'' He couldn't have sounded more irritated if she'd just lost his secret decoder ring.

She racked her brains for a plan. She could navigate the subway systems of every major city in the United States. She could even seat fifty congressmen at the same dinner party in such a way that nobody killed their neighbor. But she had no bloody idea how to get out of a jungle full of armed kidnappers.

''My cell phone!'' she exclaimed suddenly. ''Can't we just call someone?''

''And where in that tight little outfit is your cell phone hiding?'' His fiery gaze raked up and down her person, sending an involuntary shiver racing across her skin.

She realized belatedly that she was without her purse. She was so used to having it slung over her shoulder, she hadn't even registered its absence.

''Any other bright ideas, Einstein?'' he asked dryly.

At this point she was desperate enough to try smoke signals, but she could imagine what reaction *that* idea would get from him. This whole thing was just too crazy to be real.

To be real…

And then it hit her.

''Did my father put you up to this?'' she demanded.

''Your father?'' Tex all but choked in obvious surprise. ''You think your *father* kidnapped you?''

''Of course not,'' she answered indignantly. ''I think he told you guys to stage a fake kidnapping and pretend to rescue me. That way you can run around acting like the macho jerks you are and prove to me how necessary the new sniper rifle is.''

''To stage…'' Tex trailed off, sputtering. His face took on a distinct flush.

Yup. She'd caught him red-handed.

''Miss Stanton, I assure you. This is most definitely not a fake kidnapping or a pretend rescue. Actual bad guys are

chasing us as we speak, and the odds are excellent that
they'll kill us both if they catch us.''

She waved a casual hand. ''Whatever. I'm sure you guys
cooked up a wonderful training scenario. If it makes you
feel any better, I don't really care about the gun one way
or the other. The main focus of my lobbying is in disbanding teams like yours who'd use the sniper rifle in the
first place.''

''Miss Stanton.'' His voice rang with irritation. ''I don't
care one way or the other if you believe me or not. But I
do require that you do what I tell you to, when I tell you
to do it. While you float around in your fantasy world of
denial, I'm going to do my best to keep you alive and get
you home.''

She refused to play along with this whole stupid game.
She struck a disdainful pose, but when his burning gaze
locked on to her thrust-out chest, she wilted and crossed
her arms defensively across her breasts.

''Put these on.'' He tossed her a wad of fabric.

A stale, sour smell, redolent of rancid refried beans, rose
from the bundle. She held up the mess and made out a
soiled, disgusting pair of army fatigues. She didn't even
want to *think* about their previous owner. She drawled,
''My dear sir, the grunge look is so passé.''

His eyes glinted and he drawled back, ''But it's all the
rage in the jungle, my dear.''

She tossed the repulsive things back to him. ''Take
some advice from a fashion trendsetter—dare to be different.''

He shrugged as he tied them around his waist, where
they were sure to get even sweatier and dirtier. ''Let me
know when you're ready to put them on,'' he commented
nonchalantly.

She stared at him, startled at his easy capitulation. A
moment of doubt sliced through her. Maybe G.I. Joe knew
something she didn't. Maybe she should've donned the
awful things. But then she bolstered her resolve. She

wasn't going to succumb to barbarism just because he insisted on pretending they were Jane and Tarzan running
around in the jungle.

Tex's voice interrupted her turbulent thoughts. "Let's
get a move on," he ordered.

Her eyes narrowed. That was the very same tone of
voice her father used when he waxed autocratic. It never
failed to provoke her into doing the exact opposite of what
he demanded, purely out of general principles.

Tex stopped several yards in front of her and looked
over his shoulder. "You coming?"

"This is nuts," she announced, not budging. "I'm not
playing along with your stupid game."

He glared for a moment and then sighed with long-
suffering patience. "Indulge me. Let's pretend that what
I've said is true. Let's pretend someone very dangerous is
chasing us and that we need to get away."

"And then what? You'll drag me all over creation and
put me at risk of serious injury or worse?"

"You won't get hurt. I promise."

She stuck out her chin stubbornly. "I refuse to let your
delusions of invincibility get me hurt or killed."

"My what?" he asked, his voice dangerously quiet.

"You heard me. I've got you figured out. You have
some sick, hero complex thing going and need to prove to
me how studly you Special Forces guys are. I won't buy
into it."

He stared at her for a long moment. Then he turned
deliberately and began to walk away.

Even though she could still see him, the loss of his
strong presence terrified her for some reason. Regardless
of whether this was Quantico's back forty or a real jungle
the Air Force had flown her to for this little demonstration,
it still pressed in on her menacingly, squeezing the air out
of her lungs.

She lurched into motion as Tex and the safety he rep-
resented disappeared from sight. She tripped over her high

heels and went down to her knees. Abruptly the panic she'd held at bay until now tightened into a death grip. He couldn't leave her alone out here, damn him!

Scrambling inelegantly to her feet, she stumbled toward him. She rounded a big tree and there he was. Waiting.

Silently he held out his hand to her.

Disdaining his offer, she brushed the dirt off her skirt.

He shrugged and turned away, pressing forward into the morass of green.

She glared at his retreating back. There was *nothing* she hated worse than a military man who thought he could push her around. First her father and now Tex Monroe. If only she and he weren't deep in a jungle where she'd get lost in a New York minute, she'd give him a piece of her mind!

She clamped down on her ire and followed him. Lifting her skirt high above her knees, she climbed gingerly over a giant tree root in her path.

That root was the harbinger of things to come. She spent the next two hours chasing after Tex. She slogged along the damp floor of the rain forest, scrambling over more roots and fallen logs than she could count. She dodged slimy vines and hanging moss, batted aside giant fern leaves and pushed through more brambles than she ever wanted to see again for the rest of her life.

She was going to *kill* her father when she got home. Only a congressman with his clout could have arranged this elaborate a demonstration for a civilian.

Furthermore, she was going to launch a congressional investigation of the Special Forces that would make their heads spin. She'd nail them for reckless endangerment, kidnapping, misappropriation of funds in running this outrageous exercise...

As the trek rolled on, she pressed her lips more and more tightly together. Her jaw ached from clenching so tight for so long. It was all she could do to keep from railing at Tex.

The only thing that stopped her was the realization that throwing a major fit was exactly what the Air Force wanted her to do. A giant tantrum, conveniently caught on hidden cameras no doubt, would totally destroy her credibility with the press and Congress if she tried to complain about this junket.

And as if this whole stupid chase-through-the-jungle scenario wasn't torturous enough, she had to go to the bathroom. Bad.

The day grew warm, moisture dripped from the leaves and humidity hung in the air, sending her smooth hair into waves and curls all around her face. Any semblance of makeup had sweated away long ago. Not that she particularly cared about impressing Tex Monroe.

Her sweater stuck to her skin in a hot, fuzzy mess. Her feet were killing her, and her ankles hurt from countless falls off her low heels. And to think she'd chosen this pair of shoes for the outing to the firing range because they were sensible!

Finally her bladder got the best of her resolve never to speak to her lout of an escort again. "Ahem." She cleared her throat politely.

He glanced back over his shoulder. The impact of his gaze sent a hot tremor through her. "What?" he asked shortly.

"I need to make a little stop. Have a bit of privacy..." she trailed off delicately.

"Why?" he asked bluntly.

"I need to, uh, relieve myself."

"Ah. Okay, but make it fast."

She frowned. He wasn't being the slightest bit helpful, here. She had no idea how she was supposed to go about doing such a thing in the middle of a jungle. He just stood there, staring at her like he expected her to drop her drawers and go for it right in front of him.

Heat started creeping up her neck. "How do I... How does one, uh, proceed in this sort of situation?"

"In what sort of situation?" he asked innocently.

The jerk was enjoying her discomfort. Only her status as a lady prevented her from throttling him. "How does one…do the deed…in a wilderness environment?"

"Well now—" he crossed his arms in exaggerated consideration "—I just unzip my fly, whip it out, and water the nearest tree."

She clenched her fists until her fingernails dug painfully into her palms. Her whole face felt hot. "You, sir, are a boor. I would appreciate it," she gritted out, "if you would show a little respect for my feminine sensibilities."

His eyebrows shot straight up and unholy amusement lit his gaze. "Feminine sensibilities, eh?" He chuckled. A little bit more politely he added, "I suppose women out here just go behind a bush and squat. You can drip dry, or there are plenty of leaves to wipe with."

Leaves? Oh, Lord. The way this day had been going, she'd pick poison ivy for the job. What did poison ivy look like, anyway? Why, oh why, had she dropped out of the Girl Scouts? What did it matter if the uniforms had been hideous?

Somehow she got through the operation without dying of embarrassment. When she emerged red-faced from the bushes, Tex turned without comment and resumed walking.

He marched on in front of her, setting a grueling pace. Not even the ongoing view of his outrageously sexy behind alleviated her suffering. She felt rotten in just about every way a person could feel rotten. And he just kept pushing deeper and deeper into the jungle.

Dark thoughts swirled in her mind. Why stop her lobbying campaign at merely disbanding the Special Forces? She'd get all the Special Forces soldiers thrown out of the military. Heck, she'd push to have them institutionalized as menaces to society!

Fueled by her fury, she stomped along behind him. She batted away the insects that swarmed around *her* head, but didn't seem the least bit interested in him. He must be too big a jerk for even a fly to bite.

Finally, blessedly, the dense underbrush thinned out into an easy walk on a carpet of dead leaves. God, that felt good to her aching feet.

Tex abruptly veered to the right and headed for a steep, heavily overgrown slope. He started up the difficult, nearly vertical climb. She stopped in her tracks and stared in shock.

She'd marched through thorns that had ruined her clothes, put up with swarms of biting bugs, and sweltered through hours of sticky jungle heat, but she'd be damned if she'd tromp up some hill just so G.I. Joe could prove his point about some damned gun.

"What are you doing?" she demanded, outraged. "We can go this way with no hill and no wading through brambles!"

He gave her an infuriatingly bland look. "That's why we're not doing it. The bad guys will choose that path because it's easy. So, we're going this way." He pointed up the hill.

Her patience snapped. She'd had it with this bozo pushing her around practically like he was the supposed kidnapper.

"Look, mister. I've been a good sport about this little nature hike from hell, but I'm tired. I'm hungry and I'm thirsty, and I don't do mountains. The trickiest terrain men lead me across is a polished marble floor when I'm wearing three-inch spikes."

Tex turned around slowly. He stared at her coldly.

A reflexive shiver shot down her spine. Her father got that look in his eye when he was about to hit something. Or someone. Her insides quivered in abrupt trepidation.

Tex stated with ominous calm, "I don't recall asking for your opinion on our route."

She spluttered for several seconds, her intimidation rapidly transforming into indignation. Finally she found her voice. "I *beg* your pardon?"

"I don't give a tinker's damn where you walk with your prissy toy-boys back home," he said. "Right now, we're going up this hill."

Her gaze narrowed. "Feel free to climb whatever cliff gives you a testosterone rush, *Tarzan*. But I'm going that way." She pointed down the valley.

He stalked back toward her, radiating a menace reminiscent of her father's battle rages. Despite decades of experience with them, she still felt a rush of the same terror she had as a child.

But then years of bucking her father's rigid rules flowed over her and instinctive defiance kicked in. Rule number one popped into her head. Never show fear. Not to Daddy. And certainly not to Tarzan the Ape Man. She dug in her feet and stuck out her chin as Tex approached.

He walked right up to her and didn't stop until his chest was practically touching hers. His nose wasn't more than a foot away from hers and his diamond-hard gaze bore into her.

Lord, he was big. And strong-looking. And mad-looking.

Her father would have bellowed like a bull, but Tex's quiet voice fell menacingly flat upon her ear. "Let's get one thing straight, *Jane*. I'm the trained Special Forces officer. You are the untrained civilian. Until I hand you back over to the U.S. government safe and sound, I'm in charge of this operation. Got it?"

She glared back at him. Electricity crackled and popped in the air around them. The energy pouring off of him all but knocked her over.

This was no prissy toy-boy she could push around. A thrill of something spicy and dangerous raced down her spine.

Her gaze dropped to his mouth. His lips were generous, sensuous in shape. He'd be a great kisser. She could feel it. An errant impulse struck her to reach up and snatch the kiss hanging like a threat between them.

"Well?" he demanded.

"Well what?" she asked breathlessly.

He rolled his eyes. "Oh, for God's sake. Don't try those seductive female tricks on me. We're climbing that hill if I have to drag you up it by the hair. Now, are you going to come along nicely or do I have to play hardball?"

The bubble of sensual anticipation in her stomach deflated, leaving behind an unpleasant emptiness. So much for great kissing. She glared furiously at him. "Has anybody ever told you you're a sadistic jerk?"

He grinned wolfishly. "All the time, Miss Stanton. All the time."

Chapter 3

Tex tore his gaze away from the mesmerizing blaze of green leaping in her eyes. His hands itched to grab her shoulders and drag her up against him. He could all but taste the kiss she obviously wanted. Damned if he didn't want to give her a whole lot more than just a kiss.

How could a woman who was so stubborn and so troublesome make him so hot so fast? He liked his women down-to-earth and sweet. Low maintenance. This virago looked like she'd just as soon tear his head off. And she'd already firmly established herself as a royal pain in the butt.

An exercise, indeed. What nonsense. Uncle Sam would never waste good training dollars trying to impress a spoiled brat like her. Guilt pricked him for pushing her so hard, but he'd had no choice. Somebody'd gone to a lot of trouble to kidnap her, and getting her out of this jungle was going to take all the tricks in his bag, including moving unexpectedly fast.

Once they scaled this last ridge, they'd stop and take a

rest. But he wasn't about to tell her that after her tantrum. No way was he letting her think she ran this show. She had to understand that staying alive meant taking orders from him.

He gave her his best pissed off glare. "Look, lady. I'm out here busting my butt trying to keep you safe. I don't need any flack out of you about climbing hills or anything else."

She scowled up at him defiantly, her green eyes snapping and her rounded chest heaving. It figured. The woman he was stuck rescuing *would* have to have a body made for sin and wear clothes that were tight in all the right places.

He growled, "Quit looking at me like I'm going grab you and kiss some sense into you."

She blinked, startled. Her eyes widened and her pupils dilated. Her breathing accelerated even more.

Damn. His hands reached out of their own volition and wrapped around her upper arms. He watched in shock as he pulled her near. He registered vaguely that she didn't resist him at all. She was warm and supple against him. All woman. Damn.

He sighed into her hair. "I know this is hard, Princess. But you've got to trust me."

"Said the spider to the fly," she rumbled against his chest.

"Honey, you have no idea," he mumbled under his breath. His head dipped lower and, somehow, her mouth rose to meet his.

This wasn't happening. He wasn't kissing her. He knew better, and besides, she hated his guts.

But her mouth was soft and sweet and hungry beneath his. She melted against him and he pulled her close, as desperate for more as she was. Their tongues danced and clashed in erotic battle and they devoured each other, fusing bodies and mouths together voraciously. He couldn't get enough of her, of her honey taste, of the dark, wet recesses of her mouth, of the racing electric shocks everywhere they touched.

Her arms tightened around his neck, pulling him deeper into her, allowing for no escape. Not that the thought of escape seriously crossed his mind.

He had no idea how much time passed before they came up for air. He only knew vaguely that, for some reason, he couldn't carry her down to the ground and make love to her right now.

He stared at her. She looked as amazed and disoriented as he felt. There was something urgent that he had to remember. But all he could think about was the passion raging in her gaze, the burning need that matched his own.

Eventually his subconscious grabbed him by the short hairs and yanked. A rational thought finally pierced his addled brain. *They didn't have time for this.* They were being chased.

He shook his head to clear it. "Uh, we need to go," he managed to say somewhat coherently.

He watched her eyes sluggishly focus on him. "Uh, right," she mumbled. "Up the hill."

"Here. Take my hand. Let me help you."

When she complied, he smiled. This flash of cooperation wouldn't last, of course. Still, he relished the feel of her soft, slender hand resting trustingly in his. Resolutely he pulled her forward, ignoring his body's primitive and powerful demand to make this woman his. Now.

It was all he could do to fight off the urge to make love to her. His thoughts darted about in alarm. He had to think about something else! "Watch your footing," he murmured. "A misstep now could land you with a broken ankle."

"You'd better hope not," she retorted, back to her usual piss-and-vinegar self. "If you guys hurt me in this stupid war game of yours, I'll sue you into the last century."

He grinned to himself, but replied deadpan, "You signed a legal release before the firing demonstration yesterday clearing the military of any liability. I imagine it still applies.''

"Oooh!'' She glared daggers at him.

Man, she was sexy when she was mad. He tore his mind away from bedding all that passion and forced himself to think about where his feet went next. The last thing they needed was for him to get hurt out here.

But his brain betrayed him, circling back to the question of what in the hell had just happened between them. No woman knocked him off his rocker like that! He *never* let women inside his guard. He'd learned that one the hard way years ago. Kimberly Stanton, of all people, most certainly couldn't have wormed her way past his defenses.

Her dislike of the military was well known within the Special Forces. She'd made it clear to him from the get-go that she intended to take apart his own unit, Charlie Squad. After he'd sworn off women, his team had become his life. He couldn't imagine doing anything else but spending as many years as his health held out on the squad.

The last thing he needed was a high-maintenance princess with attitude to spare. Especially one who couldn't hack it when the chips were down. Kimberly Stanton was *so* not his type. His attraction to her must come from the remnants of the drugs in his system. Lord knew, he'd been off his game from the beginning of this fiasco.

He stopped twice on the way up the valley rim when her breathing became labored. The last bit of the climb was harsh, requiring them to scramble on their hands and knees, searching for footholds and handholds among the tangled roots of giant trees. He dropped back behind her to catch her if she fell.

Patiently he guided her through the remaining climb. He touched her ankle when it was time to move a foot, and sometimes moved up behind her, his belly pressing against her back, to guide her hand to the next hold.

He caught snatches of the steady stream of muttering she kept up. "…will see all you lunatics put away…make sure none of you procreate and raise any miniature psychopaths to replace yourselves…have you all neutered as a public service…''

He hid his grin and climbed silently behind her.

Every time he touched her, a sexy little hitch caught in her breathing. It just about drove him to do something drastic. *Business first,* he reminded himself sharply.

Twice he had to put his hand under her firm, shapely tush to hoist her up over a rough patch. Even he was sucking wind by the time the ground leveled out. He glanced back at the brutal hillside they'd just scaled. *Not bad for a woman. Not bad at all.*

Kimberly halted beside him, bent over at the waist, breathing hard. "If any of your imaginary bad guys want me bad enough to follow us up that hill, they can have me," she panted.

Tex snorted. "Nobody's catching you on my watch."

She looked him in the eye briefly before her gaze skittered away. "Thanks," she mumbled.

What was this? Gratitude from the princess? "For what?"

"For helping me up that hill. I can do without this whole Outward Bound experience, but if you're under orders to drag me through it, I appreciate the assistance."

Surprise coursed through him. He'd pegged her as the kind of woman who took such things as her due. "No need to thank me," he replied gruffly. "It's my job."

She continued to talk to his feet, refusing to look up at him. "Nonetheless, thanks for the help."

Fair enough. He asked, "Does this mean you'll do what I tell you to from here on out?"

She straightened until she looked directly up at him. A spark of humor lit her eyes. The sight of it made his gut clench with need. "If you ask me nicely, and you explain why I need to cooperate, I expect I'll be generally helpful."

He grinned in genuine amusement. "A politician's answer if I ever heard one."

"My father trained me well," she answered, her voice light and bitter.

His eyebrows shot up at her tone. What was *that* all about? She said that like she hated her old man's guts.

Tex sat down on a big root and gestured—politely—for her to sit beside him. He was pleased when she did. "Didn't Senator Stanton fight in Nam?" he asked casually.

"Oh, yes. He had a rip-roaring good old time over there."

Tex rolled his eyes. That was one war he didn't joke about.

Kimberly waxed serious. "He was a big war hero. Decorated six times for bravery on the field of battle. Multiple purple hearts, presidential citations, bronze stars, a silver star, the works. Made the covers of *Time* and *Newsweek*. That's what launched his political career."

Her rote answer sounded faintly resentful. He threw up a cautious trial balloon. "You don't sound too thrilled about being a senator's daughter."

Wariness leapt into her gaze. "Let's just say the senator and I have agreed to disagree on certain subjects."

The senator? Not "my father"? Tex frowned. Kimberly Stanton was famous for her clashes on Capitol Hill with her old man. But Tex had always thought they remained close outside the political arena. Certainly the press painted the Stanton family that way. But from her tone, he got the distinct impression their differences went much deeper than politics.

He changed subjects. "Any idea why someone would want to kidnap you?"

"You tell me. It's your stupid training scenario."

He exhaled in frustration. "I'm not kidding. This isn't an exercise. Can you think of any reason why someone would want to kidnap you?"

She glared at him. "Are you always this stubborn?"

His eyebrows shot up. *She* was calling *him* stubborn? "Aw, come on. Play along for fun. Can you think of anything?"

"Nope. Not a thing."

What was so special about her or her family that made Gavronese rebels kidnap her? He asked, "Do you know much about what your father's working on politically these days?"

Her eyes narrowed, giving them a distinctly feline look. She answered coolly, "My father doesn't scratch his nose in Congress without me knowing about it."

He almost felt sorry for the elder Stanton. He sure as hell wouldn't want to have to face her across a Senate chamber. "Can you think of any legislation your father's involved with, any committees, any investigations, that might be of interest to the Gavronese rebels?"

Her gaze turned thoughtful. "Is this exercise based on some threat you've received from these rebels against my father?"

"Hello. Earth to dense blonde. Come in. This is *not* an exercise!"

She just shook her head.

He had never met anyone who could so ignore the evidence staring them right in the face. She was sitting in the middle of a jungle, for God's sake!

She laughed without humor. "Maybe you should pretend to kidnap me for money. My parents are rolling in it. But I wish your hypothetical bad guys luck in prying any of it out of my father's tight fists."

Wow. So much for the cheery, All-American image the Stanton family projected to the public. He sighed. "I suppose it doesn't really matter why the rebels kidnapped you at this point. The goal now is to get you home safely."

Speaking of which, they needed to get moving. He stood up and shouldered the two rifles. He turned to head out but was forestalled when Kimberly put a hand on his forearm. Her fingers were cool against his skin, but they might as well have been branding irons the way they burned his flesh.

"Why don't we just cut to the chase and save ourselves a lot of grief, here? You do the big, fancy, save-the-girl firing demonstration you're supposed to do. I'll act suitably impressed and then we can both get out of here. If we hurry, we can be home in time for supper."

"Darlin', has anyone ever told you you're more stubborn than a constipated mule?"

She laughed, her eyes sparkling merrily. "All the time, Mr. Monroe. All the time."

"I'm a captain, not a mister. But call me Tex. I don't like titles much either way."

"Okay, Tex. And please, call me Kimberly."

Their gazes met candidly for a moment. The touch of her gaze upon him was nearly as tangible as a physical caress. The swirling currents between them began to build again and heaviness built low in his gut. Tex looked away hastily.

He cleared his throat. "I'd like to follow this ridgeline for a couple more hours. But no more climbing today, I promise. An hour or so before dark, we'll stop to hunt for food and water. Then we'll set up camp for the night. Okay with you?"

She grimaced in distaste. "Camp? Sorry. I can't stick around for a whole night of this hilarity. I've got a dinner meeting this evening with Senator Norwood. I'm afraid I'm going to have to insist that you take me home now."

"Sorry. No taxis run from Gavarone to Washington after 3:00 p.m." he replied.

She fisted her hands on her hips. "Look. Enough is enough. Take me home. Now."

"Believe me, Princess. I'm tryin'."

"Just how far away from Washington did you guys take me while you had me knocked out?" she demanded.

"Kimberly, you're not even on the same continent as Senator Norwood."

She stared in disbelief. "I'd heard you guys took things to extremes, but did you actually have to fly me to Timbuktu for this little exercise of yours?"

"Timbuktu's in Mali. Wrong continent. We're in South America. That much I am sure of."

She huffed in exasperation. "Fine. So I have to miss my dinner meeting tonight. At least get me to a phone where I can call the senator's office and cancel. I really could use a shower and a hot meal, too, while you're at it."

"If you know of any hotels within walking distance in this jungle, by all means let me know," he drawled. "Otherwise, camping it is."

She stared in dawning dismay. "You're kidding."

"Nope," he replied.

"But I don't *do* camping."

"You do now," he retorted.

She took a step backward. "You don't understand. My idea of camping is a hotel without room service."

He snorted in amusement. "Then you're going to be *real* disappointed with the accommodations tonight."

He started to turn away, but he caught a glimpse of the genuinely frightened glint in her green eyes. And then the truth hit him. Poor kid was clinging to the whole this-is-an-exercise idea because she was scared out of her mind. "Think of this adventure as a learning experience," he offered.

"I hate learning new things," she said vehemently.

"Too bad. There's a lot I could've shown you," he murmured.

Her gaze snapped to his. Damn. He hadn't meant for it to come out with quite *that* innuendo. He blinked in surprise when he actually felt his cheeks heating up. He couldn't remember the last time anything had made him blush. Particularly a woman.

Kimberly spent the next few hours more miserable than she could ever remember being in her life. *This was real.* It had to be. There was no other explanation for why Tex thought he could make her this miserable and not get the tar sued out of him.

She was still having trouble wrapping her mind around the whole kidnapping idea, but this was definitely a jungle. A jungle! Complete with bugs and sweat and scary noises and God knows what crawling and creeping critters. Insidious fear almost but not quite overwhelmed her dragging exhaustion.

Just when she was sure she couldn't take another step, couldn't withstand another jolt of fear from an unexpected noise, memory of Tex's sizzling kiss would pop into her head. Be it from irritation or titillation, thoughts of that kiss energized her, putting new life into her flagging spirits.

Most of the men she'd dated recently—okay, pretty much most of the men she'd ever dated—fell into the same category: politically correct, self-absorbed and more interested in what she could do for their careers than they were in her. Not that she went out with men she *despised*—Heaven help her if she ever got *that* jaded.

But Tex was definitely a departure from all other men who'd ever kissed her. His blunt honesty bordered on rude and he wasn't worth a darn at slippery maneuvering.

Abruptly a vine snagged her foot and she pitched toward Tex. He whipped around and his hands shot out, snagging her shoulders and stopping her from falling. The display of lightning quick reflexes left her blinking. His strong hands were impossibly gentle as he steadied her.

She frowned. No man touched a woman like that unless he was at least a little bit interested in her. Her heart fluttered.

And then her brain kicked in. She must be suffering from jungle fever. He couldn't possibly be interested in her. Two people couldn't be more different than the two of them.

What *was* it about his mere touch that sent her pulse racing like that? It was more than a little unnerving. She avoided meeting his gaze as she disentangled her foot. His touch slid away from her skin, almost like he was reluctant to let go of her. She shivered with a sharp, sexual thrill.

"You okay?" he asked. "You haven't complained for at least two minutes."

"No, I'm not okay," she snapped. "I don't like this escape-through-the-jungle thing, and I want you to make it go away!"

As he resumed walking, his chuckle floated back to her. "That's more like it."

She stared at his back through narrowed eyes. One thing was certain. Tex Monroe hadn't kissed her for political reasons. He knew she was out to take his Special Forces unit apart.

That had to gall him. No doubt he was sure the world would fall apart without men like him running around patrolling it. The idea was well and good in theory, but save-the-world heroes were purely the stuff of legends. They didn't actually exist. She knew that better than most. After all, she'd grown up with a man the whole world touted as a hero. And what a crock that was.

Tex Monroe was no different than her father. Just like William Stanton in Vietnam, he'd burn himself out chasing after an imagined destiny of saving the world. Although she doubted the hard soldier in front of her was that deluded.

Tex might act the gentleman and help her through this nightmare, but she had no illusions about his real motives. His fanny would be in a sling if he didn't keep her safe. Pure self-interest motivated him.

But, as he'd promised, Tex stopped when the light finally began to fade and the relentless steam heat of the afternoon broke. She sagged down onto a moss-covered log, completely drained. "Thank God. I don't think I could take another step."

He replied, "Rest here while I do a little scouting. Gotta be some water around here somewhere."

Water. A long cool drink sounded like manna from heaven. She pulled out the neck of her bedraggled sweater and blew down its front as Tex disappeared into the greenery. If she knew he'd be gone for a while, she'd take the darned thing off.

Her stockings were ruined, the French silk full of holes and runs. Her shoes were destroyed, too. The fine leather was badly scuffed and muddy. *Wherever you are, Donatella Versace, please forgive me for what I've done to your lovely shoes.*

The air hung on her skin like soggy cobwebs, heavy and sticky, without even a hint of movement, as she listened to the myriad exotic sounds trilling and screeching through the jungle. The day's hothouse humidity slowly seeped out of the vibrating air and the jungle's vivid hues faded to gray.

She jumped violently when a hand landed on her shoulder from behind. She lurched off the log and spun around.

Tex.

"You scared the daylights out of me!" she exclaimed. "How did you do that?"

"Hush," he admonished her. "It's my job. I'm not exactly in the Boy Scouts, you know."

Now that was stating the obvious. No Boy Scout kissed like he did, she was sure.

"I found us a good spot to sleep tonight. I also found water," he announced.

"Hallelujah," she replied fervently. But the word died on her lips a few minutes later as she stared down at a muddy pool of water. It was little more than a puddle, really.

"But it's dirty!" she cried in dismay made all the worse by her raging thirst.

"Sediment looks bad, but it won't kill you. Hell, little kids eat dirt all the time. Think of it as an extra-thin latte."

She sniffed delicately. "Shouldn't we boil it first?"

"Can't risk a fire," was his terse reply. "Here's the thing, Kimberly. Both of us have gone over twenty-four hours without water. I bet you've got a decent headache going by now."

She did, but she wasn't about to admit it. She wasn't on the verge of dying, and nothing short of that was going to get her to drink that filthy water.

"Your lips are chapped. You're not sweating enough, and you're grouchy as hell. Classic signs of dehydration. We'll die in about four more days without any water. But, any disease we pick up from that—" he pointed down at the puddle "—won't kill us for a couple weeks."

"Lovely," she muttered.

He shrugged. "That's the worst case scenario. It's much more likely that if the water's contaminated you'll only get a good case of the runs."

She looked up, appalled by the prospect. *The runs?* No thank you. "I'm not drinking that slop," she announced. "Why don't you do your Daniel Boone thing and find us some clean water." She crossed her arms over her chest for good measure.

His gaze narrowed into a dangerous calm she was beginning to recognize as a bout of bull-headed, testosterone induced, macho mad. "You need water, and you need it now," he growled.

"Not on your life."

"Look, Miss High and Mighty. I'm responsible for your welfare, and I'm ordering you to drink that!" He pointed at the mud puddle.

"Sorry," she answered breezily. "I'm a civilian. I don't take orders from soldiers."

The muscles in his jaw rippled and suddenly he seemed to grow taller and broader. Uh-oh. He looked just like he had at the firing range when he'd gotten ready to kill something. He loomed dangerously close. She took a step back. And another.

He stalked after her. He finally spoke low and silky. It positively made her skin crawl. "Am I going to have to kiss you half senseless again to get you to drink some water?"

Again… She stopped retreating indignantly. Was he implying that he'd kissed her before only to get her up that hillside? How *dare* he?

"Half senseless…me…*again?* You lout!" Fury boiled up in her gut, and somewhere very deep inside her, a kernel of hurt formed. That kiss had blown his socks off. She knew it as surely as she was standing here. He could deny it all he wanted, but she wasn't buying it for a second. "You didn't kiss me to coerce me into climbing that hill and you know it," she accused.

He lifted a skeptical eyebrow and gave her a cool-as-cucumber look. "Do you need me to prove the point?" he drawled, his leering gaze locked on her mouth.

"Don't even think about it, mister!"

He laughed and took a step forward.

"If you lay a hand on me, I'll…I'll…"

"You'll what?" he challenged.

She stared at him, her mind a blank. What did you threaten a commando with when you were temporarily stranded in the middle of a jungle with him? "I'll make you admit that kissing me completely blew you away!"

That set him back on his heels. His gaze narrowed ominously.

She glared right back.

Finally he sighed and looked away. "We don't have time for this foolishness, but I'll make you a deal. If you'll drink some of this water, I'll filter it for you and get most of the dirt out first. It won't be sterile, but it'll look better."

Part of her wanted to tell him to go suck an egg. But the other part reluctantly had to admit that he was right. Her head throbbed and her lips were cracked and parched. "Is that *really* the only water available to drink?" she asked thinly.

"It really is," he answered quietly.

"Okay." She gave in with ill grace.

He walked a few yards away and tore off several gigantic leaves from a plant. He dug a depression in the ground with the heel of his boot and lined it with the leaves. Then he pulled out the red felt beret and scooped up a hatful of the water. He held it over the shallow hole.

Nothing happened at first. But then water started dripping steadily out of the hat. As it collected in the basin it was clear, the sediments trapped by the hat's felt, more like drinking water was supposed to be.

After he'd strained a good half gallon of water, he handed her a thin reed she'd seen him pick a while earlier.

She looked at the stick blankly. It wasn't thick enough to whack him over the head with like she'd like to.

"It's hollow," Tex explained. "Like a straw."

Ah. She poked the end of the reed in the makeshift basin and drank. The water was warm and tasted terrible, but she couldn't remember the last time anything felt so good going down her throat.

Tex drank, as well, using another reed. He strained water until both their thirsts were slaked.

He stood up. "Come on. I've got to build a shelter before it gets full dark."

She'd expected him to lead her to a nice little clearing, build a cheerful fire and maybe find some logs to sit on. But instead he pushed into the thickest underbrush she'd seen all day. More of the giant-leafed plants hung low over a tangle of vines and roots.

She watched him pull a bunch of the leaves down and lash them with thin vines to a waist-high jumble of growth. Then he bent back enough of the vines and brambles below to create a tiny hollow. In a few minutes a little green cave took shape.

"Get in," he ordered. "I'm going hunting. I'll be back as soon as I can."

"Hunting? As in for food?" she asked hopefully. Her stomach growled impatiently.

He shrugged. "That, too. I'm going to do a little reconnaissance along the way, though."

Reconnaissance? That sounded dangerous. She warned him, "If you get yourself killed and leave me alone out here, I'll have your head on a platter in the afterlife."

He answered dryly. "I'll keep that in mind. Wouldn't want to jeopardize my immortal soul." Grinning, he shouldered the gun he'd called an AK-47 and pushed the other gun into the shelter. "If somebody approaches you, point this baby at them and pull the trigger once. I'll hear the noise and come back right away."

"You're suggesting I *shoot* someone?" she exclaimed.

"Keep your voice down!" he barked under his breath.

"I'm not suggesting anything. I'm *ordering* you to shoot anyone besides me who approaches you."

"What if I miss?"

"RITA doesn't miss. It's a computer-guided targeting system. You only have to point in the general direction of your target and it'll do the rest."

She recoiled from the thought of blowing someone's head off like she'd seen him do to clay targets. "I can't kill someone!"

He sighed. "Just promise you'll pull the trigger. It's the only way I'll know you're in trouble."

She eyed the rifle with deep suspicion.

"Is it loaded with real bullets or fake ones for the rifle range?"

Tex laughed shortly. "It's loaded with hydra-shock explosive rounds. They'll blow a hole the size of a basketball in anything they hit."

"What if I accidentally shoot you?"

He shrugged. "Then take the beret. You'll need it to strain your water." And with that he turned and melted into the trees.

She glared at the spot where she'd last seen him. Then

the immensity of the jungle crowded in as it hit her she was alone. She got down on her hands and knees and crawled into the shelter. Where was a four-star hotel when a girl needed one? Heck, she'd be delighted with a rat-infested flea trap right about now.

She shimmied out of her ruined sweater, so relieved to be free of the blasted thing she hardly cared if Tex came back and found her in her bra. The pink angora garment looked as pitiful as a cat who'd been caught out in the pouring rain.

The shelter's roof was too low to sit upright beneath, so she stretched out on the cool ground and wadded the sweater under her head. Relief washed over her as she finally let go of the day's tension. She'd close her eyes for just a minute.

She had no idea how long she slept. One second she was peacefully unconscious and the next she had the distinct feeling she was not alone. She opened her eyes and looked up.

A man loomed over her. His skin was dark and a red beret slouched over one eye. His eyes gleamed with hatred and lust.

She drew breath to scream, but a filthy hand slammed down on her mouth. She froze as cold steel bit into the side of her neck.

Chapter 4

Cold-blooded, killing-on-his-mind rage surged through Tex at the sight of the soldier holding a knife to Kimberly's neck. He lunged through the thicket at the rebel, snarling low in his throat. The soldier spun away from Kimberly and sprang into a fighting stance. A knife glinted faintly in the guy's right hand.

Blood roared in his ears and Tex didn't mess around with any finesse moves. He charged forward, grabbed the slashing wrist and slammed his fist into the guy's face as hard as he could.

The rebel dropped like a rock.

Jeez. That had been close. Way, way too close.

"Kimberly, honey, are you all right?" he panted.

She crouched in the opening of the shelter, her eyes huge and frightened as she peered up at him. He held open his arms and she all but leapt into them. She hung on like her life depended on him. Of course, it probably did.

Her shudders gradually subsided and she looked up at him. "Did you kill him?" she choked out.

He glanced down at the unmoving rebel. They guy's nose was mush. He'd probably cracked a few of the dude's facial bones and the guy'd probably lose a couple teeth out of it. Not that it was going to matter when he was done with the bastard.

His first inclination was to cause the rebel a whole lot of pain before he waxed him. But, given the need for quiet, he'd have to settle for slitting the guy's throat. He realized Kimberly was staring at him, waiting for an answer to her question.

"No, I didn't. But I'm going to."

"You're going to…" Her gaze flickered to the unconscious man at their feet, then back up at him. "You wouldn't!" she accused.

He leaned down and plucked the bowie knife out of the guy's limp fingers. "I'll drag him away from here before I slit his throat because the smell of blood's going to attract some nasty visitors. I don't want packs of predators parking on the front steps of our shelter."

Her eyes went wide and black, and fine trembling enveloped her entire body. Good. Maybe the seriousness of their situation was finally starting to sink in. He pressed the point. "I'm not going to bother burying him because it would take too much time. And besides, when the animals are done with him, nobody will be able to tell if he was human or not."

Even in the near total darkness, he saw her face go white as a sheet. He hoped she didn't faint on him. He already had his hands full with the rebel.

Kimberly grabbed him by the arm. "Tex. You can't kill this man!"

"Sure I can. Besides the fact that he deserves to die for attacking you, I can't let him run back to his buddies and tell them where we are. I've got to silence him."

Words tumbled out of Kimberly's mouth, stumbling over one another as she spoke urgently. "I believe you.

This is all real. You don't have to kill that guy to prove it to me.''

"I'm not killing him to prove anything," Tex answered reasonably. "I'm killing him because he found us and he represents a threat to your safety."

She wrung her hands, keeping pace beside him as he commenced dragging the soldier's limp body out into the jungle. "Tex. You can't kill a man on my account. It's wrong to slaughter another human being like this! I couldn't live with this guy's life on my conscience. Please. For me. Don't do it!" she begged.

Tex let the guy's feet drop to the ground with a thud. He stared hard at her. She looked desperate. "Are you for real?"

She nodded frantically. "Yes. Absolutely. For God's sake, don't kill this man!"

He closed his eyes for a moment in sheer frustration. "You're asking me to make a huge tactical mistake. My job is to keep you safe. At all costs. Including this guy's life."

"I understand. But spare him anyway. Please?"

Her eyes were so soulful, so pitiful. He felt his resolve slipping. And then she put her soft, supplicating hand on his arm. He cursed viciously under his breath. "Mark my words, I'm going to live to regret this," he rumbled. He tucked the knife in his belt and pulled out a length of rope. "Help me tie him up, will you?" he asked in resignation.

She took breath to speak and he interrupted her before she could say a word. "There's no way you're talking me out of this, Kimberly. I *am* binding and gagging him so he can't get loose for a day or two. By then we'll have a big enough head start so he can't give away our location. I hope."

Kimberly flung herself around his neck. "Oh, thank you, Tex." She planted a big, enthusiastic kiss on his mouth.

Hell, for a thanks like that, he ought to spare bad guys' lives more often. He tied and gagged the soldier quickly, securing the guy's hands around a rough barked tree. If the fellow rubbed the ropes on the tree for long enough, the cord would fray and he'd get loose. If not... Tex shrugged.

"Come on," he growled. "Let's get back under cover."

Fortunately, Kimberly didn't give him any more flack. He trussed up the unconscious soldier in resigned silence and then led her back to their shelter. He paused outside the entrance. "Tell me the God's honest truth, Kimberly. Are you saying you believe me about being kidnapped because you wanted to save that guy's neck or because you do accept that, in fact, you were kidnapped?"

She stared up at him for a long time. She whispered, "You were really going to kill that soldier, weren't you?"

He nodded without hesitation. "Absolutely. I can't believe I let you talk me out of it."

"If I had any doubts about it being real before, I don't anymore." She collapsed onto the nearest log and buried her face in her hands.

He sat down beside her, at a loss as to how to comfort her. He rarely hung around women. Especially crying ones. "Nothing's changed. I'm still going to get you out of this safely. It'll all turn out fine and you'll have a story to tell your grandkids."

She glanced up at him, her eyes suspiciously watery. "If only you could wave a magic wand and make it all stop!"

"I will make it stop, darlin'. You just have to bear with me for a few days. We'll be okay. I swear."

"Cross your heart and hope to die?" she asked in a small voice.

"There'll be no dying here," he replied firmly. "How about if I swear on a stack of bibles instead?"

She took a deep breath and nodded, a hesitant grant of trust.

Relief made his knees go weak for a moment. Now maybe they actually had a snowball's chance of surviving.

Worry for her safety slammed into him like a runaway train. A visceral need to protect her flowed through his veins. Damn. His reaction was a whole lot stronger than mere professional concern.

He stared down at her in the dark. Violent desire to make love with her shuddered through him. So much fire blazed in her. She'd burn the night down around them if she ever turned it loose.

I'm going to make you admit that kissing me completely blew you away. Her challenge swirled around him, more of a threat than she knew.

Except he'd met her type before. They'd wrap a guy around their little finger, wring the very guts out of him, then toss him away like an old rag. He'd been down that road before and learned his lesson. He had no interest whatsoever in being the next conquest in Kimberly Stanton's string of toy-boys.

Yeah, he'd liked that kiss. Hell, it tied him in knots just to think about it. But that didn't mean he was going back for more. He could do without the strings attached, thank you very much.

His gaze dropped to the expanse of creamy skin she'd revealed by stripping off her sweater. Her flesh glowed in the filtered darkness that enveloped them. His hands ached to stroke that satiny smoothness. Beneath his scrutiny, abrupt awareness of his attention visibly thrummed through her and goose bumps raised on her skin.

The night air suddenly felt overwarm. He spoke as much to distract himself as her from the heavy tension hanging between them. "I said I'd get you out of this alive and well, and I will."

The tension gradually drained from her and she sagged against him for a moment. She lifted her head and spit grass out of her mouth. "What in the world have you done to yourself? You're covered in mud and grass!"

He grinned. "Like my camouflage?"

"No! It's hideous."

He laughed. "But it's the latest in haute jungle couture."

"High Neanderthal fashion, maybe." She laughed. "On television, you guys use nice, civilized grease paint and a few twigs in your helmet. What's with this pig-in-swill look?"

"On television, we don't give away our secrets," he retorted. "The last thing we need is to broadcast how we really operate on the evening news for our enemies to see."

"Are you sure it's terrorists and not the rest of America you don't want seeing how you really operate?"

He paused, kneeling before the shelter entrance. He looked up at her. "The American people don't want to know how we really operate, darlin'."

She crouched beside him, bringing her into disturbingly close proximity. Close enough for him to lean forward just a little and kiss her. The memory of the warm, sultry taste of her swirled through his head with aphrodisiac intensity.

"The American people have a right to know what you do with their tax dollars," she murmured.

He frowned at her. What was going on here? She actually wanted to sit in the middle of a jungle full of kidnappers and discuss politics? An undercurrent flowed through her words. Something more personal than a mere point of view. What was it she had against soldiers like him?

"Look," he said on a sigh. "You're welcome to your opinion, and I'll stick to mine. The reason I do what I do is so you can have your opinion and express it freely."

She frowned, but he continued. "When you get back home safe and sound, you can do your worst to convince Congress to disband my unit. But in the meantime, I've got a job to do, whether you approve of it or not." He shoved the beret, which he took from inside his shirt, into her hands. "Eat these."

She picked up one of the green berries he'd collected and examined it suspiciously. "What is it?"

"It comes from a native vine. I don't know the name. The berries taste terrible, but they won't kill you. The locals distill its juice into a truly evil rotgut."

She popped one in her mouth and immediately puckered up, shuddering. "God, that's worse than a lemon!"

He made a sympathetic face. "Just swallow them down as fast as you can. You need to eat. We could be out here for several weeks."

She popped another berry into her mouth. She chewed it minimally and gulped it down.

He talked to distract her while she dutifully consumed the fruit. "I found some signs of other humans besides our visitor."

She stopped eating abruptly. "How close?"

"A couple hundred yards. Fortunately not real fresh. Probably some poachers. But tomorrow we'll need to take precautions and move more carefully."

"What sort of precautions?"

"For starters, we'll need to camouflage you, too."

She asked in dismay, "Do I have to do the whole mud-and-grass-in-the-hair thing? Couldn't I just smear on a little grease paint and call it good?"

"Sorry. I don't have any grease paint with me on this trip."

"Why not?"

He snorted. "I wasn't exactly expecting to get kidnapped and end up in a South American jungle when I went to work yesterday. As it is, we're lucky I've got any survival gear on me at all."

She frowned. "Exactly how much gear do you have?"

"Enough for us to live on, if that's what you're asking. I've got the knife I just picked off that soldier, and we have rope and a cigarette lighter from the guard in the truck. I happened to have a space blanket in the pocket of my pants, and that's a real piece of luck. Not to mention a couple ounces of DEET in my shooting gear. Plus, we have the two rifles. Although we'll only use those as a last resort.''

"What's a space blanket?"

"It's a thin piece of plastic coated with a Mylar heat reflecting surface. Folds up into a little bundle about the size of my fist. It'll keep us dry and warm in a pinch.''

"We're supposed to survive out here for weeks with a knife, some rope, a lighter and a piece of plastic?" she asked incredulously.

What did she sound so upset about? It could've been worse. Not a lot worse, but worse. "I've survived with less," he commented casually.

She looked at him in patent disbelief.

He grinned. "Welcome to some of that training you're so hot and bothered to tell the taxpayers and terrorists all about.''

She harrumphed. "What's DEET, anyway?"

"Diethyl-m-toluamide. Industrial-strength insect repellent.''

"Insect repellent? Give it to me!" she demanded.

"Easy.'' He snatched at the little bottle as she made to pour the whole thing on herself. "Just a few drops will protect you for several days. We've got to make this bottle last until we get home.'' He added, "Not that I expect to be out here all that long, of course.''

She gave him the intent look of a woman thinking hard. That just couldn't be good. She was already too smart for her britches.

Finally she announced, "You can drop the reassure-the-frightened-female act. I recognize a tight spot when I see one. And we're there.''

He considered her in turn. He had been trying to reassure the frightened civilian, but he was surprised she'd seen past her own fear to realize what he'd been up to. She might be a city slicker and out of her element, but she was no dummy. He made a mental note not to underestimate her intelligence again.

At least she finally grasped the gravity of their situation. He should probably be thankful that she hadn't fallen apart at the realization. He responded candidly. "You're right. We are in a jam. We're going to have to think our way out of this one."

She stared at him a few more seconds and then sighed. "I'm going to have to eat more of these berries, aren't I?"

He smiled ruefully. "'Fraid so. We'll need to stay on the move, and we're going to have to eat whatever we come across."

She shoved the beret and the remainder of the berries back into his hand. "Well, at least I won't need that trip to the spa I had planned for next month to drop a few pounds."

He blinked, surprised. "You? Drop a few pounds?" His gaze dropped to her bare torso. "Why? You look great."

She laughed lightly. "Thanks. I needed that."

He shook his head and mucked down the last few berries. Man, they were nasty. He waited for her to crawl inside the shelter before he shoehorned in beside her. It was a tight fit. Tight enough that her shoulder rubbed against his and her knees kept bumping into his as she shifted around trying to get comfortable.

He unfolded the space blanket and spread it out over Kimberly's legs. An image broadsided him of their smooth length wrapped around his waist, urging him on. He cleared his throat huskily. "You should probably put your sweater back on. It can get cold at night out here."

He gulped as she twisted and wriggled in the confined space, slipping the fuzzy sweater over her head. It hung up on her breasts, highlighting the swelling cleavage in a way that made him break out in a sweat before she yanked it down into place.

Hands off, pal, he ordered himself.

Yeah, right, his libido retorted.

Damn. He had a sinking feeling this was going to be a long night. He laid back and closed his eyes.

"What are you doing?" Kimberly demanded.

He cracked open one eye. "Going to sleep. And I'd recommend you do the same."

"You're going to sleep in here?"

He opened both eyes all the way. "Where did you think I was going to sleep?"

"Well, I just assumed you'd have your own bed or sleep across the entrance, or something."

"Darlin'," he drawled, "this ain't no double queen bed suite. Besides, we're going to need to share body heat to stay warm."

"Share..." Her eyes widened.

"We're both adults. What's the problem?" he asked.

"Somebody out there's trying to kidnap me, and you're just going to lie here and sleep? Aren't you supposed to protect me?"

He could try to explain the vital strategic importance of sleep in a situation like this, but he doubted she'd hear him past the panic darting in her eyes. He'd learned long ago that fear made people act stupid faster than just about any emotion except lust. What she needed was a good dose of riling up to chase that stark terror from her gaze.

He grinned up at her. "What ever happened to making me admit I liked that kiss?" He held out an inviting arm. "Now's your chance, or did you give up on your threat already?"

She spluttered, "Aah! You think I'll just fall into your arms if you so much as—"

He cut her off. "Get over yourself, Princess. I'm perfectly capable of sleeping beside you without giving in to uncontrolled lust." He added for good measure, "You're not that irresistible."

Her gaze narrowed. Ah, yes. That pushed her mad button but good.

Slowly she stretched out beside him. Her hand landed

in the middle of his chest and began wandering over the suddenly tight muscles there. Her leg rubbed against his. And then her thigh started to climb his, inching toward parts of him that were abruptly at full attention. Her body moved sinuously against his side.

"What in the hell are you doing?" he growled.

"Sharing body heat," she answered, all innocence.

Damn. Maybe he shouldn't have riled her up quite so much.

Kimberly huffed. Not that irresistible, indeed. She'd felt the surge of sexual heat from him when he kissed her earlier, and it was pouring off him again now. She'd show him, by golly. She traced his rib cage, counting the bones beneath slabs of heavy, hard muscle. Everywhere she touched him he was like steel.

The men she knew wore suits and battled with words and money and power. But Tex was a throwback to another time. He was a warrior. He lived off his brawn and quick thinking. A thrill of purely female appreciation swept through her. Whoa, more than she'd bargained for, here.

Her inner thigh swept high along his leg and she started as she encountered the heavy bulge of his desire. A low, warning growl rumbled in his chest.

She ignored a thrill of trepidation. She'd make him admit he wanted her one way or another.

His pectorals leapt under her hand as it slid upward. The muscles and tendons in his neck formed tense cords when she scratched her fingernails lightly across them. She ran her fingers around his ear, revelling in the shudder that rippled through him.

The motion of her arm moved her breast back and forth across his chest, rubbing her sensitized nipple against his unyielding strength. She gasped at the sensation, galvanized by the ripples of pleasure that shot through her belly and tingled out to her fingertips. It was absolutely indecent

to crawl all over a man like this. Shameless. *Delicious.*
She moved her arm again. Oh, that was very nice.

This time the warning came from inside her own head.
She was in danger of losing control, in danger of giving
in to him completely, of begging him to make love to her.

*In danger of breaking out of your shell and finding some
real pleasure for once,* a little voice whispered in her heart.

That gave her a start. Was she that inhibited? That much
of a control freak? Did she never let go of herself and just
enjoy the moment? She became aware of Tex once more,
stretched out rigid on the ground beside her, breathing
heavily. His self-control was a palpable thing between
them, a fragile barrier he was determined not to cross.

But what if he did cross it? What if they both did?

The possibilities spun in her head until she could barely
see straight. Abruptly she knew. With utter certainty. They
would create a passion between them that was so hot, so
overwhelming, they'd bring the jungle crashing down
around them.

She moved against him, seeking more of the piercing
pleasure touching him gave her. She lifted her mouth to
his neck, tasting the salt on his skin, smelling the lightly
musky scent of him.

She couldn't get enough of it. She pressed even closer
to him, dying for more. His jaw was as hard as a rock as
she explored it. Tension rolled off of him in thick waves
that made her giddy with anticipation.

He lurched and somehow she was abruptly on her back
with him looming above her, his hands pinning her arms
to the ground. "Enough," he growled. "No more games."

She stared up in the darkness at the black, unreadable
shadows enveloping his face. His breathing was ragged,
like he'd just run a race. So much for him claiming to be
able to resist her. Triumph coursed through her.

The way he collapsed back onto the ground beside her
with an arm thrown over his eyes was solid evidence that
he knew he'd given himself away. He might not have ad-

mitted out loud that he wanted her, but he didn't need to. She'd felt his heart racing, his body's reaction to her, the tension in his jaw.

She settled down beside him, snuggling against his warmth. After all, she could be patient. She knew off balance when she saw it, and she had Tex Monroe reeling. He blew first hot then cold, and went from nice to nasty in the blink of an eye. He obviously didn't know whether to clobber her or kiss her senseless. No doubt about it. He wanted her. As much as she reluctantly wanted him.

He'd eventually admit that he couldn't resist her. And when he did, she'd bring him to his knees!

"Is everything about power with you?" Tex asked her abruptly.

She started at the uncanny accuracy of the question. Had he read her thoughts? "Isn't everybody ultimately chasing after power of one kind or another?" she retorted.

He rolled on his side to face her. "That's where you and I are different. I see the world in black and white, and you see nothing but shades of gray."

She frowned. "That's not true."

"Sure it is. I know your type. You think nobody's a good guy just for the sake of being a good guy. Everyone's working an angle of some kind. You see a world where everybody's out to feed their own greed and lust for power."

"Try living in Washington, D.C., for a while," she replied. "It'll make a cynic out of you in no time."

"Maybe you need to get out of D.C. more often," he murmured.

"I'm sure as heck out of there right now."

His slow-as-molasses smile unfolded, warming her all the way to her toes. "You are at that. Maybe I should readjust your outlook on life while you're out of the asylum."

"My outlook's just fine, thank you very much," she said tartly.

"I dunno. You're wound about as tight as a bronc with his bucking strap cinched too hard. From where I sit, you could use a little unwinding."

"And you think you're the man to do it?" she challenged.

His eyes gleamed like black diamonds. "I've tamed wilder fillies than you, Princess."

And with that he rolled on to his back and promptly went unconscious.

Fillies? Fillies! He'd compared her to a horse? He was the one who resembled a horse. Or at least the hind end of one. In a huff, she turned her back to him. Tame her, indeed. She'd show him.

Chapter 5

Kimberly eased out of a deep slumber to the tantalizing sensation of Tex's lips moving against her ear. Mmm, that was nice.

He breathed, "Someone's out there. Don't move and don't make any noise. Understand?"

She jolted wide-awake. Adrenaline slammed through her bloodstream. She nodded fearfully, holding her breath and listening hard. A hundred completely unfamiliar sounds disturbed the night air. There was a low, loud buzzing noise, like a cricket on steroids. Something clicked rhythmically. Probably another insect of some kind. A bird, or maybe a monkey, screeched in the distance.

And then she heard it. A swishing noise, just like the one she'd made all afternoon as the leaves and branches rubbed against her.

It was close. Really close.

Oh, God. What if whoever was out there found the guy that Tex had tied up? As soon as the rebel was cut loose, he'd tell his buddies where they were hiding! Tex must be regretting his decision not to kill the guy.

Tex moved very slowly beside her. He eased one of the rifles across his body into a firing position.

The swishing noise retreated a little ways. And then it stopped. She could picture someone out there, standing stock-still, listening as intently as she was.

A quiet mumble of Spanish.

An answering mumble.

If only she spoke that language! She spoke Italian so beautifully it would make the Pope weep, but that didn't do her a darn bit of good right now. Frustration mingled with her helpless terror.

She glanced over at Tex. His jaw rippled with tension and his expression was grim, but he didn't show the slightest sign of fear. Thank goodness he seemed to know what to do, because she was clueless.

She blinked, startled by the thought. Never, ever, had she been able to tolerate helpless females. Her mother had been that way in the face of her father's aggression. Revulsion at the memory of her mother's biddable meekness surged through her. She'd sworn ever since she was a little girl that no man would ever have such power over her. But here she was, perfectly happy to have a strong, macho, *armed* male beside her.

She really hated the idea of depending on Tex. But what choice did she have? She had no idea how to survive out here, let alone how to evade her would-be captors.

The whole idea of being chased by kidnappers had seemed distant and surreal even after she accepted that this wasn't a training exercise. And then a rebel put a knife to her throat. And now these quiet Spanish voices nearby. The danger facing them was suddenly very real indeed to her. Fear clogged her throat and made her light-headed. She struggled to breathe normally but only marginally succeeded.

The swishing started again. She inhaled on a gasp and

held her breath until she thought she'd pass out. The noise moved away until she couldn't make it out anymore. Tex continued to lie still. She took her cue from him and made like a statue.

While she waited a dozen lifetimes for Tex to call the all-clear, she prayed frantically that the bad guys would go far, far away from them. She prayed that Tex had the skills to get them out of this alive, and she prayed for a second chance to stay out of his hair and not give him any grief as he tried to save her neck.

Finally he eased the gun back down. "They're gone," he murmured.

"Who was it?" she whispered. "Could you understand them?"

"Yeah. They were poachers. Talking about their prey."

She sighed in relief. Thank God it hadn't been the Gavronese rebels chasing after them. "What were they hunting?"

"Two Americans."

"What?" Her heart battered against her ribs like a panicked bird trying to escape a cage.

"There's probably a reward out already for anyone who brings us in or sights us."

She gulped. There was a bounty on their heads? "What are we going to do now?" she whispered desperately.

"First, talk low under your breath like I'm doing. The sound of it carries less than whispering. Second, we're going to take down our shelter and get moving."

"Now?" she asked in surprise. "It's pitch black out. And those poachers are still out there!"

"Now," he answered firmly. "They won't expect us to move until morning, and it'll put some distance between us and them that they won't be counting on."

She gulped and crawled gamely out of the shelter.

"Put these on." He handed her the dirty fatigue pants. She scowled at the Almighty's rotten sense of humor.

Did those gnarly pants *have* to be the test of her resolve
to cooperate with Tex?

With a sigh, she shimmied out of her skirt and hose and
slipped on the pants. She then took one step away from
Tex and promptly tripped on a vine. Even though his back
was to her, he whirled and grabbed her before she hit the
ground. Lord, he was fast.

"Give me your shoes," he ordered.

"I beg your pardon?"

"You heard me. Pass them over."

Bemused, she sat down on a log and passed her shoes
to Tex. She winced as he used the knife to saw off most
of each heel. She was all in favor of anything that helped
her move more easily, but she'd really liked those shoes.
Not to mention they'd cost a small fortune. She sighed and
slipped them back on. They felt a hundred percent more
stable beneath her.

"There. Now you can walk a whole lot faster and
safer," he said quietly.

"How am I supposed to move at all when I can't see a
thing?" she murmured in consternation.

"I'll go first." He moved in front of her. "Put your
hand on my back if you need to. Slide your feet forward.
Don't pick them up. Feel your way with the soles of your
feet."

She glided forward awkwardly.

"Good," he murmured. "There'll be a little more light
once we get out of this thicket."

He was right. Once they pushed out of the thick stand
of plants, she was able to make out vague shadows along
the ground. It was still very dark and made for slow going,
but she managed to pick her way over and around obstacles and stay close to Tex.

Before long the uncomfortable chill in the air felt good.
How long she stumbled along, balancing herself against
Tex's powerful back, she had no idea. But eventually she
became aware of a faint gray tinge to the darkness around

them. Panic tickled her stomach. Daylight meant the kidnappers could see better.

"Tex, it's getting light. Shouldn't we take cover or something?"

"I wish," he murmured back. "But we've got to keep moving. It's our only chance. If we sit still, they'll throw a ring of hunters around us and close the net until they find us."

Abruptly the fatigue of a short's night sleep dissipated. Lovely. Now they were prey to a veritable army of hunters. More edgy than ever, she jumped at every noise.

Tex stopped suddenly and turned around. "Kimberly," he said very calmly, "I need you to do something for me."

"What is it?" she asked nervously.

"I need you to take a couple deep breaths and relax. You're kicking in your adrenaline, and you need to save it for when we really need it."

She frowned. "How do you know that?"

"Your hand is shaking on my back and you're breathing at about twice your normal rate."

"Oh." She had to give him credit for being observant, at least. She took a couple deep breaths. And didn't feel any calmer.

Tex reached up and pushed a stray lock of hair back from her face. The gentle gesture startled her. It was incongruous coming from such a hard man.

He spoke quietly. "Whoever's hunting us probably figures we'll panic and run if we hear them. They aren't going to make much effort to be quiet. In fact, they'll probably make noise intentionally to scare us into bolting."

She frowned. She wished she knew more about how this life-and-death game was played. She looked at him questioningly.

He elaborated. "We'll hear the bad guys coming long before they see us. You don't need to worry about them jumping out from behind a tree and shouting 'Boo!'"

Ah. Well now, that *was* reassuring. Her breathing settled down a bit and her heart eased out of her throat.

"Just so you know the plan. If we do encounter the rebels, we're going to hide, wherever we are, and wait them out. Okay?"

She nodded.

"If they find us, I'll take them all out with the rifles. After that, we'll run like hell. But we'll worry about that when the time comes."

The reminder about the pair of deadly rifles slung over his shoulders made her feel much less like a cornered rabbit. Her pulse started to calm down. What exactly did he mean by "taking their pursuers out," though?

Her mind skated away from the obvious answer to that one.

Tex walked along ahead of Kimberly, more worried by the minute. Each time her hand settled lightly on his back, lust shot through him like an armor-piercing round. Each time it happened, it got harder and harder to fight off an urge to turn around and kiss her senseless. Fear of that urge gave him a nearly uncontrollable need to cut and run from her and the sexual shocks tearing through his gut.

That had been a close call back at the shelter. Too close. Not the soldier putting a knife to her throat, although that had been dicey, too. But the way she'd crawled all over him, teasing his body to a fever pitch of desire...he'd very nearly rolled over and ravaged her. He'd walked a razor's edge of self-control and had almost lost it.

What in the hell was he going to do with her?

He pondered the question grimly as they marched onward through the night.

He'd loved two women in his lifetime. And they'd both cut and run when the going got tough.

There was his mother of course. He vaguely remembered her face. She'd been blond and beautiful, too. And she couldn't deal with living way out in the middle of nowhere on a lonely cattle ranch. She'd lasted until he was seven years old and his sister, Susan, was five. And then she'd bailed on her husband and two young children. He was still embarrassed to think about how old he was before he stopped crying himself to sleep each night, his face buried in a pillow so no one would know.

And then there was Emily. His childhood sweetheart. He'd dated her from the moment his dad said he was old enough to have a girlfriend. They were together all the way through high school and college. He always assumed they'd end up married someday. She'd been sweet and gentle, a nice girl. Loyal. Or so he'd thought.

And then he'd come home from his first mission for Charlie Squad, full of pride and still on a high from pulling off a near miraculous mission to capture a dangerous drug lord. He'd never forget the look on Emily's face as he described the details of sneaking close to the guy's compound, shooting all the guards dead, rushing in and arresting the drug lord, and then airlifting him out by helicopter while under fire.

She'd recoiled from him in horror, distaste written all over her face. "You actually enjoyed all that violence and killing?" she'd asked with utter loathing.

She didn't get it. No matter how hard he tried to convince her that he was one of the good guys and was making the world a better place, after that day she only saw a violent, brutal thug when she looked at him. She'd been gone—packed up and moved out—before he got home from his second mission.

After that, he went strictly for groupie chicks who got a thrill out of sleeping with dark, dangerous guys like him. They hung out at all the bars near military bases, waiting to pick up soldiers just in from the field or just about to go out.

They wanted rough sex, a wild ride, and no commitment whatsoever. They didn't give a damn about him or who he was. They just wanted the fantasy of the he-man lover.

It didn't take him long to get sick and tired of them, either. He mostly avoided women now. They either didn't have staying power for when times got tough or were only out for themselves.

Kimberly's hand landed harder than usual against his back. He slowed down until she regained her balance and her hand retreated. Desire shuddered through him.

Kimberly Stanton was the worst of both female worlds. She was appalled by what he did *and* she wanted no part of sticking around. Worse, she was turned on by him. She'd use him and lose him without a second thought. Clearly she was a woman he'd be well advised to stay far, far away from.

A new sound disturbed the usual noises of the jungle. He spun and yanked her down beneath him, rolling with her until they lay under a thick stand of brush.

Her breasts pressed against his chest, her long legs tangled with his. Her belly contracted hard against his and the blatantly sexual position they lay in made his breath come in short bursts.

He listened intently.

There it was again. A rustling. Sudden silence from the birds. Three, maybe four, people moving off to their left on a parallel course. They lay there for many minutes, long after the noise had faded away and the birds had resumed their regular cacophony of sound.

He looked down into Kimberly's terrified eyes. "You okay?" he murmured.

"I'm slightly crushed, but otherwise fine, thank you."

He rolled off of her immediately. "Sorry. It's part of my training to put myself between hostile shooters and whoever I'm protecting. I do it without thinking."

She gazed at him intently. "You jumped on top of me to shield me?"

Inexplicably he was embarrassed. "Well, yeah," he answered gruffly.

"That's so sweet."

"Honey, I'm a lot of things," he growled, "but sweet sure as shootin' ain't one of them."

She laughed lightly and sat up. "I'll be the judge of that."

He stood up cautiously and had a look around before reaching down to help her to her feet.

"What's this?" she murmured at his extended hand. "Are you actually displaying civilized manners to me?"

His attention jerked from the jungle around them to her. "Contrary to what you seem to think, I am not a Neanderthal," he bit out.

"Oh, so it's just kissing me that brings out that side of you?"

He scowled at her smiling face and spun way. What could he say to that? Kissing her did bring out the caveman in him.

What did he care anyway about what she thought of his manners or lack of them? His job was to get her the hell out of this jungle, send her back to her hoity-toity life, and get on with his.

He picked up the pace, angling their course away from the last position of the people they'd just encountered. They walked until late in the afternoon, stopping only to drink water when they came across little pools of it, and to catch their breath. He didn't even take time to smear her in the mud-and-grass camo he'd promised her. Visibility wasn't their problem. Time was.

Tex stopped abruptly when he noticed a tall cluster of dried mud towers off to their right. Bingo. He veered toward the man-high, cone-shaped structures.

"What in the world is that?" Kimberly asked as they approached it.

"Supper," he replied jovially.

"We're eating mud for supper?" she asked skeptically.

"Nope, we're eating the termite grubs inside."

Shock apparently rendered her speechless and she watched in rather comic dismay as he found a long, sturdy stick and began digging at the base of the tower. When he'd dug down about three feet, he found what he was looking for. Fat, white, inch-long, termite larvae. He picked up several and held them out to her.

"You've got to be kidding," she declared in disbelief.

"Not at all. They're a good source of protein." He popped one in his mouth and swallowed it. "No need to chew it. Just toss it down like a pill."

She glared at him darkly. "You're doing this to get even with me for crawling all over you last night, aren't you?"

"I don't have any idea what you're talking about," he answered evenly.

"You know exactly what I'm talking about. This is petty and it's beneath you, Tex Monroe. I insist that you get me some decent food to eat."

He stood up to his full height slowly. "Kimberly, this is a South American jungle. The Russian Tea Room is not just around the corner. If I had all damn day to hunt for something tasty, and I don't, I *might* be able to come up with something higher class than this, like maybe a rat, for you to eat."

Her delicate jaw set in stubborn lines.

He'd had just about enough of her aristocratic, holier-than-thou routine. He stepped close and growled down at her through clenched jaws, "There are people, probably a lot of them, hunting us right now. This situation is dangerous and the cards are stacked way against us. I'm out here, completely unprepared, busting my ass to save your tush, and I'd appreciate it if you could see fit to give me a little cooperation."

Her eyes abruptly filled with tears, their emerald depths swimming with misery, fatigue, hunger and fright.

Aw, hell.

He pulled her close, wrapping her in a tight hug. She sobbed against his chest, muffling the sound for the most part. He hated the feel of her shaking in his arms, her whole frame trembling as she cried out her fear and stress.

He wanted to make it all better. But there was just no easy way out of this. Frustration twisted his gut.

It was a couple minutes before she lifted her head and looked up at him. Tear tracks streaked her ivory cheeks. Somehow she managed to look beautiful even with red, puffy eyes and a runny nose. Hell, she even cried classy.

"Feel better?" he asked gruffly.

"Not really. But at least I'm not holding all that in anymore."

"Well, that's something," he replied wryly. He looked down at the ground and then back up at her. "I wish I could wave a magic wand and make this all go away. But I can't. We've just got to press on and do the best we can."

She nodded on a wobbly breath.

"I'm in this with you to the end, Princess. Whatever happens to you happens to me. We either make it out together or we go down together. Okay?"

She gazed up at him seriously. "You know as well as I do that you could make it out of here without any trouble if you were alone. If the situation becomes hopeless, why wouldn't you cut your losses and at least get out yourself?"

He blinked in surprise. "That's not how we do business in Charlie Squad. We all make it out together or not at all."

"You honestly wouldn't abandon me if it came down to a choice of both of us dying or saving yourself?" Disbelief filled her voice.

What or who had turned her into such a cynic? With a finger under her chin, he tilted her face up and forced her to look him in the eye. "Kimberly, I am a man of my word. I have told you the way it's going to be and I mean it. It'll be all or nothing with us. Got it?"

She stared at him with a combination of skepticism and pain. "Heroes only exist in comic books, Tex," she whispered in a choked voice.

He snorted inelegantly. "Heroes are all around you, every day. They come in all shapes and sizes. Sometimes they perform tiny acts of courage and sometimes they pull off stunts so spectacular you wonder where they even got the notion to try."

She shook her head, denying the truth of what he said.

His gut clenched with a need to convince her she was wrong. "Heroes are the family members who've lost loved ones to tragedy but go on. They're the teachers who work with kids society's given up on." He cast around for more examples. "What about single parents? Hell, people with lousy jobs they hate, but who go to work every day rather than take a handout. The world is full of people doing decent, brave, honorable things."

She answered quietly, "That's where you and I are different. You look for the best in people and I see the worst."

"Who did a number on you to make you like this?" he asked angrily.

She shrugged. A world of pain—and the unspoken answer to his question—shone in her eyes. She knew who'd made a cynic out of her, all right. Ten to one her old man had something to do with it.

But he'd pushed enough for one day. He backed off, literally and figuratively, and kicked the termite mound. He ate several more handfuls of the larvae quickly. If he found some "real" food for Kimberly, he'd let her have all of it.

"Let's get going," he said quietly. "There's another hour of good light left."

She sighed and fell in behind him.

He added over his shoulder, "I'll keep an eye out for something non-disgusting for you to eat."

Her hand touched his back lightly. "Thank you," she murmured.

He wasn't entirely certain what she was thanking him for, but he nodded in response.

They'd walked about twenty minutes when, abruptly, he heard noise. Off to their right this time. He hit the dirt with Kimberly until the sound of people passing retreated.

A sinking feeling settled in his stomach. This was not good. Not good at all.

Chapter 6

Kimberly sensed the tension in Tex as they crouched behind a bunch of roots. Something was seriously wrong. Well, in the current context, more wrong than usual.

She listened hard and heard the faint sounds of people passing by, more muted conversation in Spanish. They sounded farther away than the last bunch who'd come close. Why was Tex so much more uptight about it this time?

She opened her mouth to ask him, but then caught the expression on his face. Oh, God. He looked worried.

He gestured at her with his hands. She got the impression he wanted her to stay put while he went and had a look around. She nodded uncertainly. He moved off in a crouch, disappearing into the heavy undergrowth.

She curled up in a little ball, hugging her knees to her chest. She'd thought she knew what fear was before this jungle adventure. But she'd been wrong. This gut-wrenching, deadly serious, life-on-the-line stuff brought her concept of fear to a whole new level.

Had her father been this afraid in Vietnam? Had he ultimately cracked under the pressure of living up to people's expectations after the magazine spreads raving about what a brave guy he was? Was that why he'd burst into his unreasoning rages for all those years after the war, screaming in some Asian language and attacking anything and anyone who happened to be near him?

Lord knew, she was having a hard time living up to Tex's expectations of her, and all he wanted her to do was follow along behind him and eat some bugs. How could Tex do a job like this day after day, putting his life on the line for total strangers like her? Why did he court fear like this?

He could've jumped out of that truck alone and gotten away easily on his own. Why hadn't he taken the easy way out? Was he right? Did heroes really exist? Was he one of them?

She jumped violently when a hand touched her arm.

"Easy, darlin'," Tex murmured. "There's a patrol of four guys ahead and to our right. And there are three guys paralleling our course on the left. I want to turn around and go back the way we came for a little while and see if there's anyone behind us."

She frowned. Something he'd said the night before tickled her memory. Something about a net closing in... "Have they surrounded us?" she gasped, her heart in her throat.

"Maybe. That's what I want to find out."

She looked wildly all around her.

He held her shoulders in his big, steady hands. "Don't panic on me, Princess. I know what to do in a situation like this, okay? Nothing that's happening here is beyond the scope of my training. You've got to trust me."

Like she had any choice in the matter. She nodded her understanding. She stood up when he did, and walked nervously behind him as they eased back toward the south.

Funny, but she actually did trust him. They might not

make it out of this alive, but if anyone *could* pull it off, that person was Tex. Now if only she could soak up some of his confidence. They hiked until the light began to fail and the lush green palate of the jungle had faded to gray.

Tex stopped abruptly and veered off to one side, motioning her to stay put. She saw him squat down. He appeared to dig at something at ground level with his knife. He came back in a few seconds and they continued on. What was that all about?

Her speculations were cut short by another sharp signal from Tex to get down. She dived to the ground, her heart pounding.

He belly-crawled into a thicket, gesturing over his shoulder for her to do the same. She pushed with her feet and dug in with her elbows. She moved a couple inches.

Ugh. How was Tex slithering along so effortlessly in front of her? New respect for his strength washed over her. She scrambled forward by inches, breaking several fingernails in the process of sliming along behind him. She breathed a sigh of relief when he stopped under a heavy stand of plants.

Something moved on the ground in front of her. She lurched in surprise. It moved again. It was the biggest ant she'd ever seen, dragging an entire leaf across the ground. She shuddered. At least it wasn't a snake. She hated them with a passion. Oh, she knew snakes were good for the environment and rodent control and all that, but gut-level, hard-wired terror threatened her whenever she saw one, even on television.

"Stay here," Tex murmured.

He disappeared again. He was gone longer this time and night had fallen by the time he came back. She didn't hear him this time, either, but she sensed his presence a second before he touched her arm.

He moved up beside her on the ground. His body was warm and reassuring against hers. She rolled into his strength, glad when his arms gathered her close. His hands roamed up and down her back, rubbing soothingly.

"Miss me?" he murmured.

More than he knew. And certainly more than she was willing to admit to him.

He breathed into her ear, "As I thought. We're pretty much surrounded on three sides. For some reason, the patrols are herding us to the north."

"Herding us?" she murmured in dismay. That didn't sound good at all.

"Yeah. They don't know exactly where we are, but they know the general vicinity. They've established a tight line of troops in a U-shape and are moving steadily to the north. We either keep moving in that direction or they'll catch us."

"Why do they want us to go that way?"

"Don't know. Maybe they have a camp up north, or maybe your kidnappers are waiting in that direction."

Panic clutched at her. "We're trapped?"

"Not by a long shot, darlin'."

"What are we going to do?"

"For now, we get some rest. The patrols I saw have camped for the night and they won't be closing in on us anytime soon. You're dead on your feet, so we're going to take a break."

He sat up and reached into his shirt. "Speaking of which, I found these for you." He held out several gnarled sticks the thickness of her wrist.

She sat up beside him and took the dirt-encrusted objects. "Uh, thank you?" she said questioningly.

He grinned, a flash of white in the dark. "They're edible roots." He took one from her and peeled it with the knife, exposing pale flesh.

"The plant it comes from is related to ginger. Tastes pretty good. It doesn't have a lot of nutritive value, but it'll fill your stomach."

Right now, that was just fine with her. Her stomach felt about ready to gnaw its way through her spine.

She took the hunk he sliced off for her and put it in her mouth. It did taste faintly of ginger. It was the texture of a raw potato and hard to chew, but she felt worlds better when she'd finally eaten her fill of it.

"Come here," he said, holding out an arm to her.

She sank gratefully into his embrace. His chest was a warm, reassuring wall and his heart thumped slow and steady underneath her ear.

His arm settled comfortably around her shoulders. "Get some sleep if you can. We're going to move out hard in a few hours."

She groaned into his shirt. He reached up to massage her neck and shoulders. His strong hands used just the right amount of gentle pressure to melt away the kinks in her muscles.

"Don't think about it now," he murmured. "It'll be time to go soon enough. Just concentrate on relaxing and staying in the moment."

The moment frankly wasn't that bad. Tex was warm and strong and relaxed. Her last thought before she drifted off to sleep was that, for a trained killer, he wasn't such a bad guy.

It seemed like only minutes later when he gently shook her awake with a murmured, "Time to go."

She groaned under her breath. Her back, legs and shoulders ached like she'd been lifting rocks.

"How long was I asleep?" she mumbled.

"Four hours. It's midnight. Time to rock and roll."

The tension in his voice sounded almost like enjoyment. Nah. Nobody could get a rush out of running for their lives in a pitch-black jungle in the middle of the night.

Tex sprang to his feet energetically.

Darned if he didn't look hyped up about the trek to come. "You're not actually enjoying this, are you?" she asked in amazement.

He blinked down at her. "This is what it's all about. I don't enjoy being in danger, but..." He searched for words. "This is the moment when I show those bastards out there why I'm the best and they're not."

Thank goodness he was on her side in this game of cat-and-mouse.

"Grab on to my shirt and don't let go," he instructed. "We're going to move fast tonight. I'll try to describe what's coming by way of terrain if nobody's close. But if I hear anything and go silent, just try to feel through my movements what's coming in front of you."

Fast didn't do justice to the way they tore through the jungle. It was like riding a roller coaster with her eyes closed.

She had to hustle to keep up with him, and more than once found herself hanging on to his shirt and practically letting him drag her along. The big sniper rifle banged into her wrist until she shifted her grasp to Tex's belt. That worked well and they settled into a rhythm together. She did, in fact, learn rapidly how to gauge what obstacle came next by how the muscles in his back contracted or stretched.

She felt like an extension of his body and they moved practically as one. They settled into an almost sexual rhythm of Tex leading the way and her mimicking his every movement down to the smallest nuance.

Kimberly reached out with her mind, trying to "see" the movement of Tex's body. She felt his every breath, his every tensing at a new sound, his total awareness of everything around them. His essence flowed over her and through her until she felt him in her blood, in her bones.

He stopped now and then for brief rest breaks. But even then, the deep connection between them didn't cease. She felt it each time he lifted his head to listen, each time he used his intuition to test the jungle around them for the presence of others.

The hunter in him permeated her. The way he embraced

the velvety-black darkness, became a part of the night, she sensed it all. It was completely unlike anything she'd ever experienced before. It was primitive and wild, a heady thing to have power over. No wonder Tex relished this.

He didn't have to tell her when he was ready to head out again. She just knew. She stood up with a quick stretch of her tired back muscles.

Big, hard hands settled on her waist and slid around to her back. His knuckles dug deeply into the muscles there, wringing a groan of delight from her. His arms tightened, pulling her close. He picked her up easily and held her against him for several seconds, her feet dangling just above the ground. Her spine creaked and stretched deliciously. It felt wonderful to be surrounded by so much male power.

"Better?" he murmured.

She blinked. Better? Most definitely. "I could use some more of that," she purred.

"When we stop for the night, remind me to pick you up again. It helps align the spine."

Her spine… Right. Her spine. She frowned at his shadowed form.

A brief flash of his teeth. "That was what you were talking about, wasn't it?" he murmured.

"Of course," she mumbled.

"Mmm, hmm," he replied with laughter in his voice. "Come on, Princess. Let's shock the hell out of these goons and really put some distance between us and them."

Tingling from head to foot, she grabbed on to his belt once more and resumed the trek. The psychic link between them now held a distinctly sexual edge. Every time her hand rubbed along his spine, every brush of his leg against hers, every abrupt halt that brought her chest into contact with his back took on new sizzle.

The chemistry between them grew until its carnal energy buffeted them both in its grasp.

Finally, Tex stopped again. "Time for a rest break." He

listened for a long moment and Kimberly felt the release of tension as he heard nothing untoward.

"Come here," he growled low under his breath.

She stepped forward, unable and unwilling to deny the power of what had been building between them for the last several hours.

"This is insane," he mumbled as his arms swept around her, "but damned if I can hold out any longer."

She exhaled on a breath of laughter. "If we're going to die, we may as well snatch what pleasure we can from the jaws of death."

He apparently bought that logic, because his mouth closed on hers voraciously, devouring her with raging hunger.

She flung herself into the kiss with abandon. Everything else had been stripped away from her in the past couple days, and only two things remained. Life and Death. Within that elegantly simple framework, their relationship became equally simple. He was Man and she was Woman.

She reveled in the way her body cushioned his, how her soft curves molded to his hard angles. Their mouths and bodies melded together like two molten bars of steel, flowing into one another until they became a single burning pillar of desire.

He carried her down to the cool ground, but it did nothing to slake the fire or temper the steel of their lust. They burned on, tongues and lips mating wildly, their arms and legs in a tangle, their bodies fitting to one another with seething, liquid perfection.

He pushed her hands up over her head, pinning her in place while his mouth slid down her throat, branding her his. His free hand slid under her sweater, pushing aside the soft knit and plunging into her bra to cup her flesh.

She arched up into him, frantic for more of his skin against hers. She felt the hard ridge of his desire and clasped her upper thighs around his heat, desperate to pull him into her, to make him part of her and her part of him.

His mouth closed on her breast and she bucked against the fiery heat of his mouth on her skin. His hips moved against hers and she matched the movement, their bodies completely synchronized over the last several hours.

She ached to cradle him even closer, to grasp his hardness with secret muscles, to wrench groans of pleasure from his throat that would mingle with the ones he was tearing from hers.

She yanked her hands free and ran them up under his fatigue shirt, relishing the smooth glide of flesh on muscle. She memorized the feel of him under her hands. Her palms slid to the small of his back, urging him nearer, pressing him closer to the aching, liquid core of her.

She wriggled beneath him and reached for his belt buckle. The clothes had to go. She wanted to feel all of him against her naked skin.

His hands closed over hers, his palms swallowing her fingers easily. "I'd give just about anything to finish this, sweetheart," he gritted out, "but I'm not willing to give your life. We've got to stop."

She closed her eyes in anguish. For a little while, a couple blessed minutes, she'd forgotten. It all came crashing back. The return of reality was almost more than she could bear after its momentary absence.

"I'm sorry, Kimberly," he said raggedly. He didn't sound like he was in much better shape than she was.

She peered up at his shadowed face, inches above hers. "Please tell me that meant *something* to you. You don't have to admit that it blew you away. Just don't let that have been a random moment with the nearest convenient female because you think you're going to die."

"Kimberly. You are not a groupie chick."

"A…huh?" she asked, confused.

"Never mind. Believe me," he breathed, his voice laced with laughter. "You're most definitely not a convenient female."

She punched his arm lightly. "Jerk," she murmured back.

He dropped a light kiss on her forehead and pushed up to his feet abruptly. He reached down and pulled her up beside him. "We both needed that. Consider it a reminder to us of why we want to live."

Kimberly stared at his back as he turned and offered her his belt once more. Was it also a promise of things to come if they got out of this mess alive?

A relationship with Tex Monroe? Her? Abruptly the thought didn't seem far-fetched at all.

Chapter 7

That was truly insane. Tex plowed forward through the jungle, completely stunned by what he'd just done. They were running for their *lives* from kidnappers who were right on their heels! Every second, every step, counted, but he'd taken time to stop and roll around on the ground with the woman whose life he was responsible for.

He realized he was all but jogging through the underbrush. He slowed his steps to a more reasonable pace. No sense running Kimberly into the ground. It wasn't her fault he couldn't keep his hands off her.

Sexual tension had been building between them for hours. He'd finally reached the breaking point where he couldn't take another minute of the sensual promise of her fingers against his back, her knees bumping into the backs of his, her breasts pressing against him every time he stopped abruptly. It had gotten so bad he'd made excuses to stop fast just so he could feel those mounds of sweet flesh collide with him.

The precious minutes lost had bloody well been worth

it, though. He'd never experienced a kiss like that before. It incinerated him from the inside out. God Almighty, that woman drove him out of his mind with lust. Kissing her didn't just blow him away, it blew him completely out of the water. Completely out of the solar system!

Stopping her from ripping his clothes off had been one of the hardest things he'd ever had to do in his entire life. Now, *that* had been an act of heroism. He ought to get a damned medal for that act of self-discipline.

Tree branches were whipping past his face again and Kimberly was breathing hard behind him. He slowed down for a second time.

Suicide.

The word came to him unbidden. But as soon as it popped into his mind, he knew it to be true. Messing around with Kimberly Stanton here and now was pure suicide.

He'd been a damned fool to give in to his lust. And he *was* going to get them both killed if he didn't pull himself together and get his mind back on business.

The kidnappers had a general idea of where they were and were using their superior numbers to surround a large area and close the net, just as he'd described to Kimberly.

Tonight's trek might buy them a day or so, but no more. She'd held up well so far and was in good physical condition for a civilian female. But there was no way she could move as fast as they'd have to for them to outrun the net behind them.

If she were a trained commando, they could double back and slip through the net of rebel soldiers. But that also wasn't an option for him with a complete amateur in tow.

Their only choice was to go along with this herding maneuver, realizing that they were headed for some kind of a trap. Their survival was going to hinge on his seeing the trap soon enough and finding a way out of it before the rebels sprung it on them.

The end game was going to be chancy at best. He was

going to have to be at the very top of his form to get them out alive.

And to do that, he damn well had to lay off of kissing Kimberly.

He dug deep for the determination that sustained him in the toughest of situations. He channeled it, shaped it into a kernel of pitiless self-discipline. He ripped every thought out of his mind but one. Staying alive.

Brutally he suppressed the feel of her soft hand at his waist, squashed the memory of her mouth opening beneath his, her tongue dancing and enticing his, her body welcoming him.

Staying alive, dammit!

Lust later. Survival now.

He pushed forward through the jungle. When his watch read 5:00 a.m., he called a halt. Kimberly sagged beside him. He didn't bother to make a shelter. He just crawled beneath an overhang of thick vines, spread the space blanket over them, and went unconscious.

His watch alarm vibrated silently against his wrist an hour later.

Grimly he fought off the insidious pleasure of Kimberly's warm, sleek body against his. He denied himself the lingering wake-up kiss that was his first impulse to give her, and he merely shook her lightly awake.

"Time to go," he bit out past the rigid wall of his self-restraint. He folded the space blanket and stuffed it into a pocket, ready to resume their flight.

Kimberly rubbed her eyes and looked around, groggy. She'd been deeply asleep and was having trouble orienting herself.

Tex was frowning impatiently.

But then, he'd been that way for a while last night. The searing kiss they'd shared took on an unreal, dreamlike quality in her mind.

Had it even happened?

It had to have. No way could she have imagined the uncontrollable passion that had consumed her, especially since she'd had no idea such sexual fury existed until Tex wrapped her in his arms and carried her to the ground.

He moved out, and she fell into place behind him. There was enough light to see by, so she didn't grab on to his belt. But she missed the subliminal link between them.

He seemed so…distant…this morning.

Maybe he was feeling the stress. He'd gotten as little rest as she had, and she was absolutely beat. The idea of even five or six hours of uninterrupted sleep sounded like heaven. She stumbled along behind him as the jungle faded from gray to pale mint to a hundred shades of vibrant green.

The rainforest was growing decidedly more moist. The ground was spongier beneath her feet, the soil black and damp. Humidity-loving orchids and ferns abounded, and the foliage became almost impassably thick at times. Even the animal noises sounded richer and more abundant.

The terrain began to slope gently but steadily downhill. It was a relief to her sore muscles, but it also worried her. Did it signal the beginning of whatever trap lay ahead of them?

Tex hadn't said it in so many words, but something bad waited in front of them. Unfortunately the rebels hadn't left them any choice but to walk into whatever it was.

Tex was grouchy and taciturn this morning, which wasn't like him at all. Something was up.

"So, Tex, what's on the agenda today? Swinging on vines and wrestling lions with our bare hands?"

He grunted and didn't deign to answer. That was odd. He was always quick with a snappy comeback. He just kept walking.

She frowned at his retreating back. She'd started to believe that he was different from her father. But this brooding mood of Tex's was very similar to ones she'd seen from her dad. Particularly right before he had one of his blowups.

The old fear tickled just beneath the surface of her thoughts. She found herself falling into old patterns of trying to become invisible, of not provoking Tex in any way.

They stopped briefly to harvest more of the ginger root, but Tex made her eat it on the move. When its pungent taste and woody texture started to get old, she thought about termites and the tough root suddenly held gourmet appeal.

They walked for what had to be several hours without any breaks at all. Kimberly began to feel light-headed. Her feet stopped cooperating, and she felt on the verge of collapse. As badly as she didn't want to trigger a blowup in Tex, she had no choice. "Tex," she called quietly.

He turned around with a scowl.

"I'm sorry," she gasped, completely out of breath. "I've got to stop."

His scowl deepened noticeably.

"Just a minute or two," she added apologetically as she sank to the ground.

He was beside her instantly. "What's up?" he asked shortly.

"I feel lousy."

"Dizzy? Sick to your stomach? Light-headed? Weak? Hot?"

"All of the above," she gasped.

"To be expected. Fatigue, hunger, stress…they're all hitting you at once. Your blood sugar's probably dropped off the bottom of the chart. We'll give your liver a few minutes to dump its emergency store of sugar and then you'll feel better. Put your head between your knees and breathe normally."

Like she could do anything normally at the moment! Her heart raced weakly. Dear God, please let him not blow a gasket right now. She was too tired to protect herself from it.

She put her head down on her knees and breathed deeply. Gradually she felt blood return to her head and the rumbling nausea in her stomach subsided.

She looked up. Tex stood over her protectively, rifle at the ready, his gaze roving all around as he waited for her to get up and get going again.

"Are the bad guys that close?" she asked.

"Close enough. I figure we'll be wherever they wanted us to go in the next twenty-four hours or so. We need to get there before they expect us to."

Wherever *there* was. Fear of what lay ahead clenched her stomach in yet another nasty knot. She took a couple deep breaths and climbed to her knees gamely. God, she felt awful. But when the choice was awful or dead, she'd take the former.

Tex held down a hand to her. Gratefully she took it and let him tug her to her feet. He didn't let go of her hand. He tugged again, pulling her gently into his arms.

"You okay?" he murmured.

Relief washed over her like cool rain. He hadn't lost control like her father would have. There'd been no raging, no frightening outbursts. Just a quiet question of concern.

"I'm better now," she breathed.

He pressed a fleeting kiss on her forehead and released her. It happened so fast, she almost wasn't sure it had happened. She blinked up at him in shock. Such a gentle gesture. One of reassurance. Affection, even.

He looked at her for a long moment with those beautiful turquoise eyes of his, like he wanted to say something. Finally he just nodded and turned around. She fell into place behind him, bemused. What in the world had that been all about? Had she read his intent correctly? Was he starting to have feelings? For her?

Tex pushed forward relentlessly. The day was overcast, which held down the temperatures, but the humidity was stifling. At times she felt like she was swimming rather than walking.

Late in the afternoon it rained. Raindrops pelted the tens of thousands of leaves around them, creating a deafening barrage of sound.

Tex, of course, took advantage of the din to go all the faster. She actually had to break into a jog to keep up with the blistering pace he set.

A stitch started in her side and stabbed her beneath her left ribs. She just gritted her teeth and kept going. How, she didn't know. But somehow she kept putting one foot in front of the other.

She slammed into Tex from behind when he abruptly stopped. The ground dropped away in front of him. Another sound became audible. Water flowing.

She moved up beside him and looked down at a good-size stream. It flowed nearly parallel to their course, almost due north. Tex nodded slowly beside her and she saw a grim smile touch his mouth. Uh-oh. She'd lay odds he was thinking up something she wasn't going to like.

"Let's go for a river walk," he murmured.

When she thought of river walks, she thought of romantic strolls down artistically lit pathways that meandered beside a river. Oh, no. Tex meant *in* the river. Above her knees in icy water.

The water was cold enough to make her bite back a squeal when she stepped in. Tex wouldn't let her take off her shoes, either. Something about cutting her feet and getting an infection from the water. She prayed her Versace shoes wouldn't disintegrate when submerged like this.

"Hey, Romeo," she called lowly. "An important dating tip. Most girls like to walk beside rivers, not in them."

He grinned back at her. "Thanks, Juliet. But I mostly stick to balcony scenes when I wax romantic."

She rolled her eyes and splashed forward. The first dozen steps or so were all right. And then "river walking" became unbelievably hard work. She had her choice of lifting her feet high out of the water for each step, which wiped out her thigh muscles, or of dragging her feet forward against the buffeting weight of the water, which was equally exhausting in its own right.

She alternated between the two methods, stumbling along the uneven bottom of the stream, the swirling water doing its best to throw her off balance.

The first time she fell down, the abrupt dunking in frigid water stole her breath away. She staggered to her feet, her clothes heavy and soaked. Shivering and miserable, she somehow managed to slog onward.

By the fourth or fifth time she stumbled to her knees, she was so cold and so soaked she no longer cared if she fell down or not. At least it was a bath of sorts. Maybe her borrowed pants would smell a little better now.

How long they walked in that blasted stream, she had no idea. An hour, maybe. It felt like a week.

She was so relieved she nearly cried when Tex finally climbed out on the far side of the water and plopped down on a low, grassy bank. "That," she said through chattering teeth, "was almost more fun than should be legal."

He nodded tersely. "In case they're using tracking dogs, that'll slow them down by several hours while they try to pick up our scent again."

"Hopefully, my scent's improved after that impromptu bath," she commented.

Another short nod. She supposed she should be consoled by the fact that the past hour seemed to have taken some of the starch out of him, too.

"Get a good drink now," he admonished. "This may be our last shot at water for another day or so."

In another day or so, they might be dead. She pushed the thought out of her head. She was just scared and exhausted.

Tex flipped over on his belly and hung his head out over the edge of the stream. Using his hand to scoop up the water, he took a long drink.

She watched, fascinated at the movement of the muscles

and tendons in his neck as he drank. The sheer power of the man was overwhelming.

She mimicked his actions. If anyone had told her three days ago that she'd be lying on her belly in a jungle, lapping up water from a river like a dog while kidnappers chased her, she'd have thought it was the most absurd thing she'd ever heard.

Her stomach ached from drinking so much cold water so fast. She sat upright and wiped her mouth with the back of her hand. Tex was craning around awkwardly, apparently patting himself down.

"Give me your leg," Tex ordered abruptly.

"Excuse me?"

He reached over and grabbed her foot, yanking her whole leg toward him. He pushed her pant leg up.

"Yup. Thought so."

She looked down at a dark brown smudge on her calf. "What's that?"

His one word answer sent chills of horror rippling up her spine. "Leech."

"Get it off!" she exclaimed.

"Hush!" he murmured sharply.

"Well, do something!" she murmured back urgently.

"Best way to get 'em off is with a little salt, but we don't have any. I could cut it off, but I don't need you bleeding all over the place and we've got no bandages. A cut like that would infect for sure."

She shuddered. "I don't care what you do. Just get it off of me."

He pulled out the cigarette lighter. "Let's see if a little persuasion by fire works. This may get uncomfortable," he warned.

"Just do it," she gritted out between her clenched teeth.

He flicked the lighter and held the flame against the leech's back. The heat burned her skin before the creature finally curled backward, releasing its hold on her. Tex grabbed the squishy thing between his fingers and flung it back into the stream.

"Let's have a look at the rest of you."

Kimberly blinked, shocked by his suggestion. Tex Monroe's eyes caressing every part of her body? The very thought pushed her body temperature into the feverish range. "I beg your pardon?"

"Strip. You fell in the water a number of times. You could have more leeches anywhere."

She shuddered from head to foot, her skin suddenly tingling with a thousand creatures crawling and sliming across her skin. She tore off her ragged sweater and cloying pants. "Oh, God," she said thickly. "Get them off of me!"

Tex inspected her closely, running his hands through her hair, and even checking her armpits. He was quick and impersonal about it, and she didn't know whether to be relieved or disappointed.

He found two more leeches, both on her lower legs. He successfully burned them both off, although the combination of the bite and the burn left ugly red welts on her skin.

She suddenly wanted a hot shower and a good hard scrub more than just about anything in the world. Her skin felt literally alive with creeping creatures, their tiny, sharp feet pricking her flesh. The horror of it nearly did her in.

When Tex finished inspecting her clothes and declared them free of vermin, she reluctantly shrugged back into the soggy, heavy garments. Their clammy wetness did nothing to alleviate the awful sensations racing across her skin.

Tex interrupted her waking nightmare. "Since you're already wet, and we happen to be near water, we probably ought to go ahead and camouflage ourselves."

"You mean, the mud-and-grass routine?" she asked in dismay.

"Yup."

How much worse could this day get? Her need to break down and sob grew nearly overwhelming. She couldn't go on. She didn't have it in her to deal with one more trial.

Tex glanced up at her, his gaze keen. After a long moment he spoke, his voice low-key, like he'd speak to a skittish horse. "You're doing good, Princess. Real good."

His simple words were soothing balm upon her soul. With a single remark he'd calmed her frayed nerves enough for her to go on. She took several deep, cleansing breaths.

She could do this. Tex wouldn't ask all this of her if he didn't think she could do it. An abrupt need to live up to his expectations spurred her to her feet.

She sighed, steeling herself for another horror. He was only asking her to get dirty. That was all. No eating termites, no more slimy, sucking creatures attached to her flesh. She could make like a pig in swill.

She followed him as he walked along the riverbank for a dozen yards until he found what he wanted. A deposit of gray-green clay. She watched in disgust as he reached down and scooped up two generous handfuls of the goop and smeared them on his face.

He looked up at her and grinned. "I always did want to make mud pies with a princess. Come on in and join the fun."

She squatted beside him. "Do I have to do the hair, too?"

"Yup. The whole deal. Head to foot. Easiest way is to just lie down and roll in it."

She scowled at him. "If you make one crack about mud wrestling with me, I'll…I'll kick your shins!"

His smile flashed white out of the wet mud covering his face. "Thanks for the warning. I'd hate to see the damage you could do to my poor, innocent shins."

Gingerly she stretched out on her back. The clay squished beneath her, making sick, sucking noises. She rolled to the side. Her hair felt heavy and wet.

Eeww.

She rolled all the way over, her eyes screwed shut. The mud was wet and cold and indescribably slimy. She wriggled around in it and then pulled herself free of the muck. She pushed up on to her hands and knees. Her sweater sagged away from her stomach, coated in the heavy mud.

The poor sweater was done for. This was the last indignity the fine angora would tolerate. But one ruined sweater was the least of her problems.

She sighed and pushed to her feet. Using her hands, she smeared more of the gunk on her face. "How do I look?" she asked, wincing.

He grinned reluctantly. "Do you really want me to answer that?"

"Not especially."

He scrubbed some mud into his hair like it was shampoo. From under his hands he commented, "I bet you've paid good money at a fancy spa to have somebody else do this to you."

"You're right." She laughed ruefully. "And you can bet I'll never do it again, either."

"Let's just get you out of here in one piece so you can reconsider that in a few years."

She nodded while he grabbed a couple handfuls of mud and hit the spots she'd missed—the back of her neck and around her ears. The sensation of mud smearing on those sensitive places was almost more gross than she could stand. But somehow she survived the operation.

Rolling around in the grass was much easier. The only problem with that was bits of it had a tendency to poke her once they were embedded in her covering of mud. "How do I look?" she asked.

"All breaded and ready to fry," Tex laughed.

She stuck her tongue out at him.

Fits of shuddering disgust plagued her for the next hour or so. Her hair dried into long, hard spikes that were almost more than she could bear. They actually rattled when she turned her head fast. The mud formed a rough crust on her skin, and her flesh felt like it was shrinking and cracking all over her body.

She was thoroughly sick of the never-ending ocean of green around them. Even the sky was nothing more than a curtain of green leaves in the canopy of the jungle, a hundred and fifty feet overhead.

And just when she thought she couldn't get any more miserable, Tex announced they were going to keep moving after dark. She staggered along behind him, so fatigued she could hardly see straight. Time slowed to a stop and her whole existence consisted of the next minute.

And then it narrowed down to the next step.

When she was sure she'd reached the end of her rope, somehow she found a few more steps in her rubbery legs. And a few more. And a few more after that.

It was, simply put, torture.

When Tex finally halted, almost twenty-four hours into their forced march, she no longer cared that she was caked in mud, hungry, thirsty, or running for her life. She only wanted to stop and never move again.

"Okay, that's enough," Tex said quietly. "Let's get some rest."

She nodded wearily. She noticed vaguely that he was looking up into the trees.

He walked over to the base of a big tree wrapped in vines and gestured to her. "After you," he murmured.

"Aren't you going to build us a shelter or find us something to crawl under?" she asked in confusion.

"Tonight we climb a tree," he said casually.

"We do *what?*" The idea refused to compute in her numb brain.

"Think in three dimensions for a minute. Everyone who's chasing us in thinking in two dimensions. They expect us to run around the jungle floor. So, we're heading up there. It'll be safer." He pointed up into the trees.

Her mushy brain saw the logic, but her mushier legs

thought it was a lousy idea. She'd reached the point where she had no mental or physical reserves left to cope with anything new he threw at her. "Tex, I've never climbed a tree in my life. How am I supposed to do this?" she asked helplessly.

"Just put your hands and feet where I tell you to. I'm coming right behind you, so if you slip, I'll be there to catch you."

That was small comfort as he talked her so far up the tree she couldn't even see the ground anymore. If she fell from this height, kidnappers would be the least of her problems.

Finally he murmured from behind her, "See that pair of branches just to your left?"

"The big ones that run side by side?" she replied.

"Yup. Straddle the nearest one, facing away from the tree trunk."

She did as he directed.

Nimbly he scrambled onto the branch beside hers and leaned back against the tree trunk. He pulled a couple pieces of rope out of a pants' pocket. "Now we're going to tie ourselves to the tree so we can get some sleep without falling out of the damn thing."

She sat still while he lashed her torso snugly to the tree and did the same for himself.

He smiled jauntily at her. "It's not the comforts of home, darlin', but do your best to get some rest. We've got about six hours of darkness left, and we won't move any more tonight."

Six hours. Of stillness. Of unconsciousness.

Heaven. Who cared if she was tied in a tree fifty feet above the ground? Her head landed on Tex's solid shoulder.

She slept extremely soundly. And that's why it took her several minutes to register that there was something warm and heavy in her lap as dawn broke the following morning.

Finally she woke up enough to open her eyes and look down.

Her scream ripped through the early morning silence, loud and piercing across the green expanse of the jungle.

Chapter 8

Tex jolted wide-awake as an ungodly screech tore apart the silence of the jungle. He was instantly at full battle alert, his gaze taking in the situation in a single quick glance of assessment.

Kimberly screaming her head off. Her hands up in the air, her body pressed back against the tree trunk. A large, bright yellow snake curled up in her lap. *Holy sh—* An eyelash viper. Tree dweller. Venomous bite, deadly to humans.

In the next millisecond, the question of shutting up Kimberly first or getting rid of the snake first popped into his mind and was answered. He slammed his hand across Kimberly's mouth, stifling the sound, even though she still screamed against his palm. She was completely hysterical.

Clearly *not* a fan of snakes, he thought dryly.

He took a moment to assess the deadly viper. Fortunately the creature, deaf like all snakes, wasn't freaking out at the sounds emanating from Kimberly. But the vibrations of her screaming and wriggling had disturbed it. The snake was alert and testing the air with its tongue.

Good news, it had been a chilly night, cold enough to make the snake's reflexes sluggish.

Bad news, eyelash vipers have lightning-fast reflexes to begin with. Sluggish for that snake might still be faster than him. Plus, it was curled up in Kimberly's nice, warm lap. He'd have to assume the snake was at full speed.

Keeping his left hand pressed tightly against Kimberly's mouth, he leaned over slowly, moving his right hand by gradual degrees closer and closer to the back of the snake's head.

When the snake finally began to turn his head, its tongue flicking to catch the scent of his hand, Tex lunged.

He grabbed the viper right behind its triangular head.

The snake went nuts. It writhed and flailed, flinging its long body every which way, trying to get loose.

It hissed furiously, opening its mouth wide to reveal a pair of curved fangs. It even spit its venom in a futile effort to free itself. The deadly, milky yellow fluid streamed down Tex's wrist and forearm.

He prayed fervently he didn't have any fresh scratches in the path of that venom, or he might as well have been bit by the damn snake. The venom would get into his bloodstream through the tiniest open wound on his arm.

If that happened, it was lights out for him. He'd go into convulsions in a matter of seconds and stop breathing within thirty minutes or so. An eyelash viper was not a snake to be messed with lightly.

The snake's whole body whipped about, its tail wrapping around Tex's upper arm in a powerful grasp. The thing had to be a good six feet long, and at its thickest was nearly the diameter of his wrist. It was a monster of a snake.

Tex paused in indecision. He had to have both hands free to wrestle with the snake and throw it away from him before it bit him. But he dared not let Kimberly advertise their position to the entire free world anymore, either.

"Kimberly," he panted urgently as he struggled to hang on to the powerful creature. "I need both hands to get rid of the snake. You've got to stop screaming." He prayed she was coherent enough to understand and obey him.

Thankfully she went quiet under his palm.

He grabbed the snake with his free hand, fighting to disentangle himself from its furious coils. Normally he'd break the neck of a snake like this and eat it for supper. But the thing was so damned big and muscular, he wasn't certain he could snap its neck. If he tried and failed, he'd get bit for sure.

When he finally managed, his arms straining, to get the bright yellow creature stretched out more or less in front of him, he threw it as hard as he could. It bounced briefly across the end of the limb he was sitting on, giving him a momentary start.

But then it wriggled and fell off the branch, tumbling through the foliage toward the jungle floor far below.

Kimberly tore at the knots holding her in place and worked the rope free. She flung herself at him. Fortunately he had a foot hooked around the tree trunk so she didn't tumble him right off his perch.

Her arms wrapped around his neck in almost as tight a hold as the snake's, choking him until he could barely breathe.

He squeezed her close against him, the adrenaline shock of waking up and seeing that deadly snake in her lap finally hitting him. His hands shook and he didn't feel all that much steadier than she. That had been a close call.

He took one deep breath and allowed her to take a couple breaths, and then he spoke into her hair. "We've got to go, Princess. Right now. Your screaming will bring every person within a mile to the foot of this tree in the next few minutes."

She looked up, disoriented. "I want to stay here," she wailed.

She was still too messed up over that snake to realize what she'd done. She had no idea she'd just brought the whole damn rebel army down on top of their heads.

He didn't waste any breath explaining to her. He yanked out his knife and slashed the ropes holding him in place. He stuffed the pieces of rope in his pocket.

"Let's go," he bit out as he started climbing down the tree. She shook her head in the negative and he let out a breath of frustration. They didn't have the time to argue about it, and he didn't have time to coax her out of her hysteria.

He figured if he left her up there alone, she'd come down after him, so he kept climbing downward. He figured right. She scrambled after him, more interested in staying close than in remaining in her leafy perch.

He dropped the last ten feet or so to the ground and looked up. She'd stopped in the branches above him. Her face had one of those looks of frozen terror on it that didn't bode well for getting her to move any time soon. Damn.

"Is it gone?" she asked in thick-throated horror.

He frowned. "Is what gone?"

"The snake," she gasped, searching the ground frantically.

"Trust me, darlin'. That li'l ole yellow snake was a whole lot more scared of us than you were of it. He skedaddled the second he hit the ground."

Still, she hesitated.

"Come on down, Kimberly," he said calmly. "The bad guys will be here any minute. We need to get out of here."

She blinked at him in noncomprehension.

Dammit.

"Kimberly, get your butt down here right now, or I'm going to climb back up there, turn you over my knee, and blister your behind," he barked.

He sagged in relief when she lurched into motion. Ten

to one her father had conditioned her into that automatic response to a no-kidding order. The bastard.

He waited impatiently for the long seconds it took her to negotiate her way down the last dozen feet. Please God, let her not flake out on him now. There'd only been a few times in his life when he'd truly needed a woman to come through for him, and this was one of them. He added a specific plea to his silent prayer that Kimberly wouldn't fail him like all the other women in his life had.

The moment her feet hit the ground, he grabbed her hand and took off running. They raced through the jungle like wild animals, leaves whipping their faces and branches tearing at their clothes. There was no time for stealth. They had to get away from that tree as fast as they possibly could.

It was only a matter of minutes until he heard gunshots and crashing noises behind them.

"Oh, my God!" Kimberly panted beside him.

"They've found roughly where we were and are shooting up into the branches," he grunted. "Keep going."

The shots spurred both of them onward. When Kimberly started to lag behind he just barged on, gripping her hand tightly and dragging her alongside him. If she could stay on her feet, he'd provide the forward speed.

He didn't know how long they ran. A half hour maybe. Even he had a stitch in his side by the time they stopped. He was in good shape, but carrying two heavy rifles and bodily dragging another human along at a dead run was taxing, even for him.

Kimberly's breath came in rasping gasps. He gave her sixty seconds to catch her breath, then he took off again. He didn't waste breath on speaking and neither did she.

Somewhere in their mad dash, she must have gotten her wits about her after the snake encounter, because she wore a grim expression of determination. She knew this was a run for their lives.

Ten more minutes of running and another one minute

break. They kept that up for an hour. Kimberly was staggering beside him, and her breath came in great, wheezing pulls that told him she was done for. He gave them three minutes to rest, and when he set off again, it was at a much slower jog.

His heart still slammed against his ribs, though, and he felt light-headed with adrenaline. The kidnappers were closing in on Kimberly, and the helplessness of being unable to stop it nearly made him sick to his stomach. The guys in Charlie Squad didn't fail. They just didn't.

And he was about to. In a big way.

He wasn't afraid of dying, himself. But he was appalled at the idea that Kimberly was going to die.

Think, man. Think!

There had to be something he could do to save her.

When they'd taken off running this morning, he'd chosen the same direction they'd been travelling all along. He hadn't expected to come this way at a dead run, but the same theory still applied. Somewhere out here was a trap waiting for them.

The fact that he didn't hear anyone crashing through the jungle immediately behind them led him to believe the captors were satisfied to let him and Kimberly continue in this direction.

He looked around, but the foliage was so dense he couldn't see more than a few yards in any direction. They were going to be right on top of the trap before they found it.

He'd been tempted to ditch the rifles during that mad dash away from the tree, but he was glad he hadn't. The weapons gave them a number of options they wouldn't otherwise have.

God, he hated being blind like this. If only he knew what was coming!

Keep going. If you stop, you'll die. Keep going…

Kimberly repeated the mantra over and over to herself

as she ran alongside Tex. It was the only thing that kept her going long after she was completely out of breath, long after her reserves of energy were spent, long after she'd run every step that was in her legs to be run.

When the idea of dying started to sound like not so bad an alternative to stopping, she switched to telling herself that if she stopped, Tex would die, too. It pushed her for another half hour or so.

When Tex finally slowed the pace to a fast walk, she nearly cried in her relief. She never wanted to experience that much agony of mind and body again for as long as she lived. However long that might be.

Chagrin washed through her at what she'd done. Tex had worked so hard to get them a head start, to buy them some time, to plan a smart strategy for getting out alive, and she'd blown it all with one good, loud scream.

It was her fault they'd had to race through the jungle like maniacs. She had only herself to blame for the misery Tex had just put her through. He was only trying to save her life.

Her breathing recovered slightly, even though the back of her throat felt raw and her lungs still felt like they might explode at any second. "I can run a little more if you need me to," she gasped.

He shook his head in the negative and gestured her to be quiet. His pace slowed down even more.

What was going on? She listened intently and didn't hear a thing. They'd long ago left behind the sounds of gunshots and pursuit.

Tex eased forward, moving as cautiously as a tiger on the hunt. She mimicked the way he glided around leaves and branches, slipping through the jungle in near total silence.

Her already overtaxed muscles protested.

Pain is better than death, she told her uncooperative body sternly. *But not by much,* her pain centers announced to the rest of her brain.

They continued onward for maybe another fifteen minutes when, abruptly, Tex crouched in front of her. She did the same. He gestured her to sit still while he disappeared into the jungle ahead.

He rejoined her in under a minute. "We've got a problem," he murmured very low.

Her stomach dropped to her feet.

"How good are you at rock climbing?" he asked.

She blinked. "Not. I've never done it."

"Well, you may be about to get a crash course," he commented. "Come with me."

"What's going on?" she murmured as she hustled to keep up with him.

"The rebels have chased us into a box canyon. We must've passed the entrance a while back while we were running like bats out of hell."

Box canyon. She remembered the term from a stray snippet of a cowboy movie she'd caught a very long time ago. It had to do with dead ends and being trapped with no place to go. Oh God.

He murmured, "There's a wall of rock ahead of us, probably a hundred meters high. It looks vertical from here, but I can't tell for sure. Without climbing gear, I don't know if we stand a chance of getting up it."

Great.

"Problem is, we can't turn around at this late date. I'm sure the rebels have the entrance to this thing sealed off in a line of men that's practically shoulder to shoulder. With you along, we don't have even a ghost of a chance of doubling back through the line."

They walked forward for several minutes, each step bringing her closer to her doom. She couldn't believe he just kept walking deeper and deeper into the trap.

Still, this supposed cliff hadn't come into sight. "How far is it to the dead end?" she asked in some confusion.

"About a half mile."

"And we're just going to keep on heading deeper into this canyon thing?" she asked in dismay.

"There's no way out behind us. That's why the rebels quit chasing us. They know they've got us trapped. I won't know if we have a shot at getting out the back door until I see it."

"But if there's not another way out, they'll have us cornered with nowhere to go."

"Honey, we've already got no place to go."

His words were like a bucket of icy-cold water. They froze her brain into momentary shock. In denial of the real issue, she latched on to an odd detail. "How the heck did you see these cliffs through all this brush?" she whispered.

"I climbed a tree and had a look over the understory of vegetation."

"And you can see a half mile away?" she exclaimed under her breath.

He grinned briefly. "Yeah. I'm a bit far-sighted. I'm the spotter for my team."

She didn't ask what a spotter was. Clearly, it took good eyesight to do the job. They had more important things to worry about at the moment.

Then she pushed aside a banana leaf, and there it was. An enormous rock cliff. As he'd described, it started behind them on their left and arced all the way around until it disappeared behind them on their right.

It was jagged and rough, with plants clinging precariously to cracks and crannies scattered across its vertical gray face. It was *huge*. The portion of the cliff in front of them disappeared somewhere above the canopy of trees far overhead.

They jogged toward it for several minutes, and it grew appreciably larger with each step she took. Finally they got close enough so she could see glimpses of pale blue sky between the looming granite behemoth and the trees growing out of the jungle floor beside her. The cliff towered overhead until she had to tilt her head back—way back—to see the top of it.

Tex thought she could climb that?

Chapter 9

Tex looked grimly at the rock face before them. If Kimberly had been a trained mountain climber, or even an experienced rock climber, it might have been okay. But as it was, he didn't stand a chance of getting her up that rocky face.

He glanced around quickly, looking for any other possibilities at all. This was the moment he'd dreaded. The end game. Now was when he'd have to outthink and outperform the kidnappers if he and Kimberly were to survive.

There was nothing for him to work with. The undergrowth was thin in this area. Nothing to hunker down and hide under. The tree-climbing gambit had worked once, but it wouldn't fool their pursuers a second time. Besides, he doubted he'd get Kimberly back up in another tree after her encounter with the snake.

Any second now he expected to start hearing the advance of the line of rebel soldiers behind them.

There was a pile of scree at the base of the cliff stones

and debris that had sheered off the cliff face, but there weren't even any boulders big enough for them to take good cover behind if it came to a firefight.

The kidnappers had picked their trap well.

He'd expected as much, given the efficiency of their initial attack at Quantico. He'd just hoped for a lucky break.

It looked like he was going to have to create their luck himself today. He stepped back several yards to gaze up the cliff face, scanning for a route that an amateur rock climber with no upper body strength could negotiate.

Nada.

But he did catch sight of a couple really dark shadows a ways up the face. Caves, maybe?

He stepped back farther, peering closely at the suspicious spots. One looked promising, but he just couldn't tell from this angle. He'd have to move well away from the cliff to see better, and they didn't have time for that.

"Tex," Kimberly murmured urgently. "I hear them coming! We've got to do something!"

He heard them, too. It sounded like dozens of men, beating the jungle methodically as they moved forward. They weren't even bothering to lower their voices as they called back and forth to one another.

He and Kimberly were out of time and out of options.

"We've got to climb the cliff," he announced.

"Climb *that?*" she squeaked, gazing up at the giant rock face.

"It's that or surrender. Your call."

She stared at him for an instant. He could see it in her eyes. She was weighing the idea of giving up.

And then she swallowed resolutely and turned to face the rock. "How do I do this?" she asked.

Sonofagun. She hadn't buckled under pressure. Pride in her surged through him. Quickly he showed her how to find and test handholds and footholds before committing her weight to them. The first sixty feet up the cliff weren't too bad. The rock was heavily pitted and cracked by erosion, and footholds were plentiful.

The sounds behind them resolved into words and orders to be thorough and make sure the Americans didn't circle back and slip through the line.

"Hurry, Princess," he urged her.

"I am," she wailed back in a panting whisper.

He looked up and frowned. The cliff wall above them had sheared away recently, leaving a nearly smooth granite surface ahead of them. It wasn't far beyond that he'd seen the shadow that might be a small cave.

He glanced back. They were maybe eighty feet above the ground. From his vantage point, he glimpsed the red berets that formed the human net. Once the rebels broke out of the trees, they'd have a clear shot at him and Kimberly on that smooth cliff face. The two of them would be easy pickings.

Since most politically motivated kidnappers expected to kill their hostages anyway, he didn't hold out much hope that they wouldn't kill Kimberly, too. They had to get to that cave before the rebels got out into the open at the foot of the cliff.

"Let's go," he urged her.

"Where?" she screamed in a bare whisper. "I'm stuck. I can't find anywhere to grab on."

He looked over at her. Like him, she'd reached the base of the sheared area.

To his experienced eye, he saw the tiny handholds and footholds that he'd need to scale the surface. It was going to take a lot of strength to pull himself past some big gaps in the footholds, but he could do it.

"How are your arms holding out, Kimberly?"

"They feel like rubber," she grunted.

Damn. Just as he'd thought. Even perfectly fresh, she probably didn't have the upper body power to brute force her way up this stretch of rock. And after their earlier run, she was toast. He looked up, gauging how rough a climb it would be.

No way around it. That was going to be one hard stretch of climbing.

He looked back over his shoulder at the line of red berets. There wasn't time for him to go on ahead and drop a rope to Kimberly and haul her up. Besides, if her arms were as tired as he expected they were, she wouldn't be able to hang on to a rope anyway.

Maybe he could fashion a foot harness for her to stand in and haul her up that way.

A soldier shouted out in Spanish.

Tex grimaced. They'd been spotted on the cliff face. The line of soldiers broke into a run.

He didn't have the strength left to haul himself, all his gear and Kimberly up the cliff. He could drop one or both of the rifles or abandon Kimberly. Christ, what a choice. Drop the gear they needed to stay alive or sacrifice a human life. *Kimberly's* life.

"Hang on, darlin'," he grunted as he wiggled out of the sling for the heavy sniper rifle. He popped out the clip, pocketed it, and then let the weapon go. It fell with a clatter behind him. Sixty-five pounds less.

Every second counted now. He worked his way horizontally across the cliff face to where Kimberly clung to the vertical wall. "I need you to climb on my back, honey," he directed with urgent calm.

"What?" She looked at him blankly.

"I don't have time to explain. We've got to get up this stretch of rock and you're not strong enough to do it. Climb on me piggyback and hang on tight."

"I'll throw off your balance!"

"They're going to shoot us off this wall like flies. Now *move!*" he ordered her.

Her eyes went wide. She spared one glance for the sheer wall above her and then did as he'd ordered. It was a dicey moment when she let go of the rock face and transferred her weight to his shoulders.

He had no idea if he could do this, but it was their only hope.

"Wrap your legs around my waist and hang on tight, sweetheart. Lean in close to me so your weight's right against my back."

He'd never rock climbed with over a hundred pounds on his back before. The balance was completely different, and every few seconds he felt on the verge of oversetting and falling over backward.

His fingers cramped, then his entire arms cramped. Even his toes were knots of pain before long.

More crashing in the trees behind them. The rebels had to be almost close enough to break out into view.

The next handhold was over his head. He was going to have to do a chin-up without any footholds at all, and then let go with one hand, reach up, and pull himself another two feet or so vertically before he could catch another crack with his foot.

"Hang on tight," he grunted.

She plastered herself against him, her face pressed tightly against his neck.

He exhaled hard and began to pull. He thought of every pull-up he'd ever done. Of the ones he'd gutted out in Special Forces training when he was so tired he couldn't stand up. Of the dozens of them he'd popped off to show the new recruits how soft they were. He thought about failure and the flat refusal of the men of Charlie Squad to give up. He thought about Kimberly's mouth on his, of how bad he wanted to make love to her someday.

A groan of Herculean effort slipped out from between his clenched teeth.

And somehow he gutted through pulling three hundred combined pounds four feet up a cliff by nothing more than his fingertips and brutal determination.

He blew hard, took one breath and shifted all his weight to his right hand. He threw his left hand up.

It missed the handhold!

His fingernails raked the cliff and he and Kimberly lurched precariously. His right hand cramped with the effort of hanging on.

He flung his left arm up again. His fingers caught in a tiny crack. He reached deep in his gut and found one last bit of strength even he didn't know he had.

He pulled one more time for all he was worth.

His right foot scrabbled frantically at the cold rock wall. He was losing it. He couldn't hang on for much longer.

His toe caught. He shoved hard with his thigh, taking the weight off his trembling arms. Another foothold, two more hand shifts and they were past the granite sheet.

Shouts from below.

"Oh, God, they've broken out of the jungle," Kimberly sobbed in his ear. "They're going to shoot us!"

A small ledge came into sight at eye level. He pushed, pulled and scrambled the last few feet and fell onto the tiny shelf with Kimberly sprawled on top of him.

A bullet zinged past them, nicking the rock and sending sharp bits of rock flying at them. His cheek stung from where the debris hit him. "Is there a cave?" he panted, too spent to turn his head and look for himself.

Kimberly scrambled off his back and lay flat beside him. "There's an opening of some kind," she panted back. "It's pretty small, though."

"Can we get through it?" He was too focused on the soldiers pouring out of the jungle below and on pulling out his AK-47 to spare a look at it.

"I'll fit. It'll be tight for you."

"Go. I'll hold them off until you're inside."

She scrambled toward the opening behind him.

The best way to slow down an army was to take out its leaders. He studied the posture and body language of the men pouring into the clearing. Then he took careful aim and shot the soldier all the others seemed to be looking at. The guy dropped like a rock, shot through the head.

He ducked back as an answering volley of fire sprayed more shattered rock all around him.

A grunt and an oompf from behind him and then Kimberly's voice. "I'm inside. It's pretty big in here. You'll be able to stand up."

Praise the Lord.

He wiggled backward on his belly as the soldiers congregated below. They buzzed like a horde of angry hornets. They'd stepped away from the guy he'd shot and were ignoring the body. A clean kill, then.

They looked like they were waiting for someone else to arrive who could give them orders before they attempted to follow him and Kimberly up the cliff.

His feet hit rock. He glanced back over his shoulder. It was more of a slit than an opening.

Good thing he hadn't eaten much for the last couple days or he probably wouldn't fit through the narrow gap.

He slid back until he could stand up beside the opening. By shimmying sideways and sucking in his gut like crazy, he managed to squeeze through the jagged opening.

He got stuck momentarily, but with a hard tug and the rending of his shirtfront, he popped through the entrance. He didn't look forward to squeezing back out of there. Please, he prayed, let that be a problem he had to face.

A narrow shaft of light fell on the floor. The cave was probably thirty feet across and fifty or more deep, based on the echo from his movements.

Using a cigarette lighter, he did a quick sweep of the cave. They had five, maybe ten, minutes before soldiers would start popping up over the edge of that granite wall.

"Do you see another way out of here?" Kimberly asked hopefully out of the darkness to his right.

He swept the flame along the cave's walls, floor, and ceiling. Nothing but solid rock.

"Nope. Nothing."

"How are we going to get out of here, then?" she asked. Desperation coursed through her voice.

He thought fast. He had twenty-two rounds left in the AK-47. If he was conservative, and lucky, he could take out roughly that many men before he ran out of ammo. But the twenty-third guy up that cliff would kill them.

There'd been at least fifty guys at the base of the cliff when he'd ducked in here. The rebel soldiers were expendable to their leaders. He had no illusions about the twenty-third guy. He'd get sent up the cliff. It was just a matter of time. He needed a different plan.

"Okay, Kimberly, here's what we're going to do. The first guy up that cliff is likely to be a scout type. He'll have more training than most of the other grunts down there. I'm banking on the fact that he'll have some sort of radio with him for reporting back in to his bosses."

She nodded, listening intently.

"You're going to sit in the back of the cave where he can see you if he points a flashlight through the entrance. You're going to act scared and indicate that I've left you here and climbed on up the cliff. You're alone."

Kimberly frowned.

"You've got to make it look convincing. Play the helpless female to the hilt. Make him think all he has to do is waltz in here and tie you up. Do you think you can do that?"

"Yes," she answered crisply, all business.

Thank God, she apparently wasn't one of those women who fell apart in stressful situations. Snakes excepted, of course.

He continued. "I'm going to hide over here by the entrance. When the scout comes in, I'm going to jump him and take him down. I'll search him for his radio. When I find it, I'll toss it to you. In a minute I'm going to give you a series of radio frequencies to memorize. Whichever one works on his radio, you dial it up and start shouting for help to whoever answers you. With me so far?"

She nodded.

"Once we've got a radio, I'm going to take the gun back from you and hold the doorway. I'll pick off whoever pokes their head up over that ledge with the AK-47."

"Until when?" Kimberly asked innocently.

"Until I either run out of ammo or somebody answers your radio call and comes to rescue us."

"What if—" she started to ask.

He cut her off. "Let's cross that bridge when we get to it." She frowned in consternation and he added, "I'm trained in hand-to-hand combat and I've got a knife. Any guy topping that granite face is going to be easy to push off the cliff. We can hold out here for a good, long while."

She nodded, her expression uncertain.

He rattled off a series of emergency radio frequencies, all monitored by satellite around the world, all fed directly into Charlie Squad's headquarters. He made Kimberly repeat them back to him until he was sure she had them down cold.

He gave her the final instructions. "If I go down before I find a radio, fire the gun at anyone who steps through that opening. Work your way over to the corpse and search for a radio. Got it?"

She stared at him, her eyes wide as he shoved the AK-47 into her hands. "Don't go down, Tex," she murmured.

He moved into position by the door and grinned back at her briefly. "I'm not planning on it, darlin'."

She took her place on the floor directly across from the door. As his eyes adjusted to the dark, he could see her seated there bravely, the rifle hidden out of sight beside her.

He took his place on top of a boulder just inside the entrance. From there he could jump down on top of anybody who stepped through that opening.

"Kimberly," he called low across the space.

She looked up nervously.

"In case I don't get another chance...well, just in case,

I wanted to tell you how well you've done the last couple days. Not too many women could've rolled with the punches the way you have. You did good.''

Her smile warmed him all the way across the cave.

"Thanks," she replied simply. "I couldn't have made it without you. I owe you my life."

The sound of voices drifted up from below. It sounded like an argument of some kind, but the acoustics of the cave distorted the sound so much he couldn't make out what they were saying. He glanced at his watch. About two minutes and somebody'd be climbing through that opening.

Four minutes passed. He strained to hear the telltale scrabbling sounds of people scaling the cliff.

Nothing yet.

His watch hit the six-minute mark.

Still nothing.

He glanced over at Kimberly, who was alternating between staring at the door and glancing fearfully at him. He saw her lips moving periodically, reciting the radio frequencies to herself. Or maybe she was praying, too.

He didn't have the time for prayer on most missions, and he preferred to put his stock in being better prepared and trained than the other guy. But as long minutes of waiting ticked by, he found himself offering up a plea for their safety to whatever higher powers that were.

Ten minutes passed. *Still nothing.* What the hell was going on? He didn't hear any voices at all now.

He waited another five minutes. No army was dead silent for that long. Kimberly was starting to fidget on her side of the cave. He gestured her to stay put and risked moving into the opening to see if he could hear something from there.

Silence.

In fact, a few birds were starting to call out again.

What the…

He moved over to Kimberly's side. "Give me the gun," he murmured.

She handed the weapon to him.

He gritted his teeth and faced the cave opening again. He really hated tight spaces. He steeled himself and squeezed out through the narrow gap. He felt like dough squeezed through a pasta maker. An angel hair spaghetti-maker. He dropped flat and inched over toward the edge of the cliff.

Very carefully he peered over the drop-off.

The soldiers were gone. All of them. Except the one he'd shot, who still lay sprawled where he'd fallen.

Cold bastards. Didn't take their dead with them. Charlie Squad never left one of its own behind, dead or alive.

He scanned the jungle below. There wasn't a single glimpse of a soldier anywhere at all.

That was completely bizarre. Why would they just give up and go away all of a sudden? They had their quarry trapped. All they had to do was come up and get her. It made no sense whatsoever.

He stared down at the dead guy speculatively. Was this another trap of some kind?

And then something struck him.

Something that made him sick to his stomach.

He scanned the ground around the base of the cliff quickly, not finding what he was looking for. He searched again, slowly and with careful thoroughness.

He pushed back from the edge of the cliff in complete and utter disgust.

Sonofabitch.

Chapter 10

Kimberly waited in an agony of suspense in the dark cave. What in the world was going on out there? She had visions of a sniper picking Tex off as he peeked over the edge, stranding them both up here with no chance at all of getting down that cliff alive.

He'd die horribly from his injuries, suffering greatly as he gave up life inch by inch. She couldn't bear the idea of not being able to help him if, God forbid, he got hurt. Not to mention she'd die of dehydration and starvation and her corpse would wither away into a dried-out mummy long before anybody found her in this remote spot.

Tex's voice interrupted her morbid thoughts. He sounded totally disgusted. "You can come out now."

She frowned confused. The soldiers were gone? Why would they walk away at the very moment they had her trapped and within their reach?

She wiggled out through the narrow cave opening. It was a tight fit for her. How Tex mashed through that gap with his size and muscle was a mystery to her.

She crawled over to Tex on her hands and knees and stretched out on her stomach beside him to look down. Her insides lurched at how high up in the air they were.

He was staring at the ground below in utter chagrin.

"Where'd everybody go?" she asked in confusion.

"They left. They got what they were after," he bit out.

"I don't understand…"

He turned his head to stare grimly at her. "They weren't after you at all. They never cared about kidnapping you. They were after *me* when they landed that helicopter at Quantico. Me and the RITA rifle."

She frowned. They weren't after her? She wasn't the target? Confusion swirled in her head until she was almost dizzy. She pressed herself flat against the solid rock until the sickening feeling that she was about to fall over the edge passed. "The sniper rifle? Why would they go to all this trouble over a gun?"

He snorted. "Weren't you paying attention to the briefing I gave you and all your reporter flunkies?"

She answered him honestly. "Not really."

He laughed shortly, without humor. "Figures."

He rolled on his side to face her. "The RITA rifle has a smart targeting system that locks on to a target and then tracks the target all by itself. RITA's computer makes corrections hundreds of times a second for movement of both the target and the gun, weather conditions, the wind, you name it."

She gave him a blank look.

He translated into plain English. "Once you point the RITA rifle at a target and its computer locks on to that person, the gun doesn't miss. Ever."

"That's impressive and all, but can't a good sniper do pretty much the same thing?"

Tex scowled. "There's something else about the RITA rifle I didn't tell your journalist buddies about because it's classified. Highly classified, in fact."

Her gaze swiveled to his. What could be so special about a rifle that it merited its own security rating?

"When we get back home, you're going to have to sign a bunch of documents promising not to reveal what I'm about to tell you."

She nodded impatiently. "I know the routine. I've sat in on classified sessions of Congress before."

"Oh, yeah. I forgot. Daddy pulls strings for you, too, doesn't he?"

"My father doesn't lift a finger to help me," she retorted, stung. "Truth be told, he'd be happy to see me crash and burn."

Tex looked at her a long time, his mental wheels clearly turning over that tidbit of information. Eventually he shrugged. He was close enough for her to feel the heat from his body. As always, it lured her near with its sexual promise.

She blinked and tried to refocus on the discussion at hand. "So. What's so special about this gun?"

"It can fire through bulletproof glass."

"And?" she asked, waiting for the big revelation.

"And?" he asked incredulously. "If that technology falls into the wrong hands, nobody in the world will be safe anymore! No bank teller will be safe from robbers, no head of state will be safe in his limousine. Hell, the Pope will be at risk in the Popemobile.

"The whole nature of personal security will have to change. Any terrorist group or rich bastard with a grudge could hire a sniper with a RITA rifle, and anybody, absolutely anybody, could be killed pretty much at will. The chaos that would ensue... I don't even want to think about it. Some terrorist group with one of those rifles could knock out every key world leader and then sit back and enjoy the fun while countries scramble to secure the reins of power. Not to mention the armies and nuclear warheads at stake.... And then there are the little guys. What about DEA or FBI agents who rely on armored cars and bulletproof vests to do their jobs day in and day out? Or congressmen like your father, whose desks sit in front of bulletproof windows and who ride in bulletproof cars? Jewelry stores, security guards in office buildings, cops who rely on Kevlar vests in a firefight…. Do you have any idea how many people's lives would be put at risk if that gun's technology got out?''

''Okay, I get the point. A lot of people would be put in danger.''

He stared darkly at her. His next words, spoken flatly, without any emotional inflection at all, made her flinch.

''And I just handed that rifle over to the Gavronese rebels.''

She stared at him as comprehension dawned. While she'd been clinging for her life to the cliff, he'd thrown one of the rifles down the rock face to get rid of its weight. It had been the big sniper rifle he'd tossed.

She glanced over the edge of the cliff in reflex.

''It's gone,'' he assured her. ''Believe me, I've looked hard. They got it.''

That was bad. But there wasn't a darn thing they could do about it up here. In a perfect world, they'd walk out of the jungle and call in a small army to retrieve the rifle, walk out…

The secondary implications of what he'd said began to hit her. She gazed hopefully at Tex.

''Then, if they were really after the rifle and not me, that means they won't chase us if we get out of here. We can walk out to the nearest road and get out of this bloody jungle! Then we can call in some help and get the gun back.''

Jubilation coursed through her. Thank God. Their nightmare was over! Tex's jaw looked tight, the expression in his eyes harsh. Why wasn't he as thrilled as she was?

''Let's go home!'' she cried.

''It's not that simple.''

She stared at him, surprised. What was so hard about

going home? Okay, so maybe they'd have to avoid towns and people sympathetic to the rebels. There was probably some risk to that, but nothing like what they'd been up against.

"Why not?" she finally asked. "What's so hard about getting out of here? All we need to do is get to a telephone. A couple phone calls and it'll all be over."

"I can't leave yet," he said heavily.

"What do you mean, you can't leave?" She pushed herself up on to an elbow to stare at him.

"I mean, I can't take you home yet. My job's not over, here."

A horrible sinking feeling rumbled warningly in the pit of her stomach. "What are you talking about, Tex?"

"I have to get that rifle back."

She stared in shock. "You're one man. An army just grabbed that thing. Are you nuts?"

"Maybe. But I have to try. I lost it, I have to recover it."

No. No, no, no. He couldn't detour to chase after a gun. He had to get her out of this mess first. She tried to reason with him. "That's crazy, Tex. Let's walk out to the nearest town. You can call in the Marines, and they can go get the darned thing back."

He shook his head. "The United States has a strictly hands-off policy down here. If we brought in Marines, both sides in the Civil War would accuse us of interfering and they'd both turn on us. It'd be another Somalia all over again."

Panic shortened her breath. But they had to get out of here! "So, call in the rest of Charlie Squad. Don't you guys sneak around in war zones all the time? Don't you specialize in doing stuff like taking on entire armies?" Desperation pulled the muscles across the back of her neck tight. She wanted to go home. To safety. Now!

"It'll take Charlie Squad a while to get down here. For all we know, the rebels will ship RITA out of here the second they get back to civilization. Some off-continent manufacturer could take it apart and learn its secrets in a matter of days.''

''Surely you're exaggerating the threat…''

He cut her off with a withering glare. ''Besides, deploying Charlie Squad down here could be, uh, a bit sensitive. We were down here not too long ago and made quite a splash. Neither side in the Gavronese war likes us a whole lot.''

''What did you do to tick everyone off?''

''We blew up Gavarone's only international airport in its entirety, which the Gavronese government is miffed over. Then we killed a couple hundred rebels on the roof of the American Embassy while we rescued the U.S. Ambassador, preventing him from becoming the rebel's juicy political hostage. For some reason, the rebels are pissed off at us over the incident.''

She stared at him. ''How do you destroy a whole airport?''

He grinned briefly. ''We blew up the above-ground fuel storage tanks. They ignited a secondary blast that blew all the underground fuel pits. The whole tarmac and a couple big chunks of the runway are smoking craters now. Most of the Gavronese Air Force was parked on the ramp when it blew, too.''

She shook her head in amazement. ''Six guys did all that?''

''Six guys and one woman. An American military attaché was with us. It was her idea. I'll introduce her to you when we get home, if you'd like.''

She blinked at the way he said it. As if there was a tacit understanding that they'd see each other again once they got out of here. His voice rang with straightforward certainty, as if there was no question about it.

Suspicion flared in her gut. She'd spent a lot of years in Washington learning that anyone who pretended to be that sincere, wasn't. In fact, in her experience, the more honest a person seemed, the more dishonest they usually were.

She'd been a naive, idealistic kid once, who might have bought that utterly convincing ring in his words. But that had been a very long time ago. He was running a con on her. She just didn't see his angle yet.

Tex's voice interrupted her turbulent thoughts.

"The U.S. government promised the Gavronese government that it wouldn't send Charlie Squad into Gavarone again for a good, long time. Which leaves just me on the ground and in place to deal with this."

"Alone," she retorted. "Why can't they come in here in the role of a rescue team?"

"By the time you and I can contact them, we probably won't need to be rescued."

She rolled her eyes. "A technicality. Tex, I'll be the first to admit that your skills and training are impressive. But come on. You're not John Wayne! You can't do this by yourself!"

He lifted a single lazy eyebrow at her and drawled, "Are you offering to help?"

"Me?" She recoiled. "Certainly not. I'm going home. To a hot shower, clean clothes, new shoes, and dinner at the best restaurant in Washington. And I'm never setting foot in another jungle as long as I live!"

Tex gestured with his hand at the ground far below, hard cynicism in his eyes. "Be my guest, Kimberly. Nobody's forcing you to stay with me. Feel free to go home right now, by yourself. But even in a best case scenario, it'll take Charlie Squad some time to get down here, and every second may count right now. I'm going after that rifle now."

She glared at him, severely annoyed. "This isn't fair! I'm stranded up the side of a cliff, and you know darn well I can't get down it by myself."

"Fine," he snapped. "I'll take you down. Let's go."

He picked up the AK-47 from the ground beside him

and stood up. He rigged some sort of harness out of bits of rope and tied it around her. She watched dubiously while he secured the end of the longest rope to an out-cropping of stone behind him.

He moved over to the edge of the cliff and gestured expansively. "Your ride awaits you," he said with false politeness.

She glared at him and shimmied over to the edge of the cliff.

"Hang on to the rope and use your feet to hold you away from the cliff. I've got enough line left to lower you past the vertical face. When you get to the broken rocks beyond the smooth stuff, step out of the harness and free climb the rest of the way down."

She looked up at him in dismay. "You're not coming with me?"

"I need to bring the rope along. We don't have much gear, and I don't want to waste what we do have. Once you're down the cliff, I'll untie it and climb my way down."

"Isn't there another way? That sounds awfully danger-ous."

"Darlin', I free climbed up the damn thing carrying you. Going down it is going to be a cinch."

She supposed he knew what he was doing.

She paused in the act of lowering herself over the edge. "By the way, Romeo, girls like balconies that won't break their necks if they fall off them."

His grin flashed. "Picky, picky, picky."

Pushing any thoughts about what she was about to do out of her mind, she took a deep breath and slipped over the edge of the wall. She hung on to the ledge for as long as she could, easing her weight gradually into the make-shift harness. She held her breath as the rope accepted her weight, stretching and creaking ominously. Oh, God.

She hung on for dear life as Tex lowered her slowly down the granite wall.

Yet again her safety and well-being rested completely in his hands. The vulnerability of owing her life to him like this was incredibly intimate. It struck her anew how deeply she trusted him. Earlier, on the way up the cliff, she'd let go of that rock face and climbed onto his back. And just now she'd stepped, literally, off the edge of a cliff without hesitation because Tex said it would be all right.

How could he make her so mad one minute and then command total trust out of her the next? He was the most confusing man she'd ever met, with the possible exception of her father.

Her father and Tex. Boy, now there were two birds of a feather. Military men, driven by some inexplicable, demonic need to be heroes. Her father had broken under the strain of the demands he placed upon himself and had spent years lashing out in unreasoning anger over it.

And here was Tex, losing himself in his own hero complex before her very eyes. The idea that he could find that rifle and get it back all by himself was patently absurd. The fact that he'd even consider trying it astounded her. And she was helpless to stop him, to protect him from himself. He'd end up just like her father.

The rope hung up for a moment, then lurched as it jerked free from a snag in the rock. Her heart raced and she felt light-headed with the burst of adrenaline that hit her.

The rope felt pitifully thin in her hands, not nearly strong enough to support her weight. She squeezed her eyes tightly shut and added rock climbing to the list of things she was never, ever, going to do again as long as she lived.

Finally her feet struck a protruding rock and the wall grew uneven beneath her cheek. She'd made it past the worst part. She shimmied out of the rope harness and called up to Tex, "I'm clear of the hard part and the rope's free."

The line disappeared quickly as he hauled it back in. Now that there was nobody chasing her, she took her time climbing down the rest of the wall. She tested each hand-hold and foothold carefully before shifting her weight lower.

It seemed to take forever to get down the cliff. How had they ever gone up it so quickly before?

Finally her feet touched solid ground once more. She'd made it. She sighed in heartfelt relief. Suddenly her arms were so exhausted, she didn't think she could lift them if she had to.

She looked up the wall and saw Tex clinging to the smooth granite cliff. How he was staying on the rock face, she had no idea. He looked like he ought to slide off it any second.

She held her breath each time he moved. Fear for him surged through her and she felt like she'd made the descent again by the time he dropped lightly to the ground beside her.

For some reason she was struck anew by how big and powerful a man he was as he strode up to her.

"Still here?" he growled. "I thought you'd be on your way home to D.C. by now."

She scowled back at him. "I don't happen to know which way it is to Washington or I would have been gone already."

He pointed over his shoulder toward the cliff. "North's that way."

"Gee, thanks."

He turned and walked away from her quickly. He glanced up once at the cliff, as though taking a bearing, and veered off into the brush.

"Where are you going?" she called after him.

"To search the guy I shot."

She made a face of distaste, but morbid curiosity propelled her after him. She pulled up short when she burst into a clearing. Tex was kneeling over the body of the

Gavronese soldier, going through the guy's pockets. The sight turned her stomach. There was something really wrong about touching a dead person.

"Bingo!"

She jumped at Tex's sharp exclamation. He held up a small, black object. It looked like a cell phone.

A rustle sounded in the bush close by. Tex threw her the phone and whirled, the AK-47 coming up into a ready position in his hands, almost as if by magic.

"Make the call," Tex ordered tersely over his shoulder as he plunged into the brush toward the noise.

Frantically she dialed the phone number he'd made her memorize. Static filled her ear. Please, please, please, let this thing work out here in the middle of nowhere.

A faint ring sounded. God bless communications satellites!

"Identify yourself," a man barked in her ear.

She jumped at the sharp command. "My name is Kimberly Stanton. Tex Monroe gave me this phone number."

"Jeez! Stand by." There was the tiniest pause and a clicking noise. "You're on speaker phone. Go ahead with your location."

"Uh, I don't know. Tex thinks we're in Gavarone. We've been walking north for three days."

"Say your status," a deep voice cut in.

"My status? Uh, we're both fine. Although soldiers—rebels—wearing red berets have been chasing us."

"You've escaped your kidnappers, then?" the deep voice asked.

"Yes. Tex did that right after he woke up. He freed us before I regained consciousness."

"Stay on the line, ma'am. We're attempting to locate your signal as we spea—"

A burst of static filled her ear.

"…old model…no triangulation. Still there, Miss Stanton?" the deep voice asked urgently.

"Yes."

"Can you put Captain Monroe on the line?"

"He's not here. He heard someone in the brush and went after them. We got this phone off a dead guy—"

She waited out another burst of static.

"...and Tex threw it at me and said to call you."

"Did he ask for any support?"

"No, he said there'd be some problems sending any help for us into Gavarone." She hesitated. "Something important has happened that I think he'd want you to know about. Can I say something classified, at least I think it's classified, over this line?"

Surprise resonated in the deep voice. "This is Charlie Squad headquarters, and I'm Colonel Folly, the commanding officer of Charlie Squad. Anything he said to you, you can say to me. Your phone line isn't secure, but under the circumstances I'm willing to take the risk. Go ahead."

"Tex thinks I wasn't the target of the kidnapping. The RITA rifle he had with him was. When the rebels caught up with us this morning, Tex dropped the rifle. They took it and left, even though they had us cornered."

A long silence greeted that announcement.

"Are you still there, Colonel Folly?" she asked in dismay.

"Yes, ma'am. Did Tex say what his intentions are?"

"He said he's going after the gun to get it back. He said he thought the U.S. government couldn't send in Marines after the gun, and he didn't think Charlie Squad could get here in time."

"If you're in Gavarone, Miss Stanton, we can be there in eight hours. But we need an exact location on you. Do you have any idea where you are? Have you passed any distinguishing landmarks in the last few days?"

"No. Just tons of jungle. We crossed a little stream yesterday afternoon that flows to the north. I'm standing in front of a really big granite cliff. It's part of a box canyon the rebels used to trap us. The cliff wall faces south."

"How big's the canyon?" the colonel asked.

"It took us over an hour to run the length of it, I think."

"Anything else, Miss Stanton?"

She racked her brains but couldn't think of a thing to help. The static was getting worse.

She barely made out Colonel Folly's voice as he said, "Tell Tex we'll be in theater tonight. As soon as he can get us a position fix, we're coming in to provide support to him and pull you out. Tell him to get the gun back..."

She couldn't make out any more. A beeping sounded in her ear. The connection had been lost.

She stared glumly at the phone.

How could Tex's own commander send him on a suicide mission like this? What was it about soldiers that made them all believe they were super heroes? Didn't the colonel realize the odds they were up against out here? How could this Colonel set Tex up to fail, or even die, like that?

Was this what had happened to her father? Had he sold his own heroic persona to his superiors so well that they demanded too much of him? Had he broken himself on the rocky cliffs of their expectations?

And then something rustled in the brush behind her. She looked frantically in both directions and dived under the nearest bush.

Chapter 11

"Dammit, Kimberly. Where are you?" Tex called lowly. He didn't have time to play these games with her. A second's panic hit him. What if she had called his bluff and walked off into the jungle by herself? He moved faster toward her last position.

He let out a relieved huff when she crawled sheepishly out from under a bush.

"I thought you were the rebels," she confessed.

He shook his head in disgust. "They're long gone, the bastards."

"So what was that noise?"

"A jaguar. Probably smelled the blood from the dead guy and came to investigate."

She glanced around in consternation. "There are jaguars out here?"

"Yeah. Not many, but they're here, all right."

She shuddered visibly. "Now what?"

"Now we track down the rifle. Any luck with the phone?" he asked.

"Yes. I talked to a Colonel Folly."

Just hearing his commander's name made him feel better. He and Kimberly were overdue for a good break. Eagerly he asked, "What'd he say?"

"He said he'd position the team in theater by tonight. As soon as you get an exact position fix, contact him with it."

Disappointment coursed through Tex. "He couldn't locate us from the cell phone?"

Kimberly shook her head. "He said something about it not having a triangulation capability."

"Too bad. Did he have any instructions for me?"

She answered reluctantly. "He said you're to go after the rifle and get it back. As soon as we figure out where we are, he'll send in some guys to pick me up and to help you."

Tex nodded grimly. Just as he'd thought. Getting that gun back was a top priority. At least he still had the clip. It'd take the rebels a couple days and a good weapon smith to fashion a new clip for it. He *had* to stop the rifle from falling into the wrong hands. The hands of people who'd take it apart and learn how to duplicate its amazing technology.

He glanced at his stolen watch. "It's about noon. We've still got plenty of daylight left to track the rebels."

"Wonderful," Kimberly rumbled under her breath.

"Let's see if we can lift anything else useful off the dead guy's body."

Kimberly grimaced.

He didn't particularly enjoy poking through a dead man's pockets, either, but they had precious little gear. Anything they looted could be useful.

Flies were starting to buzz around the corpse as they approached it. It didn't take long for Mother Nature to claim back her own out here. With a shudder of horror, Kimberly stood well back and let him do the honors.

She was authorized to be grossed out. She'd held up

shockingly well through the morning, first on that long run and later climbing the cliff. He'd never have guessed a spoiled little rich girl like her could gut it out like that.

Methodically he stripped and searched the corpse. He took off the guy's camouflage fatigue shirt. Too small for him, but it would work for Kimberly. A cigarette lighter. Half a pack of smokes.

"This guy's carrying Gavronese cigarettes," he commented.

"Great! At least we know what country we're in now," she responded dryly. "Now if only we knew where in it we were."

He grinned at her sarcasm. "It's a dinky little place. We're bound to run into someplace I recognize sooner or later."

"You've spent a lot of time here?" she asked.

He grunted. "That's putting it mildly. I spent two months earlier this year in this very jungle, doing surveillance on the rebels before they attacked. Then we got trapped in St. George and had to egress right through the middle of the damned revolution."

"Sounds like fun," she commented.

He looked up at her and grinned. "That was the mission where we blew up the airport."

"What ever happened to the woman with you guys?"

"My commander married her."

"Love in a war zone? How romant—" she broke off.

He looked up at her sharply. If he wasn't mistaken, she was blushing. Hell, the back of his own neck abruptly felt hot.

He lowered his head and got back to work. The dead soldier had a utility belt. Tex unbuckled the wide webbing and pulled it from underneath the guy. He started opening its pockets.

"Jackpot!" he exclaimed.

"What?" Kimberly stepped closer.

He held up a tiny brown glass bottle, not much bigger than his thumb for her to see. "Water purification tablets."

"Hallelujah." Kimberly sighed in relief.

"He's got a canteen, too. We can fill it and have a little to drink between water sources." The guy had all sorts of useful bits and pieces in the belt's half-dozen compartments. Knife sharpener, compass, needles, fish hooks, hell, even condoms. He stuffed those back into their pouch hastily.

Kimberly's mouth curved into a beautiful smile that warmed him from the inside out. "Who'd have thought I'd be so thrilled with a canteen and a bottle of iodine pills a few days ago?" she asked, shaking her head and sending her mud-caked hair rattling like a pile of bones.

He gazed up at her. Even coated in mud and grass, she was beautiful. Her bones, the shape of her face, were exquisite, and the bright green of her eyes matched the jungle around them.

"Survival scenarios have a way of stripping everything down to the bare essentials."

She stared back at him. Something electric sprang up between them, pulling him slowly to his feet. "They do, don't they?" she murmured.

He'd never thought much further than food, water and shelter before on a survival trek. But abruptly, a need to kiss her became absolutely necessary to his long-term survival. He stepped forward slowly. He didn't care if her clothes were brittle with dried mud, if her face was coated in the stuff, if he couldn't get his hands into her hair, let alone run his fingers through it. He needed this woman. Now.

She moaned as his arms came around her. Their mouths met and they melted into one. One body. One soul.

Her hands skimmed up his ribs under his shirt, sliding around to his back to pull him closer. "I was so scared this morning," she murmured, her breath a warm caress on his lips.

"But you fought through it," he murmured back.

Her lips softened and molded to his, cutting off any further conversation. He felt the aftermath of her desperation coursing through her, a wildness that reached out to him and called forth his most basic responses.

He slanted his head, his tongue slashing past any resistance she offered, plundering her mouth with reckless abandon. The way her breath caught in her throat drove him wild, and he could think of nothing but having her, all of her, right now. Nobody was chasing them. They could afford to steal a moment for themselves.

She arched into him, her body strung as tight with need as his.

"Please, Tex," she murmured. "Take me away from here."

Her words registered as love talk. "Together," he mumbled back against her lips. "We'll fly all the way home."

His hands fumbled at her sweater, pushing it up toward her neck.

"You'll take me out of the jungle now?" she asked hopefully. "Home?"

He froze in the act of lifting her sweater off of her.

"Not until we've got the rifle back," he mumbled. His brain felt dull, like an unsharpened knife.

She pulled back, looking up at him keenly. "I want to go home."

"So do I. But what does that have to do with what we're doing right now?" *Come on, brain. Get in gear, here!*

She stepped completely away from him and yanked her sweater down. "Fine. Let's go get the damned gun so we can get out of this hellhole."

"Fine," he shot back.

She glared hotly at him. He glared back.

He shoved the dead man's fatigue shirt at her. "Put this on. It'll hold up better than that flimsy sweater of yours. Besides, it's not caked in mud."

She stared at it in loathing. And sighed. ''No, it's just bloody.''

She reached for it in resignation and slipped it on.

He buckled the dead guy's utility belt around his waist, stuffed everything he'd found into its pockets, and moved off in the direction of the retreating tracks from the rebels.

He didn't immediately hear Kimberly's footsteps behind him. That was just peachy with him. If she wanted to throw a tantrum and sulk at the foot of that cliff till she rotted, that was her choice.

A swish of leaves behind him told him Kimberly'd caught up. The insidious relief that stole through him startled him. Rather than examine it, he picked up the pace and continued on.

The rebels were moving as a group and not bothering to hide their tracks. It was an easy thing to follow the trail of fifty men barging through the jungle. Their machetes cleared what felt like a veritable road through the brush. He and Kimberly made excellent time.

They'd walked for two or three sullen hours when a distant sound made him pause and take note. A grin split his face.

''What?'' Kimberly snapped irritably.

''I think I hear something you're going to like.''

''A taxi cab that'll take me to Washington?''

''Better.''

She tugged on his shirt till he actually had to stop. He turned to face her. ''What is it?'' she demanded.

''Let's go find out if I'm right,'' he said imperturbably. He didn't want to get her hopes up and then disappoint her if he was wrong.

They walked another couple minutes and the sound grew into a steady roar. He pushed forward and even began to smell it. When he could feel it on his skin, they finally broke out into a large clearing. Before them stretched a pool of water, maybe a hundred feet across. A small waterfall cascaded down the side of a large outcropping on the far side of the pond.

Its crashing sound was what he'd been hearing all this time. It wasn't a gigantic waterfall, but it was plenty big enough to pound all the mud off them and out of their clothes.

He stepped aside so Kimberly could see. "Can I interest you in a bath?" he asked.

She squealed with delight and rushed forward. Then she stopped abruptly. "Are there leeches in there?"

He squatted down and stuck his hand briefly in the water. "Nah, it's too cold for them."

"Are you sure?" she asked dubiously.

"Positive. Of course, it's going to make for a wicked chilly bath."

"Can we afford the time?" she asked.

"Yeah. We're moving fast, and I don't want to run up on their heels before dark. We've got maybe an hour to get clean," he replied.

Kimberly was already tearing off her filthy clothes. She stopped when she got to her lacy pink bra and matching bikini panties.

He gulped at all those slim, tempting, female curves. Hot damn, but she had a great body. He drank in the sight of her thirstily. Her legs were just right. Slender, but muscular, like a dancer's. He felt his body getting all hot and bothered at the thought of those sleek thighs wrapped around his waist.

Kimberly stepped forward, dipping a toe in the water. She looked like some fey forest creature as a shaft of sunlight fell upon her form.

With a gasp, she eased into the water. "Oh, my gosh, it's like ice water!" she exclaimed.

He shrugged out of his shirt and pants and stepped forward. The second her gaze landed on him, he felt its heat on his skin like a laser beam.

He didn't think often about how he looked. He usually

measured his body in terms of how strong or fit it was. But for once he was glad for the bulging muscles, the flat stomach and lean hips.

Her gaze devoured him. He walked toward her, as mesmerized by her as she seemed to be by him. She'd waded out waist-deep into the pool, only a few yards from the shore. The bottom must drop away pretty steeply.

He took a running step and leapt away from the bank in a shallow dive. He knifed into the water only a few feet from Kimberly.

The frigid water blasted him back painfully to the present. Wow, that was cold!

He shivered through the first shock of it and surfaced, shaking the water out of his hair. The bottom was rocky but not jagged. He stood up.

Kimberly's nipples were tight little buds beneath her bra, which clung to her almost more revealingly than being completely naked. His hands ached to cup the soft mounds, to tease the heat back into her breasts, to tighten her nipples once more for an altogether different reason.

Kimberly ducked under the water and a pool of light brown floated to the surface around her. The mud coming off her. He dunked himself and scrubbed the mud off his body.

He didn't usually worry much about cleanliness in the field. He took it when he could get it, and he didn't sweat it when he couldn't. But today, bathing beside Kimberly, he felt every inch of her relief as she washed herself. His own skin suddenly itched with a burning need to be squeaky clean.

He swam over to the waterfall and stood up under the edge of its pounding spray. No shower had ever felt better. He stepped out of the pounding flow and opened his eyes. Kimberly stood under the water beside him with her eyes closed and her head thrown back.

She looked like a goddess. Venus rising from the sea. She looked almost fragile beneath the force of the waterfall. A pang of remorse hit him for the way he'd made her work the past few days. She deserved to be pampered and protected. She was a lady, and he wished he could have shown her proper respect. But he'd dragged her around a jungle and bullied her into feats of enormous effort like he was a drill sergeant and she was some raw recruit.

The circumstances had demanded it, but that didn't make the regret for the way he'd been forced to treat her any less keen.

He slogged over to her side through the waist-deep water. ''Turn around,'' he murmured.

Her eyes flew open and she looked up at him warily.

''I'll scrub your back for you,'' he offered quietly.

A look of surprise flashed across her face. It pained him that an act of kindness from him elicited such a response.

She turned around and he reached out slowly. Her back was slim and graceful, disappearing into the water enticingly. He rubbed her shoulders gently, massaging away the tension there while he worked the last, light brown film of mud off her skin.

He diverted falling water onto her back, rinsing away the last vestiges of filth. Her skin was a warm, ivory color like a rich ice cream. It begged to be licked and tasted in the same manner as the sweet treat. He clamped down on his libido sternly. Hadn't he just been telling himself that he should treat her with more respect?

She turned under his hands to face him. His palms came to rest on her slim shoulders.

With her wet hair slicked back from her face and not a stitch of makeup on, she was possibly more beautiful than he'd ever seen her before, including the first day he met her. Not many women got more good looking as all the artifice and primping was stripped away, but she was one of them.

He stared down at her, mesmerized by the purity of her features. In the dancing play of light from the falling water, her eyes glowed with an ethereal, emerald light with an unmistakable offer. Herself.

Chapter 12

He stared down at her in shock. The directness of her gaze threw him completely off balance.

It would be so easy to take her up on the offer, to sink into the secret garden of pleasure in her eyes. To lose himself within her. To walk away from the danger and fatigue, the filth and fear. To forget his duty. To abandon his honor…

He jerked his hands away from her with a sharp curse. She was just like Emily. She didn't get it. Didn't understand what honor and duty and doing the right thing meant to him. Hell, she wasn't all that different from his mother, either. When the first opportunity presented itself for her to bail on him and run from hardship, she'd leapt at it.

Not that he could blame Kimberly for wanting to get out of the jungle. Hell, he was seriously looking forward to a real bed and a real meal, himself. But that didn't mean he was willing to walk away from everything that mattered to him for the sake of his short-term comfort. Unlike his mother and Kimberly, he wasn't that selfish.

He sighed. "I have a responsibility, not only to myself, but to hundreds or thousands of people who will *die* if I don't get that rifle back. I'm the only person in the right place at the right time to recover the RITA, and by God, I'm going to do it!"

Her reasonable tone of voice was like fingernails on a chalkboard to him. "Tex, listen to me. You can't do this alone. It's too much for one man. You're so caught up in being a hero you're not thinking straight."

He answered bluntly. "Bull. I'm thinking perfectly straight. I *can* do this mission. You have no idea what kind of training I've got, what my skills are. You've just got a burr up your butt about this whole situation because your father was a big war hero and you can't stand anyone who's like him."

"That's not true!" she retorted hotly.

He glared angrily at her. "What's the matter, Kimberly? Can't stand being in the company of an honest man? Got tired of being the military hero's daughter, so you set out to tear down everything he stands for?"

She recoiled from that one like he'd hit a nerve. She turned and started wading toward the bank of the pool. He followed after her, splashing loudly.

"Is that why you're so bent on stopping me?" he taunted. "Don't want to have to stand in the shadow of another war hero? Well, don't worry about it. I don't give a damn about being on the cover of a magazine, and I'm sure as hell not interested in politics. I'm not going to steal your precious spotlight!"

She whirled abruptly and he almost ran into her. She glared up at him, her hands planted on her hips. "I don't give a damn if you're a hero or not, Tex Monroe. I was only trying to save your life, you sanctimonious bastard!"

Oh.

He stopped. And blinked.

Her eyes snapped like sparks flying off a sword, hot and deadly. She was serious.

"Why?" he asked, feeling stupid.

"Because you've saved my life a hundred times already. Because I don't want to see your own need to be a hero destroy you like it did my father. Because…because I care about you, dammit!" She spun away and splashed the last few yards to the shore. "How in the bloody hell am I supposed to dry myself off without a towel?" she demanded irritably from the grassy bank.

He answered distractedly, "Lie down in the sun and air dry."

She cared for him?

The thought whirled around in his head with the force of a revelation. How could that be? They were so different, came from such different worlds. She was so classy, so elegant. Country clubs and cocktail parties. He was all about crawling around in filthy jungles after criminals. What in blazes did a guy like him have to offer to a woman like her?

Dazed, he flopped down beside her in the soft grass. A shaft of sunlight warmed his skin. After the icy chill of the water, it felt great. He threw an arm over his eyes to block the bright light.

What in the hell was he supposed to say in response to something like that? He cared for her, too?

It was the truth, but did he dare admit it to her? Did he dare give her that much power over him?

"Tex, would you do something for me? Could you… Never mind." Her voice trailed off without finishing the question.

What was she going to ask of him? To kiss her? To make love to her? To tell her he felt the same way? What did she really want from him?

"What were you going to ask?" he prompted.

"I was going to ask if you'd mind checking me for leeches."

Leeches? So much for declarations of his feelings. Man,

did he feel stupid. A snort of laughter escaped him. "Sure. No problem."

He hoisted himself up on one elbow and looked down at her, stretched out on the ground beside him. Good Lord, she was beautiful. Her skimpy lingerie clung to her, half dry, more tempting than just about anything he'd ever seen before. Belatedly, he checked her front for any sign of a leech.

"Roll over on your stomach so I can have a look at your back," he ordered gently.

She rolled toward him, bringing her almost into direct contact with his entire torso. His body responded with a powerful surge of white-hot lust.

He rose up on his knees beside her, fighting an overwhelming urge to leap on top of her and take her. His gaze skimmed the length of her body. No telltale brown smudges.

He placed his hands on the middle of her back.

She jumped and he murmured, "I'm going to check underneath your bra strap. Make sure nothing got under it."

She nodded, her face buried in the crook of her arm.

Her skin was warm to the touch. Like satin. He started in the center of her back, running his hands outward, underneath the elastic band of her brassiere.

He continued his explorations around her sides, underneath her arms. She took in a sharp, light breath and held it. He paused, giving her a chance to tell him to stop. But she remained silent, her face hidden.

Slowly he eased his hands farther around her, underneath her bra. The swelling flesh of her breasts came under his fingers. His gut throbbed with need and his male flesh went rock-hard. Her only response was to lift her chest slightly off the ground.

They still had a little time before they had to go. Enough time, to be precise. She moaned and his hands swept forward, cupping her breasts entirely in his hands. He

skimmed over them, encountering nothing but the silkiness
of her skin. He tweaked her nipples gently, and they tightened instantly into hard little nubs of desire. Kimberly took
another light, short breath.

He tested the weight of her breasts in his hands, massaging them and molding them lightly. He rubbed his fingers in circles around the tight tips, until she arched her
back even more, lifting her breasts even farther off the
ground, giving him even fuller access.

He teased her flesh lightly at first, and then with more
pressure until she fairly gasped with pleasure. Her whole
body undulated subtly before he withdrew his hands, retreating the way he'd come. He ran his palms down the
elegant curve of her spine, slipping his fingers under the
elastic of her panties.

Her body felt like molten silver, flowing and pulsating
beneath his touch. He cupped the warm flesh of her bottom, running his hands lightly over her hips and sides.
Nothing on her skin, he noted vaguely. He returned to the
first hint of the crevice of her buttocks and skimmed a
single finger lightly into its warmth.

Kimberly gasped, her hips lifting slightly off the ground.
He eased his finger farther along the curve of her body,
his control spinning dangerously close to the breaking
point. He wanted the tight heat of her around him. He
wanted to feel the undulations of her hips beneath his, to
feel her surging up into him like that.

Shaken, he ran his hands around her hips until he felt
the first soft rise of feminine flesh under his fingertips. He
slid his hands slowly between her thighs, which softened
in unmistakable welcome.

The incredible softness between her legs was nearly his
undoing. He penetrated the folds of velvet flesh slowly,
easing his fingers toward the very core of her. His own
breath came in ragged bursts as she moved helplessly
against his hand. With a single finger, he stroked the damp,

sensitive center of her, wringing a soft moan from Kimberly's throat.

A flush stole up her neck, and even though her face was buried in her arm, the little gasps of pleasure she took still reached him.

He spread his fingers lightly and her thighs opened for him, granting him full access to her.

He tested the smooth wetness of her entrance, driven almost out of his mind by its tight, hot promise. Her delicate muscles clenched around his fingertip, and abruptly she shuddered. Another moan slipped from her throat.

Without dislodging his hand, she rolled onto her side to face him.

He stroked her deeply, and her eyes fluttered shut in abandon. "Do you want more?" he managed to force out past his clenched teeth.

She answered on a sigh. "Oh, yes."

The relief that flooded him was so profound he didn't even want to think about what he'd have done if she'd said no.

He hooked her panties and skimmed them down her legs in a single, swift movement. A quick reach behind her and her bra fell away. He dipped his head to taste her rosy flesh, the peaks straining with pleasure as he circled them with his tongue.

Her hands speared into his hair, pressing him closer to her heated flesh. He feasted upon her breasts, relishing the dewy freshness of her skin.

And then her hands were on the waistband of his briefs. Her fingers dipped inside, clasping his throbbing flesh and threatening to send him over the edge right then and there.

He fumbled behind him for the web belt lying on top of his clothes, searching for the pouch with the condoms. He ripped open the foil packet quickly, praying the guy'd bought a decent brand that wouldn't break under the strain of what they were about to do to it.

He slipped off his briefs and skimmed on the protection

in one quick move. He gathered Kimberly in his arms and leaned over her, relishing the sexual haze in her eyes.

Starting at her brow, he ran his fingertips lightly down her cheek and throat, down her neck, through the warm valley of her breasts, across her flat stomach, and down, down, to the hot, wet core of her.

Her thighs fell open and she pulled him down to her, impatient in her need. He laughed and obliged, settling himself between her sleek thighs.

He kissed her then, melding their mouths into a heated, passionate dance of advance and retreat, a swirling, carnal waltz. Finally she tore her mouth away, gasping for him to come to her.

The slide of flesh on heated flesh about did him in. He forced himself to take her slowly, relishing every agonizing inch of the journey home. Finally he was seated deep within her, her heat clenching him more tightly than he'd imagined possible, her muscles throbbing with tremors of pleasure before he even began to move.

He retreated slowly and she surged up into him, demanding all of him. He thrust deeply into her, matching her desire with his own.

Just as they had during their midnight treks, their bodies quickly fell into sync, mirroring each other's movements with the perfection of a symphony. The music of their souls built into a towering crescendo, their bodies pounding out the rhythm with abandon, their throats singing out the glory of their passion.

In the same instant their voices broke on a gasp. They froze while the climax of their lovemaking tore them free of their bodies and flung them up into the ether, away from the material world.

They hurtled back down together, the power of their release slamming them back into their bodies with a shudder of exquisite pleasure so intense they nearly lost consciousness for a moment.

Tex became aware of his breathing. He was sucking air

like he'd run a marathon. Hell, a triathlon. Kimberly's body was damp and hot beneath his. He propped himself up on one elbow and used his free hand to push her golden hair back from her forehead.

Her chest rose and fell deeply beneath his and a rosy flush tinted her entire body. Her eyes fluttered open and she stared up at him in dazed amazement.

"Welcome back," he murmured.

"Wow," she breathed.

He smiled at the wonder in her voice. He could lay here forever, just looking down at her. The moment was perfect. She was perfect.

Carefully he memorized her down to the very last detail. For as long as he lived, when the going got tough and he needed a reminder of why he was fighting to live, this would be the moment he hearkened back to.

"What are you doing?" she asked.

"Making a memory. Next time I'm about to die, this is what I'm going to think of. It will motivate me to make it out alive. And if I do die, I can't think of a better moment in my life to have in my mind when I go."

A soft smile curved her mouth. "What if it's true that your last living thought colors your afterlife? You might end up being a totally lascivious ghost."

He grinned. "Sounds to me like a decent way to spend eternity."

She laughed up at him. "Men. You're all the same."

He rolled away from her gently and then stood up in a single move. He held a hand down to her. "Can I interest you in another bath and maybe a bit to eat? It would need to be a quick bath, but I think we can spare a few extra minutes."

"Two baths in one day? Will the luxury of this vacation never cease?" she teased.

"We aim to please. If you're real lucky, I'll catch us some fish for supper. I saw a few in the water earlier."

She groaned with pleasure. "Fish. Something that actually qualifies as food fit for human consumption. Oh, how you spoil me.''

He leaned down and dropped a quick kiss on her up-turned mouth. ''I do my best, darlin'.''

Kimberly knelt by the shore, rinsing the worst of the filth out of their clothes. She watched Tex stand motionless as a statue in thigh-deep water. He held a sharpened stick high over his shoulder. He looked like a Greek god. Apollo poised to sling his war spear.

She fed a couple more sticks into the fire he'd built before he went fishing. For some reason the very act of having a fire made her feel safer. It was an acknowledgment that they were no longer running for their lives.

She waved away a plume of smoke as an errant puff of wind blew in her direction. An abrupt flash of movement made her jump. Tex's arm had just shot down into the water.

He lifted up the spear and a good-size fish wiggled on the end of the stick. Grinning, Tex waded to the shore.

''Hey!'' she exclaimed. ''You actually caught one!''

''Being a hunter is all about patience and cunning, my dear.'' His eyes gleamed at her in a way that had nothing to do with fish. He knelt beside her, pulling the flopping fish off the spear. ''Do you know how to prepare a fish?'' he asked.

She gave him a quelling look. ''My idea of preparing fish is to go to this wonderful little private restaurant I know in Annapolis and tell the chef how I want it cooked.''

He laughed. ''I forgot. You're a city slicker.'' He picked up the still flopping fish. A flash of silver glinted off its scales. ''First order of business is to kill it. You bash it on the head with a rock or the butt of a knife.''

She winced as he demonstrated. At least the thing quit wiggling.

''Next, you chop off its head and slit its stomach from

chin to tail. Then, you squeeze out all the entrails. You can just spread it flat and cook it right there, or you can cut off the tail and fillet it if you're feeling fancy.''

She was still stuck on the squeezing-out-the-entrails part. She began to feel slightly nauseous, and much less hungry for fish then she'd been a minute or two ago.

''Here. You give it a try,'' he said, shoving the dead fish and his knife into her hands.

The fish was cold and slimy. Ick.

She looked up at him pleadingly. ''When we get back home, I'll take you to that restaurant in Annapolis, my treat, if you'll fix the fish.''

''Squeamish, eh?''

Darn him. He was laughing at her. ''Yes. Yes, I am squeamish. And I'm not ashamed to admit it.''

He lifted the fish out of her hands and knelt by a rock, which he used as a work surface. He efficiently whacked off the creature's head. She looked away hastily and busied herself adding more wood to the fire.

''That's enough wood,'' Tex commented over his shoulder at her. ''We don't want a bonfire. It'd send up too big a smoke plume.''

Alarmed, she replied, ''I thought we were safe. Nobody's chasing us anymore, right?''

''True, nobody's chasing us. But that doesn't mean we're safe.''

She turned around to face him. A neat, white fillet was falling away from the carcass of the fish under the ministrations of his sharp knife.

Now what threat did they face? Her heart raced and her stomach felt truly queasy as she asked, ''Why are we still in danger?''

Tex glanced up from the second fillet. ''Nobody in this country likes Americans. The poachers and farmers out here would have no compunction about slitting our throats just because of our nationality. More importantly, if the rebels figure out we're tailing them, you better believe they'll kill us if they can. They went to a lot of trouble to get the RITA rifle, and they're not going to hand it over without a fight.''

She gulped. What he said made sense.

He stood up and moved to her side. ''Here.'' He handed her the two fillets that, thankfully, looked like fish was supposed to, now.

''Do you think you can manage to thread those on a stick and roast them over the fire?''

She frowned up at him. ''What are you going to be doing?''

''I'm catching a couple more fish. We could both use a no-kidding, stomach-filling meal, and we can smoke any leftover fish and eat it later.''

She managed to drop the fish twice, coating it with ash, then to burn her fingers wiping the ash off, and to scorch her face from the heat of the fire before the fish was finally cooked through, but she did it.

Tex finished cleaning the four additional fish he caught and joined her by the fire. Proudly, she handed him his fillet on a stick. He took a bite while she watched anxiously.

''Well?'' she asked.

''Well what?''

''How does it taste?'' she demanded.

He grinned. ''Fine. You did a great job of cooking it. Or are you waiting to see if I keel over dead before you taste yours?''

She stuck her tongue out at him and bit into her fish. It had a strong, oily taste, but she was so relieved to be eating real food again that she didn't care. They ate another entire fish. Then Tex partially cooked the remaining fish before wrapping it in green leaves and burying it in the coals of the fire.

''That'll be ready in about an hour,'' he remarked. ''We can rest until it's done.''

She could think of something else she'd like to spend an hour doing. But even the idea of saying it out loud made her blush.

Tex hopped up and searched the edge of the woods for a moment. He stooped, picked a handful of leaves and came back to her side.

He flopped down on the ground beside her, half reclining against the buttress root of a giant tree. "Here, have a couple mint leaves."

She smelled them cautiously, enjoying the bitingly fresh odor.

She watched Tex pop several his into his mouth and start chewing. Around the leaves, he explained, "It's not exactly a toothbrush and toothpaste, but it gets the fish taste out of your mouth."

She mimicked him, gingerly nibbling the edge of a leaf. It had a rather green taste to it, but the cool, minty flavor the leaves left behind was worth it.

She watched Tex prop his hands behind his neck and close his eyes. When he relaxed like that, he looked just like a tiger, sleek and well-fed. She itched to reach out and touch him, to explore more slowly this time the expanse of muscles that was his chest and shoulders. She talked to distract herself. "So what's the plan now?"

He answered without opening his eyes. "We track the rebels until we catch up with them. Then we watch for an opportunity to move in and steal the rifle back. Once we've got it, we hightail it out of there and get back home."

She frowned. "We're going to have to run away from the rebels again?"

"'Fraid so."

Her stomach fell to her feet. Just when she'd finally relaxed, he had to go and drop that bomb on her.

He opened one eye and peered at her. "Why the long face?"

She rolled her eyes. "Do you have to ask?"

"No." He sighed.

He held an arm out to her. "Come here."

She cuddled against his powerful side, laying her head on his solid shoulder.

"Tell you what. I'll make it up to you as best as I can.

I'll try to do this mission as fast as I can, and I'll do what I can to make the trek as comfortable as possible for you.''

"I don't care how long it takes, Tex. Just as long as you're safe. If you'll be at less risk to do it slowly, then by all means, take your time.''

She couldn't believe she'd just said that. But once the words were out of her mouth, she realized they were absolutely true. She'd rather spend an extra couple weeks out in the jungle than see any harm come to him.

His hand began to move across her back soothingly. He dropped a kiss into her hair. "It'll be okay,'' he murmured.

Abrupt tingles shot across her skin. She was far from okay. She needed more of that, and she needed it right now. She should hold out against her desire. Should take advantage of his full stomach and relaxed mood to argue one more time with him. But it wasn't like he'd change his mind in this lifetime. Reluctantly, she admired his conviction and let it be.

She ran her palms over the bulging muscles of his chest, her fingers acutely sensitive to the fine ripple of response that raced across his skin.

She really ought to let him get some rest… His hands plucked at her collar, peeling the fatigue shirt off her shoulders, baring her breasts to the cool air and pinning her arms at her sides…. The thought spun away.

His fingers speared into her hair, pulling her face to his, holding her gently in place while he plundered her mouth.

Mint still lingered on his breath and she savored the taste of him. Then his mouth slid away from hers, down her throat and toward the cleft between her breasts.

Anticipation shot through her. The remembered feel of his mouth on her flesh, of the magic he wove with his tongue, tightened her nipples in response before he even got there.

His mouth closed upon a rosy peak and she was lost.

Chapter 13

How Tex managed to move around briskly, putting out the fire and packing up the smoked fish after what they'd just spent the past hour doing, she had no idea.

When he helped her to her feet, her legs felt virtually boneless. Heavy languor weighed down her limbs, and it was an effort to follow him back into the jungle.

Her brain felt drugged. All she could think about was the way his mouth and hands had moved on her skin, the way his flesh had filled her, hot and hard and pulsing. Even now, the thought of it made her go weak at the knees.

Fortunately the pace he set wasn't too awful. Wearing her pants from the first guard and the newly washed and semi-dried shirt from the second soldier, she found the going much easier. She was free to climb and scramble over and around obstacles without worrying about catching or tearing her clothes.

They picked up the trail of the rebel force where they'd left it off. Instead of just running through the brush this afternoon, though, Tex stopped now and then. He'd point out a footprint in the mud, or the way the twigs were broken to indicate which direction the rebels were moving.

He even stopped once to pick a gorgeous white orchid for her. Its deep throat was scarlet edged with yellow, its feathery petals a pure, brilliant white. After inhaling its sweet, exotic scent, she tucked it behind her ear.

They hiked until nightfall. Tex picked out a camping spot, then hacked the lower limbs off several trees and dragged the pile of boughs over to where she sat. In the settling darkness she made out his hands, weaving the boughs in some intricate pattern. He laid the resulting frame on the ground and then tore off a dozen giant banana leaves to lay over it.

When she stretched out on the makeshift mattress, its springy support held her a good six inches off the ground. It wasn't quite her own bed, but it wasn't bad. It was a heck of a lot more comfortable than the damp, cold ground they'd been sleeping on.

The boughs gave as Tex's weight eased down beside her.

She snuggled against him, enjoying their newfound intimacy. For the first time she didn't lie in the dark listening fearfully for the sounds of men hunting them. She noticed the jungle's nighttime symphony and was amazed by its variety and richness.

A deep popping noise sounded nearby.

"What's that?" she asked, startled.

"A frog," Tex murmured easily. "About the size of a bullfrog. Lives in the trees and eats bugs. I don't know its name."

She subsided, relieved. A few moments later a sibilant hiss startled her. "What's that?"

"A coatamundi. Looks sort of like a raccoon. Good eating if you can catch them, but they're fast little suckers."

She subsided yet again. And then a terrible screech rent the night air. She lurched against Tex. "My God, what's that?"

"A big bad jaguar that's going to come eat you if you don't quit asking what all the noises are."

"Really?" she asked breathlessly.

He chuckled and ruffled her hair. "Jaguars don't eat people. They're too small to attack humans, and they're terrified of us, anyway. I think that was a monkey."

A couple more strange noises erupted and she jumped, but she didn't ask about them.

Tex's smooth, deep voice caressed her out of the darkness. "Do you need some distracting from all the noises, darlin'?"

"That would be wonderful," she answered, relieved.

"Any preferences on how we go about it?" he asked.

She smiled against his chest. "It's my turn to taste you all over, this time."

His whole body clenched beneath her. He cleared his throat. "That sounds, uh, fine."

She smiled at the way his breath caught when her mouth slid across the rippled washboard of his stomach. And when her mouth slid even lower, she loved the way his groans rose to join the other untamed sounds of the night.

The muffled alarm of his stolen watch beeped and he fished around in the cloth he'd wrapped it in to mute its noise. He turned it off and swam slowly toward consciousness. Something warm and sleek and female pressed against his side. A smile curved his lips. She'd about killed him with pleasure last night. But what a way to go.

Reluctantly he disentangled himself from Kimberly and sat up. The jungle was quiet. The night creatures had retired for the evening, but the first hint of dawn hadn't arrived yet to wake the chorus of daytime creatures.

He leaned over and kissed her smooth shoulder. She groaned and rolled over onto her stomach. He eased the space blanket down her back, kissing the curve of her spine as he went. She stretched with the lazy contentment of a cat.

She mumbled, "It's still nighttime. I thought we were going to take it easy from here on out."

"This is taking it easy. I let us sleep a whole extra hour."

"What time is it?" she asked sleepily.

"Four-thirty. Time to rise and shine."

She groaned and rolled over. Her breasts gleamed, pale in the darkness, and his hands started to reach forward. God, he couldn't get enough of her.

He fisted his hands until his nails bit into his flesh. They were never going to catch the rebels if he spent every waking moment making love to her.

He sighed and pressed to his feet. He pulled on his clothes and helped Kimberly into hers. He packed up their gear, kicked apart their bed and moved out.

The rebels were making no effort whatsoever to conceal their movement and it was a no-brainer to track them through the dense jungle. Thank God. Without a machete to slash a way through the underbrush, this stretch of jungle would have been nearly impassable. They'd have ended up crawling forward on their hands and knees most of the time.

He'd done that before, the last time he'd been in Gavarone with Charlie Squad. They'd been watching the rebel army prepare for war. An army shockingly well-equipped and trained for a bunch of locals in a rinky-dink South American country. He and the team were pretty sure a guy named Eduardo Ferrare was backing them, although they didn't have any solid proof.

Charlie Squad had run a surveillance op on Ferrare a few years back and heard enough of a meeting between Ferrare and a bunch of Gavronese terrorists to conclude they'd asked him for money. With a lot of zeros in the sum. Enough to fund an army.

As Tex followed the rebel trail, he turned over the question of why some rich crime lord would buy himself an entire army? What purpose would it serve Ferrare to take over a tiny chunk of South America? Free money laundering? An ego rush? Something more sinister?

He frowned, pulling his mind back to the business at hand. He'd leave the analysis to politicians like Kimberly's father. His job right now was to make sure the Gavronese rebels didn't add the RITA rifle to their arsenal.

Around midmorning, his stomach began to rumble. "Hungry?" he asked Kimberly over her shoulder.

"Starving. With all this fresh air and exercise, I'm working up a big appetite." She laughed.

He sat down on a high root and pulled out the smoked fish from the day before. It didn't taste half-bad prepared that way. They ate their fill and he passed her the canteen.

He watched her slender throat work, recalling memories of pleasure so intense last night that he thought he might pass out from it.

Before yesterday, he only had to touch her to be so turned on he was ready to explode. Now, just looking at her did it. How in the hell was he supposed to get through the next few days in such a state? For her sake, he had to find a way.

He cast about for a topic of conversation that would take his mind off of throwing her down and making love to her until she screamed. "Tell me, Kimberly. What is it you have against your father?"

She stopped drinking abruptly. "Why do you ask?"

"Well, you accused me of being like him, and you obviously hate his guts. I'm trying to avoid making the same mistake with you that he did."

She stared off into the jungle. Her answer was a long time in coming. "Vietnam changed him."

He snorted. "It changed everyone. Hell, any war changes a guy."

"No, I mean really changed him. He was seriously messed up when he came home."

"Physically or mentally?"

"Both. He got shot in the back and barely missed being

paralyzed. That's what got him sent home for good. It got him his fourth Purple Heart, too."

Tex whistled. Not bad. "What did he do in Nam?"

"He's never said a word about it."

Tex frowned. Most vets eventually got the war out of their system and were able to at least talk about it. "He's never talked about it because he can't or because he doesn't want to?"

Kimberly shrugged. "I don't know. I do know he worked in some sort of special expeditionary force. I think he went to some weird places."

Tex was intrigued. "Why do you say that?"

Kimberly seemed to withdraw into herself. He put a casual hand on her leg to let her know he was here for her. Eventually she continued.

"When he came home, my father had developed a bad temper. A really bad one. We never knew what was going to set him off. The silliest little things could completely freak him out. When he blew up, he used to yell in some Asian language. My mom taped it once and found out he was speaking Laotian.

Laotian? Damn. Most of the Americans who operated in Laos during Vietnam were Special Forces types doing very, very dirty work. No wonder the guy was messed up. Tex's hand tightened on her leg. "Did he hit you or your mom?"

She shook her head in the negative. "He put his fist through a wall a couple times, and he used to throw stuff like chairs and books. When he got that wild, Mom and I would leave and go shopping or get an ice-cream cone or something. He probably would have gotten physical with us if we'd have stuck around."

"How long did he stay mad?"

"A half hour, maybe. He was usually calmed down by the time we got home."

Tex frowned. "I don't mean to ask a strange question, but did he remember his episodes?"

Kimberly's gaze snapped to his. "How did you know that? He rarely remembered getting mad."

Tex shook his head. "Poor bastard was having flash-backs, wasn't he?"

Kimberly shrugged. "We weren't allowed to call them that."

"Why not? Did he get help? Some decent counseling at least?"

Kimberly laughed shortly, without humor. "Are you kidding? He was a junior congressman in a tightly con-tested district. He didn't dare go see a psychiatrist. It would've ruined his career."

"So he ruined his family instead?" Tex demanded.

"It got better over time. By the time I was twelve or so, he'd pretty much stopped having his episodes."

Tex ran a hand over his face. "It's called post-traumatic stress disorder."

Kimberly replied bitterly, "It was nice of Uncle Sam to give it a name twenty years too late. Meanwhile the gov-ernment sent thousands of young kids like my father off to war and destroyed them."

He stared at her in dawning understanding. "And that's why you're an antimilitary lobbyist on Capitol Hill, isn't it?"

She shrugged. "I don't believe any government has the right to put people in situations that will wreck their minds and souls."

"What if someone volunteers to serve? Is it okay then?" he asked.

She shook her head in the negative. "It's still wrong."

He frowned, considering her. He flatly disagreed with her point of view. But given the emotional cost to her life already, he doubted he'd change her mind. "That's why you're so bent out of shape over me going after the RITA rifle. You're worried I'll crack up under the stress."

"Something like that." She frowned. "You're an intelligent guy. How can you buy into the whole military brainwashing thing?''

''What brainwashing?'' he asked, surprised.

''This business of being a hero for your country. Mom and apple pie and Fourth of July.''

''What's wrong with that?'' he challenged.

''It's a lie. You don't come home all proud and happy from war. You come home totally screwed up in the head.''

''Am I screwed up in the head?'' he asked.

She glared at him. ''Not yet. That's why I want you to get out now, while you still can.''

''Kimberly,'' he said quietly. ''I've been on over thirty combat missions every bit as harrowing as this one, if not more so. And I'm okay. You said so yourself.''

''Oh, yeah? If you're so fine, why do you keep going back out? What makes you go on the next mission? And the next? And the next? You're chasing after some elusive dream that your own government has fed you of being a hero and saving the world.''

He jumped up and paced a few steps, then turned around to face her. ''What I do is important. I make a difference. I *do* make the world a better place.''

She threw up her hands. ''See? They've got you just where they want you. Believing your own press releases.''

He scowled and stuffed the canteen back in the web belt. She was wrong. He and the men he worked with *were* heroes. It *was* real. And it *was* necessary.

He wasn't about to let her plant any insidious doubts in his mind. Doubt led to weakness and weakness led to hesitation. And hesitation led to death.

''Let's go,'' he said shortly.

They walked for most of the afternoon in silence. It was a little after 5:00 p.m. when he stopped abruptly, cursing.

Kimberly came up beside him, peering over his shoulder. ''What's wrong?'' she murmured.

He pointed down at the ground in front of them. "The trail forks."

"And the significance of that is…what?" she asked.

"Ten, maybe twelve, of the rebels split off from the main party and headed to our left, while the other thirty or forty guys continued on that way." He pointed straight ahead.

"Oh." She stared down the two convergent trails on the ground. "Which one are we going to follow, since neither one is the path not taken?"

He snorted. "Robert Frost ain't gonna help us now, darlin'. We're gonna follow whichever one has the rifle."

"And how do you know which group that is?" she asked, her voice already impressed at his ability to read that from the tracks.

"I don't."

"You don't?" she echoed. "Then which way should we go?"

He shrugged. "The main road's still off to our left by a mile or two if I don't miss my guess. The smaller group has no doubt peeled off to head for it. There's probably a camp of some kind straight ahead of us, and that's where most of the rebels are headed."

Kimberly's next question followed his thought process exactly. "Where would they take the rifle?"

"I can make an argument for either group. The smaller group takes its prize to the road where it can be picked up and whisked off to some overseas producer to be copied. Or, the main group keeps its find and takes it to the rebel bosses at their jungle headquarters to show it off."

Kimberly frowned. "Either logic makes sense."

"Agreed." He looked at both sets of tracks and neither gave him any clue which way they should go. He looked up at Kimberly. "So. Which set of tracks would you follow?"

She looked down both trails. "If I had to choose, I'd

head for the road. If we don't find the rifle, then at least we can hitch a ride to a city and get out of here.''

He chuckled, genuinely amused. He had to give her credit for her persistence. "Problem is, if we don't catch the rebels before they get to the road and get picked up themselves, we'll completely lose their trail and we'll have no way of following them. Then we'll have to backtrack and pick up the trail of the guys who headed deeper into the jungle.''

"How much of a head start do the guys going for the road have on us?'' she asked.

"Good question." He walked several yards down their trail and knelt, examining the ground closely.

"They're about an hour ahead of us," he announced.

Kimberly lurched. "I had no idea we were so close to them after that long break we took!" she exclaimed quietly.

He stood up and rejoined her at the fork in the paths. "An hour is too big a gap for us to overcome before they get to the road. We'll never catch them. And by the time we come all the way back here, the trail deeper into the jungle will be cold. We're better off following the larger group of soldiers toward wherever they're going and hoping they've got the rifle.''

Kimberly sighed. "Somehow, I knew you were going to say that.''

He grinned at her dismay.

And then a sobering thought struck him.

The smaller, splinter group of rebels had hacked a clear trail through the jungle that Kimberly would have no trouble following all the way to the main road. If she wanted to leave him now and head for home, she'd probably be able to do it by herself. Somebody was bound to stop and pick her up. Lord knew, she could charm a dead man into taking her wherever she wanted to go. Odds were she'd be fine. Even if there was a risk she could be assaulted or raped...

It crossed his mind not to mention it to her. He hated the thought of her being harmed, not to mention being away from her. It was more than the mind-boggling sex he'd miss. He'd gotten accustomed to her presence. He even liked arguing with her. She was smart and articulate, even if some of her ideas were full of crap.

Dammit, he felt protective of her. He wanted to take her all the way home to Washington by himself, to personally tuck her back into her safe little world before he left her side. In the meantime, he wanted to keep her right here with him where he knew she'd be safe.

Except he couldn't promise to keep her safe in the days to come. His mission was an extremely risky one.

He cared about her too much to be selfish.

He sighed and looked her straight in the eye. "Kimberly, if you want to, you can follow that group of soldiers. They've made a clear path you'll have no trouble following. If you take it slow, they'll be long gone by the time you reach the road. You can flag down a truck or a bus and get the hell out of here right now if you want. It could be dangerous, but you could be home tomorrow."

Her green eyes darkened nearly to black as she stared back at him. She swallowed convulsively. "Do you want me to go?" she finally whispered.

"Hell, no, I don't want you to go!" he exploded.

She stared at him a little longer, her expression softening until he swore he saw tears glistening in her eyes. "If you don't object," she said quietly, "I'd rather stay with you."

His chest felt tight but he managed to squeeze out an answer. "I don't object."

Sonofagun. Who'd have thought she'd voluntarily stay for more of the misery and danger she had to know was coming? Decidedly un-Emily. Relief flooded his gut and he avoided examining her motives too closely. *She wasn't bailing out on him when she had the chance.*

Their gazes locked and strong emotion swam in her gaze. Something passed between them. An awareness. An understanding. An acknowledgment that their relationship had changed. They were in this together now.

He didn't know why in the hell she'd made that choice, but he wasn't about to question it right now. All that mattered was that she'd chosen to stay. With him.

"Ready to go chase us an army?" he asked lightly.

He grinned at her answering look of dismay.

"Cheer up, darlin'. We should catch 'em within twenty-four hours or so." He added, "If you're lucky, they won't have the rifle and we can go home."

She looked at him keenly. "Just out of curiosity, do you know what will happen if you go home without the gun?"

"Yeah, that's easy. I'll be court-martialed."

Chapter 14

Kimberly gulped. "Really?"

He answered casually, "Yeah, really. Colonel Folly gave me a direct order over the phone. He was explicit. Get that rifle back. That's my duty."

"It's not fair!" Kimberly exclaimed. "That's too difficult a mission to assign to one guy. Isn't there some law about not having to follow illegal orders?"

Tex grinned. "Yeah, there is, but this isn't an illegal order. Like I keep telling you, I've got the training to carry out the order."

She huffed. "I realize you've got the survival skills of Daniel Boone, and the rock-climbing skills of Spider-Man. But that doesn't mean you can take on dozens, if not hundreds, of rebel soldiers by yourself."

"Why not?" he asked blandly.

"This is just the sort of brainwashing I was talking about! Your boss has you convinced you're some sort of superhero, and you're not!"

He looked back over his shoulder with a wide grin. "Wanna bet?"

Oo-oh! Sometimes she just wanted to wring his neck.

They walked until early evening and stopped by mutual consent to camp for the night. They fell into the usual routine of Tex going hunting for a spot to sleep while she harvested what berries and ginger root she could find.

She looked up from where she dug as he approached a little while later. He moved with panther-like grace toward her, perfectly at home in this tropical wilderness. His male beauty was stunning.

"I found us a sweet little camping spot," he announced.

She sighed. "Too bad you didn't find us a sweet little four-star restaurant while you were at it."

"All in good time, darlin'. Think how much more you'll appreciate a fine meal when you get home."

She rolled her eyes. "I'll appreciate a greasy burger from a fast-food joint when I get home."

"You're on. I know a little hole-in-the-wall that serves the best burgers on the east coast."

She looked up at him sharply. There it was again. The casual reference to a future for them after they got out of here. She couldn't afford to think beyond the present. Each hour, each minute, was enough of a challenge to get through already.

"Come on," he said quietly. "Let's bed down early tonight. Tomorrow could be a long day."

She didn't need to ask why. He expected to make contact with the rebels tomorrow.

He led her into yet another thicket, but she was surprised when a small clearing opened up in the middle of it. She set up a real camp while he went hunting for water. She set to work weaving a bed like she'd seen Tex do. She had room to lay a small fire so she took care of that, too. Tex had the cigarette lighter, so she'd have to wait until he got back to light it. She laid out the roots and berries she'd stuffed into her shirt over the past couple of hours.

She stood back, pleased by her efforts. She hoped Tex would be, too. Who'd have guessed it was possible to wax domestic in the middle of a tropical jungle? She wasn't usually the fussy, frou-frou type under any circumstances. Besides, she wasn't actually being domestic. She was just helping with the chores.

The night noises gradually started up around her. One by one, the different creatures of the dark added their chorus to the overall din.

Tex had been gone a long time. She wasn't exactly worried about him, but she was concerned at what snag he'd run into that had slowed him down.

For once she actually heard him coming. He pushed through the wall of brush, his head emerging at knee level into the little clearing. She lowered the heavy stick she'd held poised over her head

"Hi, honey, I'm home," he announced.

She put an irate hand on her hip. "Did you go out with the boys again after work for a drink? I told you to call me when you're going to be late, Ward."

He stood up, grinning. "Sorry, June." He looked around the clearing at the camp she'd built. "Nice job."

She felt warm all over.

Tex continued. "We may be staying here for several days, so get comfortable and knock yourself out giving it all the comforts of home."

She frowned. "Why are we staying here?"

"The rebels are camped about a mile away. They've arrived at wherever they're going."

"Really? And where's that?"

"A big encampment. Tents enough for something like two hundred men."

"Is this the rebel headquarters you've mentioned seeing before?"

"No. Their headquarters had a compound of permanent buildings. This is a temporary deal. But I'm guessing they've been here for several weeks and plan to be here a couple more.''

"Doing what?" she asked curiously.

"That's what we're going to find out," Tex replied grimly. "You're about to get a crash course in covert surveillance."

"I don't think I like the way you just said that," she responded cautiously.

"It's tedious work under the best of circumstances, and because we don't have any binoculars or optical gear, it's going to be dangerous, too."

She looked at him intently. "How dangerous?"

"Depends on how close we have to get to see and hear what they're doing."

She gulped. That didn't sound encouraging at all. "Is this the part where we crawl around on the ground with twigs and grass in our hair and make like snakes?"

"Yup."

"Does this mean more mud?" she asked in resignation.

"Yup. Not the full body deal like before, but on your face and hands for sure."

She sighed. Well, at least she could scrub that amount of mud off herself on a daily basis.

"Normally a full team would set up a watch rotation where we each take turns observing. Since there's only me, I'll have to do all the watching and you'll have to do the hunting for food and water."

"Why can't I take a stint at the watch?" she asked.

He blinked at her in surprise. "You don't know what to look for."

"So teach me. How hard can it be to make a list of stuff that I should come get you if I see?"

He considered her idea. "I suppose I could do that. You're highly intelligent. You'd make the right call…"

. A burst of heat spread through her. He thought she was highly intelligent? Cool.

"Even if you just relieved me a couple hours a day, it

would let me hunt for real food for us and catch a little nap.'' He nodded. "That would help out a lot.''

She grinned and stuck out her hand. "We have a deal, then.''

He took her hand in his, the firm grasp sending shivers across her body. But instead of letting go of the handshake, he tugged her close. "I'd rather seal the deal with a kiss, myself,'' he murmured.

She laughed up at him in the gloom. "Why am I not surprised?''

His lips were warm and gentle against hers, kissing her with tenderness tonight. He lingered over the moment and she savored the unhurried mood of the evening.

He ran his hands up and down her arms, chasing away the chill of the night air before he pulled her slowly into his arms. His mouth molded to hers as he enfolded her in his slow heat and easy strength.

She murmured against his chest. "Do you have to go watch the rebels tonight?''

He answered into her hair, "I got close enough to hear that they're going somewhere nearby tomorrow to enter the last phase of preparations for something. We'll need to follow them then. But for tonight, there's nothing pressing going on. They were all more interested in getting drunk and sleeping in real beds than anything else.''

She groaned quietly. "I don't even drink, and that sounds great.''

A chuckle rumbled against her ear. "That bed you made looks pretty comfortable. Have you given it a try yet?''

"Nope. For all I know, it'll collapse the moment we sit down on it, or it'll poke us all night long.''

He eyed it over her shoulder. "Nah. Looks good from here. Did you learn to do that just by watching me yesterday?''

She nodded.

"Are you the arts and crafts type back home? Weaving? Knitting?''

"Heavens, no! I can't sit still long enough to do anything like that. I don't have the patience for it."

"Then I'm doubly impressed at how fast you picked that up. I learned it from bush people in Brazil. They're very primitive, but unbelievably intelligent when it comes to living in the jungle."

"Do they wear clothes?" she asked innocently.

"No, as a matter of fact, they don't for the most part. Fabric rots too fast in the heat and humidity to bother with it," Tex answered laughingly. "Are you proposing that they may have stumbled on an important survival concept?"

"Maybe we should test the theory."

She felt Tex's grin against her ear. "I like the way you think, Miss Stanton."

She ran her palms appreciatively over his solid chest. "I like the way you feel, Mr. Monroe."

Tex was leisurely about everything he did this night. It even took him a maddeningly long time to take her clothes off. He paused between every button, kissing her and tasting the new bit of flesh exposed as he slowly peeled back her garments.

By the time she managed to push his hands aside and divest him of his clothes, she was ready to tear them off his back. But even then, he caught her hands in his and restrained her from following her urges.

And then he laid her on the bed. If she didn't say so herself, it was pretty comfortable. The boughs cushioned her body, their resilience absorbing her weight gently.

Tex's knee landed beside her leg and he loomed over her, a black shadow in the dark. "Ah, yes," he remarked. "Just the way I like my beds. A little spring and a lot of woman in them."

She smiled up at him, reaching for the width of his shoulders. But he forestalled her.

"I found something while I was out. See if you can tell

what it is by feel.'' He put one hand across her eyes, blocking out what little light there was.

Her other senses leapt to heightened function. Cool air caressed her skin, and the jungle sounds seemed even louder. She waited, curious. And then something trembled against the back of her hand so lightly she could barely feel it. It touched her again, on the stomach this time. It was impossibly soft. Weightless. It tickled.

She squirmed under the sensation. ''What is it?'' she asked as it trailed down the length of her arm, raising goose bumps as it went.

''A peacock feather,'' Tex murmured.

He trailed it up the inside of her calf this time. Her legs fell apart at the gentle caress and the feather continued its path up the inside of her thigh. Tex touched her all over with the feather, tantalizing her with it until her whole body was hyperaware, hypersensitized.

And then his fingertips replaced the feather, touching her lightly, unpredictably, all over her body. Her skin tingled. Her breasts ached. She burned from head to toe. And then she lurched practically off the bed when his mouth closed on her most private places without warning, his tongue swirling hot and wet over the swollen throbbing of her core.

She groaned deep in the back of her throat.

His hand reached up and closed over her mouth. ''Shh, we're very close to the rebels,'' he murmured.

But then his mouth closed on her again, driving her out of her mind. She bit down hard on her lower lip to keep from crying out as he drove her over the edge of pleasure again and again.

Her limbs trembled all over and she had no strength left to move by the time he rose up over her. When a burning sword of steely flesh replaced his mouth, she thought she'd die from the pleasure of it. Somehow her body began to move again, responding to the pulsing intensity of his. Her limbs wrapped themselves around his heat and strength, clinging to the solid bulwark of him in a storm-tossed sea of desire.

Their desire churned and surged around them, and he became the wild waters, climbing to impossible heights and crashing down in breathtaking drops that tore the breath out of her lungs. Their bodies lunged and pounded into each other like wild flowing rapids. She gasped for air and he was there, taking her cries into his mouth, devouring her with savage need.

They drove each other onward, ever higher, ever more frenzied, until finally their desire broke upon itself and exploded in a rush of sparkling droplets and white foam.

Slowly the waves of pleasure retreated, leaving behind the bedrock of Tex's shoulders, the solid, reassuring presence of his big, warm body. He was an island of humanity in the midst of this alien, inhospitable place. She clung to him, even after the tremors of excessive pleasure ebbed and departed from her body.

He was her sanity. Her touchstone in the midst of this madness. No matter how angry she got at his misplaced hero complex, or how much his ''I'm in charge'' attitude irritated her, he was always there for her. Steady. Smart. Strong. Solid.

How could such a dangerous man feel so safe to her?

She'd seen the results of his work already. He'd shot and killed a man without so much as flinching. He could undoubtedly kill with his bare hands. Heck, he probably had. But when he laid those hands on her, touched her and held her, she felt more sheltered, more protected, than she had in her entire life. It was amazing having someone look out for her for a change, someone who believed she could do a tough job, but who was there with a helping hand whenever she needed it.

He rolled onto his back and she settled into the crook of his arm.

Her first day in the jungle seemed like a distant memory

to her now. She'd been so afraid. So out of her element. So completely clueless.

It wasn't like she felt totally at one with the jungle now, but she knew what to expect. Knew how to react. So slowly and quietly that she hadn't really even noticed it, Tex had taught her how to survive out here.

If something happened to him tomorrow, she had enough faith in her new skills that she'd make it out alive one way or another. When had that happened?

Tex had the same quiet confidence about him, too. She'd labeled it being a chauvinistic jerk initially. But that wasn't it at all. He knew his capabilities and had faith in them. Could she put the same trust in his skills as he did?

"A penny for your thoughts." His smooth voice drawled like honey in her ear.

"I was thinking about whether or not you're as good as you think you are."

"At what?" he asked, sounding distinctly alarmed.

It dawned on her that saying something like that to a guy immediately after making love with him maybe wasn't exactly the best timing. Giggling, she clarified, "I was thinking about your combat training."

He subsided beside her. He was silent for a time and then asked, "Do you trust me with your life?"

She answered without hesitation. "Absolutely."

"Then why don't you trust me with my own life? I have a pretty powerful vested interest in keeping me alive, you know."

She sighed. "Yeah, but in my case, your duty is to keep me alive. In your case, I think you consider death to be a viable alternative in certain situations. That's what scares me so bad."

He shrugged casually, belying the tension in his voice. "But there *are* some situations worth dying for."

"I've never seen one. So I have a hard time agreeing with you on that."

He grunted. "Lucky you. I've seen more than I care to count."

"How is it you're still alive, then?" she asked, perplexed by his logic.

"Because of superior training, teammates who are completely loyal to one another, and a good dose of luck."

She flinched. "That whole luck thing makes me nervous. I hate the idea of your life hinging upon luck."

He laughed quietly. "So do I. That's why I work so hard on the training part and on having the best possible teammates."

"Some teammate I make," she mumbled half under her breath.

His arm tightened briefly around her shoulders. "Don't sell yourself short. You've held up better than most of the civilians I've rescued over the years."

She blinked, surprised. That was a high compliment indeed, coming from him.

"Speaking of which, we both need to get a good night's sleep. The next couple of days could be pretty rough."

She groaned against his chest. She had enough perspective now on his concept of rough to translate his comment in her head. What he'd meant to say was that the next few days were going to be a living hell on earth.

Tex awoke before dawn the next morning to the sound of raindrops splatting on the space blanket he'd spread over them sometime in the night.

Kimberly's bed held them off the ground, and the plastic sheet over their heads kept off the rain. All in all, it was tempting to just hunker down in this warm, dry cocoon and bag chasing rebels for the day. He'd love nothing better than to make love to Kimberly in the rain for, oh, twelve or fourteen hours.

But duty called.

He dug out the watch and had a look at the time. Another half hour until his alarm went off. He rolled on his side, gathering Kimberly close and checking that the space blanket was tucked in well all around her.

She murmured in her sleep and snuggled closer.

Contentment welled up in him. The deep, bone settling kind of contentment of having found his life's purpose.

His life's purpose? Kimberly Stanton?

He literally froze in shock at the idea.

Gradually he forced his muscles to relax. But his mind whirled in near panic. His feelings were probably just the result of some rescuer-and-victim psychology at work.

He cast back through his training for recollection of what this was and how to deal with it. The Helsinki Syndrome related mainly to hostages beginning to sympathize with their captors. She was definitely not his hostage. Especially not after he'd offered her the chance to leave.

No applicable syndrome came to mind.

Could it be that he'd actually developed real feelings for her?

He hadn't seriously cared for a woman since Emily, and that was over ten years ago. He'd figured for the last couple years that he just wasn't the type to fall in love since it hadn't happened again in all that time. He just didn't have enough faith in any woman's staying power to give his heart to one and have her walk off with it again.

But, Kimberly hadn't left him today, and Lord knew she could have. Did she have some hidden agenda in staying with him? But what could she possibly have to gain by staying out here with him? *Was she for real?*

Were his feelings real, too? Damn, if they didn't *feel* real.

The way his gut wrenched when she was mad at him or when her face lit up in pleasure... The way he craved the touch of her... The way he looked forward to just being with her... The way he stored up things to tell her when he was away from her...

Crap.

It was the real deal, all right.

He was in trouble now.

Deep, deep trouble.

Chapter 15

Kimberly woke up to the smell of something cooking over a fire. It sizzled quietly like frying bacon. She opened her eyes, disoriented for a second at the silver plastic over her face.

Tex looked up when she pushed back the space blanket. His gaze was serious, guarded even, this morning. "Hey, sleepyhead," he murmured. "I caught us some breakfast."

The skinned carcass of some rabbit-size animal was turning slowly on a spit over the fire she'd built but they hadn't lit last night. "Smells good," she commented. "Looks disgusting."

He grinned. "I'll slice the meat off the bones for you so it looks like chicken by the time you have to eat it."

"Does it taste like chicken?" she asked dubiously.

"Actually, it does." He chuckled quietly. "It was this or snake. I figured you'd prefer the furry mammal over the snake."

A residual shiver of terror from the eyelash viper incident whisked down her spine. "Good call," she said dryly.

She noticed belatedly that he was soaked to the skin. "Why are you all wet?"

"It's been raining the last couple hours. I took a peek at the rebels, who are hunkering down in their tents like I thought they might today, and then I went hunting."

"The rebels aren't moving? Does that mean we might get the day off?"

He shook his head. "I doubt it. Now that it's stopped raining, I figure they'll pack up and move out."

Her hopes fell. "At least we're getting a hot breakfast out of it."

He tested the carcass with a stick. "Done to perfection. By the time you get dressed, it'll be cool enough to eat."

She turned away as he reached out with his knife to carve the animal. She'd have to give serious consideration to becoming a vegetarian after she got home. The repeated, graphic demonstrations of what it meant to be a carnivore were getting to be a little much for her.

The rabbit—as it turned out to be—was delicious. Her standards in food had certainly taken a nosedive during the last few days. She'd never thought she'd live to see the day when a plate of French fries swimming in grease and ketchup sounded like ambrosia from heaven. Fortified by the hearty breakfast, she followed Tex out into the jungle.

Before long she was as soaked as he was. Every leaf she brushed against was drenched, every branch she bumped showered her with water. Fortunately the air was warm, so she wasn't unduly uncomfortable.

And then Tex slowed down abruptly. She mimicked the way he set each foot down carefully, easing forward in complete silence. She wasn't as good at it as he was, but she managed to creep forward with relative quiet.

He eased down into a crouch and waved her to join him. She moved up cautiously beside him.

Slowly he pushed a big leaf out of the way.

She stifled a gasp as a large camp spread out before her. People scurried in all directions. Eventually a knot of fifty or sixty men formed in the middle of the tent city. They milled around, tension evident in their movements.

Tex breathed in her ear, ''That's the group we'll follow.''

She nodded infinitesimally. Yup, whatever was up at this camp, that buzzing group of soldiers was at the heart of it.

A man in a full-blown military uniform emerged from a tent and strode toward the group. Tex tensed abruptly beside her as if he recognized the guy. The leader shouted a couple sentences in Spanish over the crowd of men. She didn't hear any responses, but the guy nodded like he'd heard what he wanted to hear.

The officer spun and headed toward the opposite side of the camp. The motley line of soldiers piled after him. They reminded Kimberly of a pack of dogs, all yipping and nipping at each other's heels, moblike, but somehow managing to all head in generally the same direction.

Tex tapped her shoulder. He eased off to their right, around the perimeter of the camp. The wet footing made for exceptionally quiet going, and they moved past the camp quickly.

Even she could've picked up the trail of the rebel unit. They talked and laughed loudly among themselves and walked along an actual path through the towering trees. Someone had hacked the overhanging branches and encroaching brambles well back.

Tex paralleled the path through the much slower going of the jungle, but that was fine with her. The last thing they needed was to walk right up on the heels of the rebels.

They'd been walking for about a half hour when Kimberly jumped at a sudden, sharp crack of sound. Tex bit back a cry of pain and crumpled to the ground.

Kimberly lurched toward him, panic surging. Oh, God. Had someone shot him?

She dropped to her hands and knees and crawled forward, frantically searching the thick curtain of green all around them. She didn't see anyone. As she approached Tex, she heard him sucking air in and out between his teeth. He was folded around his lower left leg, writhing on the ground.

"What happened?" she whispered in panic.

He ground out a single word between his clenched teeth. "Trap."

She looked down at his leg. Around his ankle was a vicious-looking steel trap, its teeth buried in the leather of his combat boot. She reached down to tug at the two halves of the trap.

Tex grunted and grabbed at his ankle. "Find the release mechanism," he groaned.

She examined the contraption to see if she could divine how it worked. And then something else intruded upon her consciousness. Another sound. A dangerous sound.

Men crashing through the jungle.

Coming toward them.

Ohgod, ohgod, ohgod...

She searched the trap frantically, looking for a lever, a handle, a hook, a catch, anything to release its deadly jaws. "Tex, I can't find it!" she cried under her breath.

The breaking of branches and swishing of leaves was getting closer.

He reached down to pull at the trap. She put her hands beside his, and they both pulled for all they were worth. The spring eased up a bit, but not anywhere near enough to pull his foot free.

Several male voices talked quietly, agitatedly, in Spanish.

Any second now they'd burst into the little clearing.

Out of her mind with fear, she yanked at the chain securing the trap to the ground. The stake it was secured to didn't budge.

Tex pulled urgently at her sleeve. "Get behind me. Now. Let me do the talking. Or the shooting." He fumbled in one of the pouches on the web belt and slammed the red beret on his head.

She looked up and realized he had the AK-47 out and across his lap. She slid behind him.

Four men burst into the clearing, all holding rifles at the ready in front of them. Their clothes were filthy and ragtag. They were ill kempt and had terrible teeth. They reeked of poverty. These weren't rebel soldiers. She nearly sobbed in her relief.

At the sight of Tex and her, the men stopped in their tracks.

Tex burst out in rapid, angry Spanish, gesturing at his foot. She knew only about a half dozen words of Spanish, and they were all curses. She heard every single one of them sprinkled liberally in whatever Tex was saying.

She stared in shock as the four men laid down their ancient rifles. Tex did the same with his weapon, although she noted it wasn't more than a couple inches from his fingertips.

One of the men walked forward and knelt beside Tex's foot. He fiddled with the trap for several seconds. Kimberly noticed that Tex went white around the mouth, but by no other gesture did he indicate that he was in any discomfort.

Finally, after what seemed like an hour, the metal jaws fell away from Tex's boot. The guy stood up, shrugging apologetically. Tex shoved himself to his feet. She jumped forward to steady him, but he brushed her hand away.

She'd heard him gasping in agony only a minute or two ago. She knew how much pain he was in. Why wouldn't he let her help him? She opened her mouth to ask, but caught the warning glare he threw her. She bit back the words and held her tongue.

Another conversation in Spanish, more casual this time, between Tex and the four men. Whatever story he was telling them, they seemed to be buying it. In fact, they all looked over at her and laughed at one point. She had a feeling she didn't want to know what Tex was saying.

Tex asked some sort of question, and the men gestured in the general direction that the rebels had been heading. A quick map even got drawn in the dirt with a stick.

Tex said something else and the men laughed heartily again. There was one last exchange that sounded like farewells and the four guys moved off into the jungle. She stood behind Tex and watched them go. When silence had settled around them once more, Tex abruptly sagged.

She dove forward and caught him under the arm with her shoulder. Staggering under his weight, she eased him to the ground.

Big beads of sweat popped out on his forehead and he closed his eyes. He was as white as a sheet. "Don't take off my boot," he breathed. "But could you check out my ankle?"

"Uh, sure," she replied. "I don't have the slightest bit of first-aid training, though. I couldn't tell a sprain from a break if my life depended on it."

He grunted in what might pass for humor. "Your life may very well depend on doing just that. Tell me what you see. Start with the damage to my boot."

She pushed up his pant leg gently and had a look. "There's a line of little punctures running along both sides of your boot. The front two inches and the back two inches or so don't have any marks."

"Good. That means my Achilles tendon probably isn't damaged."

She gulped. Yikes. That sounded serious.

"Stick your fingers into the top of my boot and tell me what you feel."

She had trouble getting even two fingers past the heavy swelling of his lower leg. A matching row of puncture wounds marred his skin.

Tex groaned faintly under his breath as she eased her

fingers deeper into the boot. "Can you feel my ankle bone?" he bit out.

"I feel the outside one."

"Try the other side."

She carefully pulled her fingers out and eased them down the other side of his boot. "There's more swelling on this side. It's over the bone."

"Push on it. Can you feel the bone?"

She did as he directed, wincing as her probing pulled a sharp inhalation from him.

"Yes, I can feel the bone," she announced.

Tex sagged back against a tree. "Thank God."

"What?" she asked in desperation. "Now what am I supposed to do?"

He opened his eyes. "The good news is that trap closed just above my ankle. I don't think the joint itself is damaged. The bad news is my leg's swelling like crazy and the drainage from that will run down into my ankle and immobilize it if I don't keep the damned thing propped up for about two weeks."

She gulped. They didn't have two weeks. "What are we going to do?" she whispered.

He tossed her gray wool skirt to her. "Tear off a half-dozen, three inch or so, wide strips from that."

Using the knife he handed her, she sawed on the fabric, tearing it into long strips.

"I'm going to take off my boot," Tex gritted out, "and as soon as I do, I need you to wrap my ankle. Tight. Have you ever done anything like that?"

She looked up and met his grim gaze. "Nope. But if you can explain it to me, I'll give it my best shot."

He demonstrated on his good ankle with one of the strips of cloth. She watched carefully until she thought she had the hang of it.

"Ready?" he asked her.

She nodded gamely.

He untied his boot laces quickly and slipped the boot

off his foot. As fast as she could, she wrapped the first strip of cloth around his ankle the way he'd shown her.

"Do the next one a little tighter," Tex directed.

Following his instructions, she swathed his foot and ankle in the makeshift pressure bandage. She leaned back on her heels when the procedure was done. He slipped his boot back on and laced it loosely.

"By the way, who were those guys?" she asked.

"Poachers. That was a jaguar trap."

"I thought jaguars are endangered," she replied.

He looked up at her grimly. "They are. That's why their pelts are worth a fortune, and that's why poor schmucks like those guys hunt them."

She felt ill at the thought of an innocent animal getting caught in the same monstrous, inhumane trap Tex just had.

His voice yanked her back to the present. "Help me up. Time for the acid test."

She awkwardly helped him stand up. Gingerly he placed a little weight on his leg. More sweat popped out on his forehead and she saw the muscles in his jaw ripple. But he nodded grimly at her. "It'll do," he announced.

She frowned at him. "Could you be more specific, please? I'm worried sick here and I want to know exactly how hurt you are."

He looked at her candidly, his eyes a clear, glittering shade of blue. "The leg is not broken. But there's serious tissue damage on both sides of my leg, just above the ankle. Hopefully your pressure bandage will protect my ankle from accumulating so much fluid that I can't use it."

"Can you walk? Run if you have to?" she demanded.

"Yes, and yes."

She didn't know whether to believe his confident tone of voice or not. It would be just like him to put on a brave front so she wouldn't get upset. "Do you need me to find a spot and make us a camp for the next couple days?"

He shook his head in the negative. "No. We go on. The

poachers said the rebel training facility is about a half mile that way.'' He pointed over her shoulder.

She stared. ''What do you mean, 'we go on'? Are you nuts?''

He looked down at her in surprise. ''No, I'm not nuts. I'll be okay. My leg's going to hurt, but it's still functional.''

She gazed at him narrowly. ''You *are* crazy. I think you're delirious from the pain. In fact, I think I should take over making the decisions here, and I say we get you off your feet and get you some rest for a couple days.''

He grinned. ''You and what army are getting me off my feet?''

She raised an annoyed eyebrow. ''Don't tempt me to go get the rebels. Or I can chase down those poachers again.''

Tex's gaze went sober. ''Don't ever mess with poachers by yourself. The only reason we're standing here alive right now is because my AK-47 could've mowed them all down where they stood before they got off a shot at us.''

Her eyes went wide and she nodded.

Tex looked around the clearing, obviously hunting for something. He hobbled forward and pulled out his knife to slash at a sapling. He finished whittling at it and brandished a reasonable facsimile of a cane in his hand. ''Are you ready to go?'' he asked lightly.

She glared at him. ''I suppose if I refuse to move you'll just leave me here in this clearing and go on by yourself.''

He grinned. ''You catch on fast, darlin'.''

She stomped forward until she was just behind him in her usual position. ''Lead on, oh, foolish, crippled one.''

He hobbled out of the clearing and she followed in no small disbelief. After a few minutes she noticed his stride evening out like he was walking off some of the pain. Or maybe he was just going into shock.

At least he had to go slow. For once she had no trouble keeping up with him. He slowed down even more as they heard noise in front of them. After a few yards he eased down to his hands and knees and she did the same.

He crawled forward a little farther and then lowered himself all the way to his belly. She groaned mentally, but mimicked him. Low crawling, as he'd called it, sucked.

They eased forward a few feet. She pulled up beside him, shoulder to shoulder.

Gradually he lifted aside the thick fronds of a fern to look at the rebel training facility before them.

The view that met her eyes was the very last thing she'd ever expect to see in the middle of a South American jungle.

Even Tex gasped beside her.

She stared in total, riveted shock. A single thought pierced her numbed mind.

Oh. My. God.

Chapter 16

A full-size mock-up of the White House loomed before them.

In utter disbelief, Kimberly stared at the south facade of the famous building. The rebels had it correct down to the very last detail. Even the cast iron chandelier on the south portico was accurate.

The jungle pressing in on it from all sides looked out of place, surreal even.

The several-story-tall structure stood on the far side of an enormous clearing in the jungle that reached nearly to the top of the canopy of trees. Far overhead, a huge blanket of camouflage netting lay draped over the trees, covering the whole site.

The scale of the setup overwhelmed her. Someone had gone to enormous expense and trouble to build it. But then, if the White House was the target, whoever was behind this was ambitious, indeed.

Tex let the fern fronds drop and rolled over onto his

back, clearly thinking hard. "How well do you know the layout of the White House?" he abruptly asked her.

"I've been there several times," she answered.

"The Oval Office looks out on this side of the White House, doesn't it?" he asked.

The implication of his question hit her like a sledgehammer. "Oh, my God," she breathed. "Yes, it does. When he's at his desk, the president sits with his back to the middle window of the Oval Office."

"With RITA, it'd be an easy shot. A sniper could park on the far side of the mall, a half mile or more from the White House. At that range, the RITA rifle would have no trouble penetrating the bulletproof glass."

"You think that's the plan?" she gasped. "To assassinate the president?"

"If they expected to blow the White House up, they wouldn't bother with a mock-up like this. They'd get the blueprints and figure out the structural weak points to blast. You can only blow up a model once. But you can practice taking a shot through a window a thousand times."

"Why wouldn't the rebels just hire a good sniper and tell him to go take the shot? Why go to all this trouble?" she asked.

"You only get one shot at the president. The Secret Service reacts so fast you'd never get a second shot off. And once someone shoots at the man through his office window, you can be sure he'll be working out of a bunker for many months to come."

"So, this whole facility has been set up for one guy to practice shooting?"

"There are probably several candidates for the honor of taking the shot."

She shuddered at the way he'd put it. How could killing anyone be considered an honor? "If only a few guys are practicing the shot, why all the other soldiers out here?"

"They're probably planning some sort of diversion to

draw away the attention of the Secret Service from the shooter.''

''What sort of diversion?'' she asked.

''I have no idea. But we'll watch these bastards until we find out. That's for damn sure,'' he retorted grimly.

They lay on the wet, black ground through the afternoon, observing the rebels as they moved around the huge clearing. It looked like the new batch of soldiers spent most of the day being given some sort of orientation to the mock-up and to the overall plan.

Tex grumbled about not having a parabolic microphone to pick up what the rebel leaders said. But, from the way the clump of soldiers was led from point to point around the clearing, the gist of the plan slowly became clear.

The rebels were going to use most of the soldiers to stage some kind of disturbance at the east entrance to the White House. Once they'd drawn the attention of the Secret Service, snipers at several locations around the mall were going to shoot simultaneously at the president. He'd presumably be sitting at his desk in the Oval Office.

Kimberly murmured to Tex, ''Do you think they'll try to copy the RITA rifle so each one of the assassins has one like it?''

''Depends on how soon they plan to pull off this operation. It'll take a minimum of a couple weeks to figure out how the RITA rifle works. I'd guess it'll take a master weapon smith another week or two to make copies of the rifle itself.''

''What about its fancy targeting system?'' she asked.

Tex shrugged. ''A top-flight computer geek could probably build the circuitry for the targeting system in a week. But even then, there's likely to be a few more days or weeks of tweaking on the copies to get them to work.''

Kimberly sighed in relief. Thank goodness. They had plenty of time here.

Tex interrupted her relief. ''However, it will only take

one working RITA rifle to take out the president. And they've almost got that."

"Almost?" Kimberly flashed him a hopeful look.

"I took the clip out of the RITA before I dropped it. A whole new clip will have to be fabricated before anyone can shoot the existing weapon."

Thank goodness he was so smart under pressure. She'd never have thought to unload the thing before she dropped it, let alone take the whole clip out.

Tex continued. "If we've pegged the rebel's plan correctly, they'll have the other snipers fire regular sniper rifles at the White House. The Secret Service will still have to split its response among all the shooters, and they won't know which position is using the really lethal weapon."

"Why does that matter? Like you said, the assassins will only get one shot at the president. If the snipers hit him he'll die, and if they miss, he'll be whisked away to safety."

"True, but the assassins can take dozens of shots at the Secret Service before their positions are overrun. Whichever agents approach the guy with the RITA rifle are going to get mowed down like toy soldiers. Their vests aren't going to stop its bullets."

"Oh." That would be some of the other thousands of lives he'd said the loss of the RITA rifle would jeopardize.

"Depending on the type of clip they make for the gun, one sniper could take out a big chunk of the presidential security detail in one fell swoop," Tex remarked.

"So I *was* right," Kimberly exclaimed under her breath.

"About what?" Tex replied.

"Back at Quantico. When I said that one of these rifles in the hands of the right soldier would turn him into a nearly unstoppable killing machine."

"Absolutely," Tex agreed.

She shoved up onto her elbows, glaring down at him. "Then why did you disagree with me when I said it?" she demanded.

"I never disagreed. I only frowned at you, as I recall. Besides, I'm damn well not going to let the press print something like that about this weapon."

"Why not?" she gibed under her breath. "Afraid somebody might go to a lot of trouble to steal it and use it for something dastardly like killing the president of the United States?"

He gave her a dark look. "Don't get started with me. I'm in a foul mood already and my ankle's killing me."

She'd forgotten about that. At least he'd spent the whole day lying on his belly and not traipsing around on it. "Where are we camping tonight?" she asked. "Should I go on ahead and start getting it ready?"

He sighed. "Based on what we've seen, we need to stay right here and keep an eye on the rebels at all times. Every detail we learn about their plan could be vital to the president's safety."

"I thought we were only looking for the RITA rifle," she replied.

"If we can't get the rifle back, the least we have to do is warn the Secret Service of the imminent attempt on the president's life. Anything we can tell them about the rebels and their plan will be important. It's 'round-the-clock surveillance for us from here on out."

She sighed and nodded. What he said made sense. "How about if I go find us something to eat and some water?"

He passed her the empty canteen and the cell phone. "Try to call Charlie Squad again. But make it fast. The battery's getting low. Drink your fill if you find any water, then bring me back a jug. I'll stay here and keep an eye on things."

She wriggled backward until she could stand up safely and creep away from Tex's position. She looked carefully at the trees around her, noting landmarks for finding Tex again. It would *not* be good to overshoot his position and stroll right into the middle of the rebel camp.

For once, water was easy to find. She stumbled across a little stream, barely more than a ribbon of water trickling along an indentation in the ground. She filled the canteen and dropped in a water purification tablet.

While the tablet did its work, she hunted for food. She tried the phone again. Despair welled in her throat as static filled her ear. Tex needed help out here! She pocketed the phone and glumly found more of the sour berries and ginger root, but not a lot of either. She found some small red berries and threw those in the hat with her other finds, as well. Maybe Tex would know if they were edible or not.

She returned to the stream. Girding herself for the iodine taste of the water, she drank down the contents of the whole canteen. She refilled the container and put another tablet in it. By the time she got back to Tex, the water would be ready to drink.

She headed off through the trees. The sun was setting and long shadows filled the jungle. Everything looked different than it had an hour ago.

She frowned, squinting at the tree trunks, trying to ascertain her position. She wasn't lost. She wasn't!

Stay calm. Breathe. Keep your wits about you. She'd work her way through this. She'd headed east, away from Tex's position. If she followed the setting sun—that meant toward the bases of the shadows—that would take her west. Toward Tex.

She tried to move as quietly as he did, but that just wasn't possible. She eased forward, an ominous sensation tickling the back of her neck. She ought to be getting close to the rebel training facility. Very close.

She slowed down even more. *If* she was right and *if* she wasn't lost, Tex ought to be just ahead. A big tree with a forked trunk should be on her right and a clump of banana trees should be on the left.

A clump of banana trees loomed straight ahead of her. She slid off to the right, searching for a tree with a forked trunk.

There! In the darkening shadows. She'd found it. Relief flooded her, almost knocking her to her knees.

She practically stepped on Tex when she finally found him. He'd apparently decided to adorn himself with the latest in black dirt cosmetics.

"Get down," he hissed.

It dawned on her that if she was standing on top of Tex, then the rebel camp was only a few yards ahead of her.

"Slow. Move slow," Tex ordered in a bare whisper.

She schooled herself not to drop to the ground like a rock. Rather she eased her body down until she stretched out at full-length beside Tex. She passed him the canteen and he took a long pull from it.

"Any luck with the phone?" he asked.

"Nope. Sorry." In the abruptly heavy silence, she inquired, "See anything interesting this afternoon?"

"Not really. More orientation. They're definitely planning on having five or six snipers shoot from various positions across the mall."

They'd guessed that already. She supposed it was good to have confirmed it. Now she could only hope that Tex didn't see the RITA rifle anytime soon. Maybe then she could talk him into leaving with their information regarding the impending assassination attempt on the president.

Tension rolled off Tex in palpable waves as she stretched out on the ground beside him. He snacked absently on the food, not even reacting to the violently sour green berries. Was he that worried? Or had he gone into some sort of work mode where he was blocking everything else out?

"Tex?" she murmured.

"Hmm?" he murmured back.

"Everything okay?"

He glanced over his shoulder at her. "Peachy keen. Why?"

She frowned. "Whenever you start tossing around homespun expressions like that, I get worried."

She had his full attention now. She persisted. "So, what's going on? You're wired tighter than you've ever been around me."

"Finding out that someone's trying to murder my president does that to me," he replied shortly.

She'd forgotten for a minute. He believed he could single-handedly save the world from the forces of evil. She refrained from going back over that well-worn argument.

Tex resumed observing the rebels, most of whom sat around fires eating their suppers, at the moment.

She lay there beside Tex for a long time. Night fell and the usual cacophony of noises commenced. She and Tex could probably have a shouting match right now and the rebels wouldn't hear them over the din of insects, frogs and assorted screeching things.

And then it began to rain. Nothing torrential, just a steady, slow drip that turned their resting spot into a black morass of cold and wet. Tex didn't budge. She wasn't entirely sure he even noticed it was raining.

But then he reached up, plucked a good-size leaf and covered the firing portion of his AK-47. Okay, he knew it was raining. Why didn't he take cover?

The temperature began to drop and their surveillance went from uncomfortable to downright miserable.

Tex remained completely focused on the rebels, clearly thinking intently. But what about? You could only stare at a bunch of guys huddled in tents, drinking, for so long.

Her fingers were starting to ache with the cold. She flexed the stiffness away, but it returned in a few seconds. Her curiosity won out over her desire to stay out of Tex's way. "What are you mulling over so seriously?"

She felt his head turn toward her. It was too dark under the ferns to make out his expression, though.

"I'm considering scenarios."

She frowned. "What kinds of scenarios?"

"A 'what if the rifle's in that big main tent over there' scenario. 'What if the rifle's in the commander's tent on the left edge of the clearing? What if the rifle's inside the mock-up of the White House?''

"Come up with anything interesting?" She asked more to distract herself from the water running down the back of her neck.

"Yeah. The rifle's not here yet."

She lurched in the dark. "What?" she exclaimed.

"Hush," he ordered sharply.

"What do you mean, it's not here yet?" she whispered.

"I think it's still getting modified. The rebels don't have a facility here to fabricate the replacement clip. It'll take a metal-working shop to do the job."

"Then why in the world are we lying here in the mud watching these idiots play soldier?" she demanded.

"Because if we'd tried to follow the rifle to wherever it's getting worked on, we'd have lost its trail or been caught. Based on this setup, we know the rifle's going to end up here."

"Why?" she interjected.

"The snipers will have to practice firing at the mock-up with it. They'll need to figure out how to use it and get comfortable with it before they try it out on the president."

"Then why aren't we well away from here in a safe, dry little camp with your ankle propped up and a nice shelter overhead?"

"Because anything we learn might be the one tidbit that saves the president's life."

She harrumphed. "All the rebels are safely drunk in their tents. They're not going anywhere as long as it keeps raining. Let's call it a night, and go somewhere to light a fire and get dry and warm."

She made out a glimmer of white as he smiled at her. "I agree. We'll sleep until it quits raining."

Then, to her confusion, he picked up a hefty stick and began digging a small trench around them. He spoke over his shoulder. "Help me dig. It'll go faster if we both do it."

She picked up a stick and began gouging at the soft dirt. "And I'm doing this why?"

"It'll channel the water away from our position."

Dawning suspicion made her ask slowly, "And?"

"Do you want to get completely soaked in your sleep?" he asked.

"I don't follow you," she mumbled.

"We're sleeping here," he explained.

"What about getting dry? And warm? Having a fire?" she demanded.

"Sorry. No comforts of home when we're doing tight surveillance."

"So we're going to lay here in the rain and mud and cold all night, like a couple of dogs?"

"That'd be the gist of it," he replied.

"That's ridiculous. The rebels aren't going anywhere. We're not going to miss a thing."

He rounded on her, abruptly looming over her, a dark, dangerous shadow. "Do you mean to tell me that your comfort for one night is more important than the life of the president of the United States and potentially dozens of his Secret Service agents?"

She sighed heavily. "Of course not."

"Help me spread out the space blanket." He passed her a corner of the mylar sheeting, its dull, black side facing up and its shiny silver side facing down. "Put rocks or a log over the edges of it to hold it in place. But make sure they're inside the perimeter of the trench."

She did as he directed.

"Tell me why we're not getting out of here and heading for the nearest phone to call the Secret Service?"

"No time," he replied shortly. "By the time someone else found this place, the RITA could be long gone and on its way to kill the president or someone else."

In a matter of moments, she was encased in an uncomfortable plastic shell. Then the large sheet began to rise slowly away from her. Tex had wrapped the end of a stick in leaves and used it to hoist the space blanket off them, forming a tiny pup tent.

Lying half on top of her, he reached down by their feet and propped up another padded stick. They didn't have much room, but it was enough to maneuver a little bit.

"Take off your clothes," he murmured.

"I beg your pardon!" She reared back as much as she could in the confined space, offended by the boldness of his proposition.

His answering grin was visible in the near total dark. "Don't get your knickers in a twist, darlin'. I'm only looking out for your comfort and welfare. You'll catch a chill if you stay in those wet clothes all night."

She subsided, only partially mollified.

He explained further. "I'm going to take mine off, too, if that makes you feel better. Our body heat will build up in here over the next few hours and will dry out our clothes some. It won't be like hanging them by a fire, of course. But we'll be reasonably dry and warm tonight, and our clothes will be mostly dry tomorrow morning when we put them back on."

She didn't see where all this excess body heat was going to come from, but she did as Tex requested. It was a royal pain peeling out of wet, cloying clothes with barely inches of room to maneuver. But with Tex's help and a lot of wriggling and squirming, she managed to get her clothes off.

By the time Tex had finished wrestling out of his clothes, her naked skin had dried and she did feel warmer. He gathered her close in his arms, and she snuggled against his steamy body. Given what he had to work with, she was impressed at how comfortable he'd managed to make her.

Then his mouth descended toward hers and he swept her away from their wet, cold bivouac in the jungle.

* * *

A gunshot tore apart the silence of the early morning. Tex froze as he'd been conditioned to by years of training, even though adrenaline screamed through his system.

Several more shots rang out and Kimberly lurched against his chest violently at each one. He held her tightly and rolled partially on top of her, using the weight of his body to hold her still. Abrupt movements like a person jumping at a noise could draw attention to their position.

"Good grief, what's happened?" she whispered frantically.

"Our girl's arrived," he murmured back. He'd know the unusual, singsong pitch of the RITA rifle anywhere.

"Now what?" Kimberly mumbled against his chest.

"Now we watch and wait for an opportunity to steal the rifle back."

"Sounds easy when you put it like that," she rumbled.

He grunted. "It'll be anything but easy, darlin'. Every bit of security these bozos have is going to be centered around that gun if they know what's smart."

Kimberly tensed against him.

"Good news is," he continued, "the bastards don't know we're here. We'll have the element of surprise working for us."

That was about the only advantage they'd have over the rebels, but he wasn't fool enough to mention that part to Kimberly. She was opposed to the idea of him snatching the rifle back already.

They watched a half dozen men spend all day firing the RITA rifle. Tex couldn't help wincing each time the gun jammed. And it did about every tenth shot. The clip the rebels were using didn't fit just right and it wasn't feeding the rounds cleanly into the firing chamber. Of course, he wasn't going to volunteer that information to the Gavronese.

In the early evening the snipers took a last few shots through the windows of the fake Oval Office, but finally the echoing blasts of gunfire ceased.

Dark approached gently and the verdant hues of the jungle softened to gray. Tex strained to watch where the rifle went. He tracked it as one of the snipers carried it across the compound to a fire and laid it on the ground beside his hip. The guy ate supper and chatted with his buddies, but Tex's gaze never left the bulky rifle.

The hour grew late and the night air grew cold. Colder than usual. His breath puffed in front of his face, threatening to obscure his view of RITA. He exhaled out the side of his mouth.

He grew vaguely aware of Kimberly's lips moving against his ear. With difficulty he focused on her words.

"You've got to have something to eat, or at least drink," she murmured.

Irritation swirled below the smooth surface of his concentration. She was right, but still the interruption bugged him. Absently he popped a handful of sour berries and drank a canteen of water.

There.

The sniper picked up the gun and walked toward the White House. What in the hell was the guy doing? Checking the targets inside the windows of the mock Oval Office one last time? Tex strained to keep the soldier in sight as he moved in the dark across the wide clearing.

The man disappeared into the White House.

Tex watched intently as several more men slowly made their way toward the white facade. There must be some rooms built into the backside of the structure. Given the chill of the night, they must be moving inside the solid rooms for extra warmth.

And RITA was in one of them. Along with a hefty phalanx of guards, some of whom were highly competent snipers, and one of whom wielded an unstoppable gun.

He rolled over on his back, stretching out the knots of having lain motionless for hours.

Kimberly's hands were there immediately, kneading out the kinks in his shoulders. The incongruity of getting a massage from a gorgeous blonde in the middle of a dangerous mission almost made him laugh out loud.

"There's nothing we can do about the gun tonight," she murmured. "Let's get some sleep."

"Sorry, no sleep tonight, darlin'."

"Why not?" she asked in alarm.

"Tonight we take the RITA back."

Chapter 17

"Tex, this is a bad idea. I thought so when you talked about it in hypothetical terms, and I know so now that I'm looking at a hundred soldiers who'll kill you on sight."

"Give it up, Kimberly," he rumbled to her. "I'm a specialist in covert insertions. That means I'm damn good at sneaking in and out of places undetected."

Specialist, schmecialist. What was it going to take to make him see the foolishness of his plan? She huffed in exasperation.

"Here's the drill," he barged on. "You stay here and I'll circle around the backside of the White House. I'll sneak inside, find the gun, and grab it. If I happen to find a radio, I'll snag it, too. Then, I'll back out, come get you here, and we'll leave the area."

"I don't *think* so," Kimberly blurted, irate.

He stared at her in apparent disbelief that she'd gainsay his brilliant plan.

"You expect me to lay here twiddling my thumbs while

you go crawling around in the dark, injured, among a hundred rebels, looking for a needle in a haystack?''

"Pardon me," he snapped. "I forgot you're a highly trained military strategist. By all means, General Stanton, what did you have in mind?"

Her blood boiled and she glared daggers at him, but she managed not to raise her voice. "I'm going with you."

"I don't *think* so!" he parroted back at her.

"Why not?" she demanded. "You're hurt and alone. You could use another pair of eyes and ears. If nothing else, I'll watch your back. My father always says it's safer if someone else is watching your back for you."

"You'll watch nothing but the stars floating by. No way are you coming with me!"

"Why not?" she demanded for a second time.

"Because I don't need the distraction."

"I won't be a distraction."

"Ha!"

"Ha!"

They stared at each other until she thought her eyes would fall out of their sockets. He looked away first.

"Darlin'," he sighed. "Please don't fight me on this. It's too dangerous. I've fought too hard to keep you safe to go and get you killed now."

"I appreciate your concern, Tex, honest. But I'll be okay. And you need someone watching your back!"

"Concern? This isn't concern, Kimberly. This is flat-out, pedal-to-the metal, gut-wrenching terror I'm feeling. I *don't* want you in there with me."

She exhaled in frustration. "Tex. Did you volunteer for this mission?"

"Not exactly. I was shoved into a helicopter without a by-your-leave."

"Would you have volunteered for this mission if it had been offered to you?" she rephrased.

"In a second."

"Then why can't you extend the same opportunity to me? I'm volunteering for this mission."

He stared at her in shock. And stared at her some more. Finally he managed to mumble, "Come again?"

"That's my White House standing out there, too. My president. I'm an American citizen, and it's my right to stand up for my country."

He literally choked in his shock and came up for air sputtering, "Since when? You're the original save-the-bunnies, give-peace-a-chance, flower child."

"That doesn't mean I don't believe in what my country stands for!"

"No, but it does mean you don't volunteer to go on special ops missions where blood's gonna spill and someone's probably going to die."

"Die?" she asked in dismay. "You expect to die?"

"Certainly not. But I damn well expect to have to slit a few throats before it's all said and done."

"Tex, no! There has to be another way!"

"Oh, I see. You're all hot and bothered to go with me as long as it's a stroll in the park! Don't want to get your hands dirty, do you?" he gibed.

"Of course not. I've never been a fan of violence." She sounded lame, even to her own ears. He was a Special Forces commando, for goodness' sake. What did she expect him to do if someone saw him?

"Like *I* said," he repeated dryly. "You'll stay here while I go get the gun."

"Like I said, not a chance. I'm going with you and that's that."

"Kimberly." His voice rumbled a warning deep in his chest.

"You can't stop me. I'll wait until you leave and then I'll follow you. It's too risky to tie me up or knock me out."

His scowl became an outright glare. His response was short and to the point. "No."

She crossed her arms casually. "Fine. Whatever you say. Go."

Narrow-eyed, he gazed at her suspiciously. "I'm not kidding. Stay here. It's too dangerous for you."

She nodded and watched him make his last preparations. He quickly disassembled the AK-47's firing mechanism and dried it off with a piece of her wool skirt. He put it all back together in a flash of quick fingers.

The last fires were doused and the last lights flickered out in the camp. A few guards strolled around, slow-moving shadows among the tents. Jungle sounds took over as the humans relinquished the night to them. Tex waited a full hour before he finally roused beside her.

Thank goodness. She didn't think she could take much more of this waiting. Especially with the heavy tension hanging between them.

She counted to a hundred after Tex left, then she eased backward on her belly, moving as stealthily as she could through the undergrowth. Her father might have cracked up, but he'd been a hell of a soldier in his day, and he said everyone needed someone at their back when bullets started to fly. She stood up behind the clump of bananas, took her bearings carefully and set off into the darkness.

The night wrapped around her like a velvet cloak, smothering her in its blinding folds. She froze at every little noise. For all she knew, the rebels had patrols out this far. Then there were the wild animals, the snakes— she shuddered and pushed that thought out of her head— and Tex. He'd probably kill her himself if he caught her following him.

A branch snapped off to her left.

She froze like Tex had taught her instead of dropping to the ground and cowering as was her first inclination. Whatever made the noise moved off behind her. She continued creeping forward, her heart racing.

What was she doing out here? She might be a trained predator in a congressional caucus chamber, but she had no business running around in a jungle by herself, in the dark, with armed men out there who'd kill her without hesitation. Except it was *Tex's* back without cover.

She walked until she thought she was past the clearing and then she turned left, heading back toward it. She approached slowly, peering ahead warily through the darkness. Someone moved. A man, moving left to right. She made out the shape of a rifle slung low by his hip. A rebel patrol.

She waited until he passed and eased forward, peering out into the clearing.

She was barely halfway around it!

If she didn't get cracking, Tex would already have fetched the gun and bump into her on his way back to get her. What if he missed her in the dark, and when he got back to where he'd left her, she was gone? He'd assume she'd headed for the road and would leave. She'd be all alone out here! That thought panicked her worse than all the snakes and soldiers in the whole jungle.

Tex. Focus on Tex. He needed her, whether he'd admit it or not.

She tore through the branches, shoving forward heedless of the scratches on her skin. She barely managed to stop herself in time when she abruptly stumbled across the clearing once more.

She crouched behind a bush and stared at the backside of the White House mock-up. It resembled a giant billboard with a crude, two-story, stucco structure nestled at its base. It looked like a decrepit, old apartment building that wouldn't have passed even the most rudimentary housing inspection.

Where was Tex?

He must already be inside. Should she follow him in and hope to find him creeping around among the sleeping soldiers? Her palms grew damp at even the thought of trying that by herself.

And then a movement caught her eye. She looked underneath the last ground-floor window on the right. She didn't see anything at first, but then a shadow separated itself from the blackness. It eased upward. Tex. He looked furtively over the window ledge into the room. He eased downward once more.

He must be looking for the RITA rifle.

He dropped to the ground and crawled quickly toward the left end of the building, where there was a doorless entrance. He must have already checked the other windows, for he passed them without pausing.

She looked all around and saw no other movement. Now was her chance. Crouching low, she moved forward. The second she cleared the jungle, Tex froze. And then he gestured at her with one hand. Sharply. He wanted her to join him. Pronto. And he wasn't happy.

In an awkward running crouch, she sprinted over to his position beside the building.

If looks could kill, she'd be dead a thousand times over from the glare he gave her when she squatted down beside him.

She raised her eyebrows and stared back belligerently. Their gazes clashed, warring silently.

Finally his glare faded to a scowl of resignation. She let out the breath she realized she'd been holding.

He gestured for her to follow him and to be quiet.

She needed no encouragement to stay right on Tex's heels as he eased forward and plastered himself beside the doorway. The AK-47 in front of him, he whipped around the corner, low, into the opening. He moved forward in a tiger prowl and disappeared.

Her pulse pounded until she felt light-headed. Now was a good moment for adrenaline. She let it flow through her veins, feeding on its restless energy. And then she stepped into the breach.

A hallway stretched straight to the far end of the building with rooms opening off it on both sides. The floor was dirty and littered with beer bottles, trash and cigarette butts. What idiot would smoke inside a firetrap like this? *The same kind that would contemplate assassinating a president.*

Tex's shadowed form paused beside the first room on the left. He gestured her to stay outside the door and keep a look out. She crouched down beside the doorway, in plain sight of anyone who happened to stick their head out a door. She was a sitting duck. This was beyond dangerous. It was nuts!

Her nerve failed her and her hands shook violently. She couldn't do it. She couldn't sit here and wait for someone to see her and kill her. An urge to run away as fast as she could nearly overwhelmed her. As she crouched beside that doorway, she regretted with every fiber of her being her big words about protecting Tex's back. What in the heck had she been thinking?

She hadn't been thinking. She'd been *feeling*. She'd gotten so caught up in her concern for Tex's safety that she'd let her panic drown her good judgment.

She'd been *panicked* over Tex's safety?

The truth hit her like a Mac truck right there in that dingy, dark hallway while she sweated for her life. She loved Tex Monroe. Enough to act like a complete idiot. Enough to put her life at risk for him without a second thought.

A compelling need to tell him almost drove her to her feet right then and there. In fact her leg muscles had coiled to rise when something dark abruptly loomed beside her.

She jumped violently.

Tex's hand landed on her shoulder. She fought to control an overwhelming urge to pee in her pants out of sheer terror.

He moved on to the next doorway and gestured her again to stay outside and keep watch. They repeated the maneuver on the remaining rooms on the left. Since he'd already checked out the right-hand rooms through the win-

dows, she wasn't surprised when he headed for the rickety
stairs to the second level.

He placed his foot on the first step and eased his weight
onto it ounce by excruciating ounce. He gestured her to
do the same. By the third step, she was ready to scream
with impatience. But Tex continued to move at the speed
of a glacier, sliding inch by inch up those stairs. It took
them upward of five minutes to traverse the dozen steps.

Tex cleared the last step and moved forward into the
hallway, a duplicate of the one below. She put her weight
on the last step and leapt up into the air as it squeaked
loudly. Tex dropped to the floor and she dived down beside him. Her heart had to be pushing two hundred beats
a minute. It all but choked her as it pounded frantically.

They waited for several minutes, but nobody came out
to see what had made the noise. Gradually her pulse
slowed to something less on the verge of a stroke.

Tex turned his head and put his lips on her ear. "Same
as below. You watch."

She nodded her understanding and he pressed silently to
his feet. Of course the question of the hour was, what in
the world was she going to do if someone actually came
out into the hall? It wasn't like she was going to shoot
them with her index finger.

She followed him to the first door on the right. He zig-
zagged his way down the hall checking the rooms on both
sides of the hallway as he went.

He'd been in the fourth room for just a few seconds
when she heard a noise. Somebody was moving in the next
room.

The doorknob turned. Oh, Lord. Somebody was coming
out in the hallway. Did she dare dart into the room Tex
was in? For all she knew, someone was sleeping in front
of the door and she'd trip over him and wake someone up.

She looked around frantically. Nowhere to hide. She
didn't have time to stretch out flat on the floor.

She snatched at the red beret tucked in her thigh pocket.

She slammed it on her head and pulled it low over her blond hair. She pulled up her knees and tucked her head against them, assuming what she prayed was the pose of a drunk asleep against the wall.

Footsteps stumbled past her, no more than a foot away. She held her breath, waiting for a hand to land on her shoulder, or cold lead to slam into her flesh. She peeked under her right elbow and watched the guy retreat down the stairs.

Oh, God, that had been close.

Tex materialized beside her. He gestured toward the room the man had just emerged from. Clearly he planned to check it while its occupant was out. Her knees wobbling like Jell-O, she followed him down the hall. He slipped into the room.

Too soon, she heard a squeak. And another. The guy was coming back! He was on his way up the stairs!

She didn't have time to race back to her position in front of the previous door. Surely the guy would notice if the unconscious drunk had moved twenty feet down the hall.

She slipped around the corner into the room with Tex. He whirled when she came in. Steel glinted in his right hand. She gestured frantically, praying she was relaying clearly that someone was coming.

Tex nodded and whirled back to the two lumps on the floor that looked like sleeping men covered in blankets.

He lifted his left hand across his body and then swung it downward hard and fast. It impacted flesh with a dull thud. The second guy stirred, and Tex jumped across the first body and chopped at the second guy, as well. He fell back to the floor with a grunt and lay motionless.

Tex jumped to the door and waved her to the side. She complied hastily.

The door opened.

The man stepped into the room. He looked up and his eyes locked on hers. Surprise flashed and his mouth opened.

Then Tex jumped.

This guy wasn't helpless and asleep. He also turned out to be a trained fighter. He spun and ducked as Tex's blow glanced off the side of his head. He crouched low and jumped for Tex, the momentum of his charge knocking both men to the floor with a heavy thud. They tangled in a canvas trap, and as they rolled, it shifted to reveal a pile of weapons. The RITA rifle!

Oh, no. The noise was going to wake someone else up. Not to mention the jerk might kill Tex! The two men rolled over and over across the floor, wrestling like bears in mortal combat.

Tex grunted at her, "Get out of here. Now!" He ducked the fingers jabbing at his eyes and continued in short grunts between exertions. "In the confusion…pass for a hooker…slip outside. Follow rebel trails…to main road."

"No way!" she cried under her breath.

He absorbed a body blow from the guy and then grunted, "Yes way. Go!"

She stepped forward, dodging flying feet as the two fighting men rolled over yet again. She needed some sort of weapon to clobber the guy Tex was fighting with and looked around frantically. The AK-47 by the window where Tex had left it! She dived for the weapon.

Voices sounded in the next room. Sitting on the floor by the window, she awkwardly pulled the heavy rifle up in front of her and groped for the trigger.

The door opened. She squeezed the trigger and the gun leapt in her hands, spraying bullets into the ceiling. The noise was deafening.

Whoever'd been in the doorway ducked back, slamming the door shut behind them. Shouts erupted up and down the hall.

"Christ, Kimberly, did you have to let the whole damn army know we were here?" Tex panted. He knelt above the now motionless figure of the guy he'd been fighting.

"Nice shot, by the way." She'd hit a guy only inches away from Tex? Oh God.

"They were coming in. I had to do something!" she wailed.

"Don't sweat it. They'd have figured out we were here regardless. You probably saved my neck," he replied.

He moved over to the corner and threw aside the canvas. "Come to papa, darlin'," he crowed.

She watched him scoop up the RITA rifle and throw its shoulder strap over his head. He pulled its proper clip out of his utility belt and slammed it into the gun.

The door burst open behind him and Kimberly watched in slow-motion suspension as he spun, dropped the bulky rifle to his hip and fired three times in quick succession.

Whoever'd been outside wasn't there anymore.

Tex sprinted to the door and kicked it shut. He turned the flimsy lock on the knob and wedged a chair under the doorknob for good measure. "Well, looks like we're cornered," he commented quietly as he headed for the window.

Kimberly gulped. This could not be good.

He shook his head. "You should've gone when you had a chance."

She shrugged. "Sorry. We're in this together to the end."

He sighed. "'The end' being the operative words."

Tough. No way would she have run out on Tex after all they'd been through together.

"Have a look around and see if you can find any more ammunition," he ordered. She checked the room fast and saw another blanket-covered pile beside where the RITA rifle had been.

She pulled the scratchy wool back and sighed in relief. Several boxes of ammunition lay there along with two long-barreled sniper rifles.

"Bingo!" she called.

Tex glanced over his shoulder and grinned at her find.

"That'll help." He ducked as somebody shot at the window from outside.

"Get back, Kimberly. These walls are made of spit and Kleenex. If anyone out there's got a high-powered rifle, bullets will pass right through them."

"What about you?" she demanded as she scooted back from the exterior wall.

He popped up and pulled off a couple shots of return fire. "I'll stay here and do a little fire suppression."

"But it's dangerous!" she exclaimed.

He gaped over his shoulder at her in mock surprise. "You think?"

She scowled at his sarcasm. And then she hit the floor as bullets raked through the window. "What's to keep them from shooting at us through the walls of the other rooms?" she asked frantically, visions of being pummeled by lead from all sides dancing in her brain.

Tex glanced back over his shoulder. "The interior walls are so crappy bullets could pass right on through this room and hit folks on the other side. They won't risk the cross-fire killing their own." He added, "I hope."

Great.

Tex grabbed one of the other rifles and returned a barrage of fire outside. At the rate he was shooting, the pile of ammunition in the corner wasn't going to last long. They had to do something. They were going to die if they just sat in here and waited for the whole rebel army to descend upon them.

There was a lull in the firing and Tex risked peering outside twice, from both sides of the window. "Kimberly, I've got an idea."

Why did that give her a horrible sinking feeling in her stomach?

"I need you to come over here and lay down a line of suppression fire for me."

"What in the heck does that mean?"

"Shoot out the window and make all the people out there duck so they can't shoot back."

"And what will you be doing in the meantime?"

"Climbing out the window onto the roof."

When he didn't continue, she said, "I assume you're not doing that because you plan to admire the view. What will you be doing on the roof?"

"Cutting guy wires."

Huh? She looked at him questioningly.

"The whole damn camp's going to be coming over here in the next two or three minutes, armed to the teeth. I've got to slow them down. If I cut the guy wires holding up the White House facade, I think I can push it over on to a bunch of the soldiers."

She blinked at the audacity of it. If he timed it right, he could take out a big chunk of the rebel force. If nothing else, he'd cause plenty of chaos and maybe buy them some time.

She moved over to the window beside Tex.

"Put the barrel of the rifle on the windowsill. Pulse the trigger in short bursts. The shorter the better. We've got to conserve ammo. Move the barrel back and forth across the field of fire as you shoot. Got it?"

She nodded.

"Once I'm up on the roof, fire a few seconds more to give me time to get beyond the roof peak, and then you can stop. Whenever anyone fires at you, fire back. Then randomly fire a couple bursts now and then to keep them off balance. Okay?"

"Okay. Tex?"

He paused, crouched beside her. "Yeah?"

"Be careful."

He grinned. "Count on it. You, too."

She smiled back, her fear so thick it made her light-headed.

He said briskly, "Let's do it."

Chapter 18

Kimberly watched as Tex shimmied out of the RITA rifle sling and took off the web belt. He nodded and she began to fire out the window. The AK-47 bucked and jumped in her hands, heavy and ungainly. Its cold steel felt foreign in her hands.

This was why she'd insisted on coming along. To protect Tex's back. She bit her lip and concentrated on controlling the rifle as she squeezed the trigger again and again.

Tex climbed on to the windowsill and reached up high overhead. While she fired past his feet, he hoisted himself up onto the roof.

She laid down another ten seconds of continuous bursts and then stopped firing. Conserve ammo, he'd said.

She'd been firing in bits and spurts for maybe two minutes when she began to hear noise. Lots of it. The kind of noise a hundred angry men would make as they rushed across a clearing.

Oh, God.

A new burst of gunfire caught her attention and she fired back in the general direction of the muzzle flashes. She prayed she wasn't killing anybody with her random fire. She didn't want to think about widowing young wives or making Gavronese children fatherless.

And then she heard another noise. Metallic. Like someone sawing on a piano wire.

Another burst of gunfire and she heard the piano wire noise again. And yet again. That must be Tex hacking through the guy wires that held up the tall facade.

She responded to a big burst of gunfire by holding down the trigger of the AK-47 and raking it across the line of fire. The shots ceased.

Her forehead burned and she felt warm blood trickle down her cheek. *Had she been shot?* She put her hand up and felt a splinter of wood in her hair. It must have flown off the windowsill and cut her face. She pulled it free and flung it aside.

A bullet had come close enough to knock a piece of wood loose only inches from her face? Suddenly she felt downright faint. She was *not* cut out for this sort of fun.

And then a new noise intruded upon her senses.

A tearing noise. Like wood cracking. The sound got louder and louder until it rumbled like a whole forest of trees toppling over. The building shook as the mock-up tore away from it and crashed with a thundering noise to the ground. Screams and shouts mingled with gunshots in what sounded like utter chaos.

Tex's terse voice came from outside the window. "Pass me the RITA, Kimberly."

She ran over to the weapon and picked it up. Lord, it was heavy. How in the world had Tex hiked all over the jungle with the darn thing? She stuck its muzzle out the window, grateful when its weight abruptly left her hands as Tex hauled it up on to the roof. In a few seconds she heard the distinctive whining of the RITA overhead. More screaming and more gunshots joined the general chaos outside.

Tex had bought them some time. But then what? How in the world were they supposed to get out of here? The other hundred rebels from the main camp had no doubt been notified by radio and would be on their way soon. Then she and Tex were toast.

Radio.

She looked back at the two unconscious men behind her. Quickly she moved to their sides. With distaste, she reached for the first one and searched him. She took a pistol out of a holster on his thigh but found nothing else useful.

She moved to the second guy. As she groped in his pants' pockets, he stirred. She jerked her hands back in horror. He couldn't wake up! He rolled over, his eyelids fluttering. He groaned.

Frantically she lifted the pistol and brought it down against the side of the guy's head. The sickening impact of steel on flesh nearly made her gag.

The guy sagged, out cold once more.

Quickly she felt his chest pockets. There was a hard lump in one. She unbuttoned the flap and her fingers encountered warm plastic inside. She gripped the object and pulled it out.

She nearly cried in her relief. It was a cell phone.

A burst of gunfire came out of the jungle. She jumped over to the window and snatched up the AK-47 again. Her bullets joined Tex's. With the rebels momentarily subdued, she flipped open the phone and dialed the same number she'd called before.

"Go ahead," a man's voice barked.

This time the abrupt greeting didn't surprise her. "This is Kimberly Stanton. Can you hear me?"

"Loud and clear, ma'am."

She ducked as a volley of gunshots peppered the side of the building.

"Tex and I are in trouble. We need help, now."

"Standby. We're triangulating your position off your phone. It may take a minute. Stay on the line."

"Okay," she shouted over another loud burst of fire.

"I need a little help," Tex shouted from the roof.

She laid the phone down and looked out the window. She stared in dismay. Dear God. At least two dozen men were advancing out of the jungle toward the building, their rifles blazing in a fireworks display of white-and-yellow flashes.

She snatched up the AK-47 and pressed down the trigger, raking it back and forth across the line of men. Easily half of them dropped, and the rest turned and ran. A few of the downed men crawled or dragged themselves back toward the jungle, their moans and groans ripping at her sanity.

"…still there? What the hell's going on?" somebody shouted through the phone.

She picked it up. "I'm still here," she half sobbed. "You've got to help us!"

"Miss Stanton," a deep voice said firmly. "This is Colonel Folly. We've got a position fix on you. We'll be there in thirty minutes. Are you or Tex hurt?"

She ducked as a spray of bullets flew into the ceiling of the room. "Not yet," she answered, half out of her mind with fear.

"How many hostiles are at your position?" the colonel asked urgently.

"A couple hundred."

The colonel swore under his breath. "Can you tell me exactly where you are? The more detail the better."

"We're trapped in a two-story stucco building on the north side of a big clearing in the jungle. The top of the whole clearing is covered in camouflage netting. Tex is on the roof and I'm in a second-story room."

"Which room?" the colonel asked, static half obscuring his question.

"North side. Second floor, the second room from the easternmost end!" she shouted as the static got louder and louder.

"Hang on!" she heard the colonel shout back to her. And then she couldn't hear him anymore.

She picked up the AK-47 and fired it again as yet another wave of soldiers charged the building. It rattled ominously, laying down a curtain of lead.

Abruptly it stopped firing.

She pulled the trigger again. It clicked. Out of ammunition.

"Tex," she called desperately. "I'm out of ammunition. I don't know how to reload this thing."

"I'll be right there," came his immediate reply from nearby. He must have been lying on the roof right over her window. What was he doing there? That was far too exposed a position!

And then a big black shadow swung through the window.

She flung herself at him, overwhelmed by her relief at seeing him alive again. He wrapped her in a crushing embrace. "I've got you," he murmured into her hair.

He yanked her down to the floor as a barrage of bullets splattered against the walls.

"I found a cell phone," she panted. "I called Colonel Folly. He got a position fix on us and said he'd be here in thirty minutes."

"Thank God," Tex exhaled. The stark relief that flashed across his face for just a second frightened her. She knew they were in huge trouble, but she hadn't realized how huge until Tex's brave front slipped for that brief moment.

He moved to the pile of ammunition in the corner and tossed a handful of banana-shaped clips toward the window. He came back to her side and slammed one of them into the base of the AK-47.

He pointed it out the window and swore under his breath. "These bastards don't give up easy," he mumbled.

Kimberly watched as he fired methodically out the window.

"We're gonna run out of this type of ammo in a whole lot less than a half hour, Princess," he said over his shoulder during a lull. "Pull out the other clips over there and see if any of them fit the sniper rifles you found."

While she fished through the pile, she asked, "How's the RITA holding up?"

"Just about out of ammo."

She matched up several clips of bullets to the other guns, but it was a pitifully small pile. She risked a glance out the window and saw dozens of muzzle flashes. They were severely outnumbered. How could they possibly hold out for a half hour?

Tex switched to firing single shots, aiming each one carefully before he pulled the trigger. She kept a morbid count in her head. She had no doubt Tex was killing, or at least hitting, someone with every shot.

Forty-two. Forty-three. She shuddered at the carnage, almost too appalled to function as Tex called out for more ammo periodically.

She was heading back toward the window with the last clip for one of the rebel's rifles when an arm abruptly went around her neck.

She screamed for a second before her air was cut off. She struggled, but the man behind her was big and powerful. And mad. He was going to choke her to death! Tex whirled around and her terrified gaze locked on him as spots began to dance in front of her eyes.

Tex went still. Utterly calm. He moved forward slowly, a knife held low and in front of him in his right hand. She looked into his eyes as he advanced and Death looked back at her.

The man she loved was gone, replaced by the coldest, cruelest, most focused killer she'd ever seen. He snarled something in Spanish.

The man behind her snarled something back, his spit

spraying her ear. Faint from terror and lack of oxygen, she felt her limbs going slack. She clawed at the arm around her neck, feeling rolls of torn skin underneath her fingernails. The man's arm grew slippery with blood and her fingers slid uselessly over the flesh that was inexorably killing her.

And then Tex lunged. The knife flashed past her face. A squishing sound and the arm around her neck abruptly fell away.

The rebel staggered back, screaming.

As she fell to the floor and rolled out of the way of the two men's feet, Kimberly stared up in dazed horror at the knife protruding from the man's left eye.

Tex yanked it out and slashed hard to the right across the man's throat. A fountain of blood sprayed her, warm and black.

And then she passed out.

Tex leapt to Kimberly's slumped form. There was blood all over her. He couldn't tell if it was hers or the rebel's. Frantically he passed his hands over her, searching for wounds.

"Come on, honey," he urged. "Wake up. Talk to me, Princess."

She lay there, limp and lifeless.

For the first time in his career his life flashed before him. He thought about the heartache of losing his mother. About Emily, his first lost love. He thought about the lonely nights at home, training because there was nothing else to do. He thought of the years of volunteering for missions, one right after another, because there was nobody for him to go home to, nobody who loved him. And he thought about the past few days with Kimberly. The laughter and loving. How alive she made him feel. She couldn't die!

"Kimberly, wake up!" he called urgently.

Her eyes fluttered open. Thank God.

"Are you hurt? Did that bastard cut you?"

"Uh, no. I don't think so," she mumbled.

He sagged beside her, too relieved to lift a finger. If he'd lost her… Hell, he couldn't even think about it.

"What's that smell?" she murmured groggily.

He took a sniff.

And leapt to the window.

Dammit.

While he'd been fighting off Kimberly's attacker, the rebels had sent another wave of soldiers toward the building. One of them was just disappearing around the corner with a large, metal container. Kimberly had smelled gasoline fumes.

The rebels were going to burn them out.

Not good. His brain went into overdrive. This building would go up like a box of matches.

He looked at his watch. Twenty more minutes until Charlie Squad got here.

Grimly he picked up the nearest rifle and fired at the two guys who were leaning down with a lighter toward the ground. He dropped them both, but the guy with the gas can had gotten away. It was only a matter of time now.

With their success in getting near the building, the rebels became bolder. They came at him in waves and he had trouble holding them off with the single-shot sniper rifles. Everyone he shot at went down, but there were just too many of them.

He didn't know which was going to be worse. Getting shot by these bastards and bleeding to death, or burning to death when the building went up in flames.

And then another rifle fired beside him. Kimberly had crawled over to the window and picked up the second rifle.

"Take your time," he instructed. "Aim carefully, hold your breath, and then fire. Every bullet's got to count now."

She nodded grimly and did as he said. With the two of

them firing together, they were able to back off the next couple waves of soldiers.

And then a wisp of smoke wafted up toward them from below.

"Tex, where's that smoke coming from?" Kimberly asked in confusion.

"The building's on fire. While I was taking care of that bastard who jumped you, a couple guys got to the building with a gas can."

She stared at him, stark terror in her eyes. "This place will go up in flames in no time," she breathed. "We're not going to make it, are we?"

"Yes, we are! We are going to make it, and that's all there is to it!" he declared fiercely.

She smiled at him bravely.

The smoke grew thicker and a gust of it came through the window. He coughed and fired at the next wave of soldiers that came at them. He and Kimberly repulsed the attack. And the next.

But with every passing moment, the smoke was growing thicker. The air grew noticeably warmer around them. He checked his watch for the thousandth time. Twelve minutes to go.

And then Kimberly called out urgently. "Tex! There's smoke coming under the door!"

"Watch outside," he ordered tersely. "Let me know if another wave comes at us." He jumped away from the window and stripped a shirt off one of the unconscious rebels on the floor. He stuffed it into the crack under the flimsy door and soaked it with all the water in the guy's canteen. He laid his hand on the door. It was almost too hot to touch.

"Here they come," Kimberly called.

He jumped back to the window and took up his position again. In the next lull he heard it. An insidious crackling noise. Fire feeding voraciously on wood. The floor was getting hot and smoke was pouring around the entire doorframe behind them now. Any second, the flames were going to burn through the flimsy door. The backdraft would incinerate them both.

They had to get out of here. But where? The entire jungle before them was full of armed rebels. "Come on, honey. We need to get up on the roof."

Kimberly frowned at him. "Why?"

"Charlie Squad will come in by helicopter. It'll be easier for them to lift us off the roof than for them to land and let us run out to them."

She nodded trustingly at him. It was a hell of a choice. Burn to cinders or face the bullets of an entire army. "I'll go first," he said. "You lay down suppression fire while I climb up on the roof. Then, I'll lay down a line of fire. As soon as I do that, I'll reach down for you and pull you up. We gotta do this fast. Okay?"

She nodded, clearly understanding their vulnerability while they climbed onto the roof.

It went off without a hitch. And then they were stretched out side-by-side on the roof. Smoke swirled all around them and a hail of bullets rained around them.

"Don't hold back on your fire," he shouted to her over the roar of the flames below them. "We'll run out of time before we run out of bullets!"

Doubt that they weren't going to make it flickered in her gaze, but she nodded resolutely. Pride surged through him. She was a fighter. She wasn't going to give up if he didn't.

He checked his watch. Ten minutes.

They fired down on the rebels for a couple of minutes. And then a tremendous crash sounded behind them. A wave of intense heat rolled over them. He glanced over his shoulder. A wall of flame leapt into the sky, lighting up the night.

"The fire's broken through the roof," Kimberly cried.

He looked at his watch. Seven minutes. No way was the remainder of the building going to stand up that long. He abandoned his rifle and threw an arm over Kimberly's shoulders. "Stay down. Our silhouettes will show up against the fire and make us easy targets."

She huddled against him, shaking like a leaf.

A few bullets sailed up at them, but he ignored them. At this point it might be a blessing if the rebels shot them. All he could hope for was that the smoke would knock Kimberly unconscious before the roof collapsed and flung her down into the inferno. The thought of her burning to death, of her suffering, was almost more than he could bear.

The roof shifted ominously beneath them and it was growing hot.

Kimberly rolled onto her side and wrapped her arms around him, hanging on tight. She, too, had abandoned her rifle. "Tex," she said calmly. "If I have to go, I'm glad I'm going to die with you."

"Hey, we're not done for yet, darlin'," he objected.

She looked up into his eyes, her gaze soft and wise. "You don't have to put on a good front for me anymore. I know we're not going to make it. I just wanted to tell you before—" her voice broke briefly "—before the end, that I love you."

He stared down at her, his heart expanding until his entire chest was tight. "I love you, too," he whispered back.

She smiled. "You're nice to say that. You always were a gentleman."

He shook her lightly. "I mean it. I love you. I'm not saying this to be nice. Hell, we're about to go face our Maker. I'm not gonna lie now!"

She stared back at him. And then an angelic smile broke across her face. She reached up with both hands and took his cheeks in her palms. "Kiss me, Tex. That's what I want to feel when I go. I want that to be the last thing I remember."

He swept her close and did as she asked, kissing her

with all the passion and fury and love in his heart. The flames roared around them and the building gave a great warning heave. An entire end of the building collapsed and the roof tilted dangerously in that direction.

And still they kissed, wrapping each other in the protection of their love, giving their very souls to one another in their last few moments on earth.

A thwocking noise startled Tex out of his absorption in the woman he loved. He looked up and saw the dark silhouette of a Huey helicopter race into view above the trees.

It slammed to a hover directly overhead and a cable snaked down out of it. Two men leaned out the door, one guiding the cable and the other firing a submachine gun in a continuous and deadly rain of lead.

A heavy metal object tore through the layer of camouflage netting and thunked to the roof less than ten feet away from them.

Tex jumped up, hauling Kimberly to her feet with him. "Let's go!" he shouted.

He raced to the missile-shaped extractor, yanked down on its folding seats and pushed Kimberly onto one of them. He jumped on the other seat, wrapped his legs around hers and hugged both her and the steel extractor. Before he'd barely climbed on, the winch above them whirred.

The helicopter drifted to the right, away from the burning roof as they rode the metal cable upward.

Tex looked down and the entire roof of the building was engulfed in flame. Only a tiny portion of the roof wasn't ablaze—the spot they'd been lying on seconds before.

He squinted as a whoosh of flame erupted. The remaining bit of roof collapsed, crashing all the way to the bottom of the inferno. An angry column of sparks shot up into the night sky.

He pulled Kimberly close against his chest. Needles of pain pricked him as hot embers landed on his back, burning through his shirt.

And then the skid of the helicopter came into sight from

above. Arms reached down for Kimberly and he handed
her up. Then he passed up the RITA rifle, which somehow
was still slung over his shoulder. Last, he climbed into the
helicopter, landing with a solid thud upon the cool metal
floor.

Something sleek and soft pressed against him from
shoulder to knee. An instinctive, sexual knowing of that
body flooded him and he opened his eyes.

Kimberly's emerald gaze met his. He flashed back to
the first time he'd landed in a helicopter beside her a lifetime ago. The same memory was clearly mirrored in her
eyes, too.

"We made it," he murmured to her.

In the orange glow from the mayhem he'd wrought below, he saw her gaze cloud over. A tear slid down her
cheek.

He reached up to wipe it away, but Charlie Squad's
medic, Doc, intervened, asking her about her health. And
then Doc was talking to him, asking him about his injuries.
All he wanted to do was wrap Kimberly in his arms and
never let her go, but too many people were in the way. He
already missed her. And there wasn't a damn thing he
could do about it.

Chapter 19

Tex stood stiff and uncomfortable in an ornate room about to do the thing he'd once dreaded. Face Kimberly Stanton across a Senate hearing chamber. His dark blue Class-A uniform felt tight across his shoulders and his starched shirt and tie rubbed his neck. *Time to pay the piper.*

Kimberly'd done as she promised and, with her father's help, launched a congressional investigation into her kidnapping and subsequent rescue. This afternoon he and she would both be allowed to testify about it before the Senate Arms Committee. Or ordered to, in his case.

Tex's chest tightened as a dozen senators filed into the room and made their way toward their places. God, how he hated having his future rest in their hands. Unfortunately in his line of work, controversial missions and occasional political fallout came with the territory.

Colonel Folly touched his elbow and directed him toward the table where he'd sit with the lawyer the Air Force had provided for him. His back was to the door when

Kimberly walked into the room, but he felt her presence as surely as if she'd grabbed his belt again. He turned around.

The whole room came to a momentary halt as she stepped in, such was the impact of her beauty. And then the low buzz of muted voices started up again.

She looked stunning. Her hair was twisted up into some sort of knot, every golden strand perfectly in place. Her makeup accentuated her features and a dark green suit made her eyes glow as bright as the morning jungle. Every inch of her was cool and elegant, classier than he'd ever imagined she could clean up. And he had a pretty outrageous imagination.

Tex's gut twisted into a hot knot as a good-looking, power-lawyer type took Kimberly's elbow to guide her across the polished marble floor. Tex looked down. Yup. Three-inch spikes.

He glanced up and she was looking at him. Her lips curved in the faintest of smiles and she nodded coolly at him.

She remembered, too.

He remembered everything about her, about their time together. He missed the feel of her sleek body against his. He missed kissing her. Hell, he missed fighting with her. He'd slept lousy every night of the two weeks since they'd been rescued. He kept hoping she'd call, even though his lawyer told him the two of them couldn't have any contact until after the congressional hearings were over.

He lay awake until all hours wondering what she was doing. Wondering if she thought about him at all. Or if she'd slipped right back into her hoity-toity world without even a backward glance for him.

As she slid gracefully into her seat, every inch of her perfect, he supposed he had his answer. She couldn't even see a grunt like him from the stratosphere she orbited in. Grimly he sat down beside his own lawyer as the session was called to order. He half listened to the drone of the chairman reading into the record the reason for today's hearing.

And then Senator Norwood addressed him. "Captain Monroe, the members of this committee have read and reviewed your report concerning the kidnapping and rescue of Miss Stanton. Do you have anything to add to your statement at this time?"

Tex winced. Even in the dry language of official reports, his mission report made for condemning reading. Attacking and looting the guard in the truck, assaulting another soldier and tying him to a tree, and killing a third rebel outright from the cliff. And then came the good stuff—assuming incorrectly that Kimberly was the target, handing over the RITA rifle, and the night they got rescued—hell, he'd slit a man's throat while Kimberly looked on.

He didn't even want to guess how many men he'd shot. The damage estimates suggested in excess of a hundred dead and twice that many wounded out of that one night's work.

He leaned toward the microphone and cleared his throat uncomfortably. "The only thing I would like to add to my report is how relieved I am that Miss Stanton was unharmed throughout her ordeal. If I had it to do all over again, I would do the very same things I did in order to secure her safe return."

He caught Kimberly's startled glance at him over her lawyer's shoulder.

"Ahem, well yes, Captain," the senator responded. "So noted." And then the gray haired man turned to Kimberly. "During your unfortunate absence, this committee had ample time to review your proposal for the disbanding of Special Forces squads like the one that rescued you. In light of your recent unique opportunity to observe a member of one of these units at work, do you have anything to add to your recommendations to this committee?"

Her voice slid across Tex's skin like velvet. "Yes, Senator Norwood, I do."

Here it came. Tex steeled himself for the charges he'd been told by his lawyer to expect her to level at him. He glanced at the pair of federal marshals positioned by the doors. He fully expected to leave in their custody this afternoon.

"My attorneys have written a complete brief that goes into more detail. We will file it after this session. But I have prepared a short summary of my observations and recommendations for you."

The senator gestured for her to read it.

With a quick shuffle of her papers, she began. "'During my time with Captain Monroe, I witnessed the full extent of his training. It encompassed skills in survival and camping, escape and evasion, hunting and tracking, and multiple demonstrations of his physical prowess. He is highly intelligent and extremely resourceful, particularly in violent or dangerous situations.

"'Additionally, I saw Captain Monroe engage in hand-to-hand combat, knife fighting, sniper shooting, and mass weapons combat. In short, he demonstrated amply to me that he is, in fact, the nearly unstoppable killing machine I once accused him of being.'"

Tex couldn't help but flinch. To hear the woman he loved speak so emotionlessly, so damningly, of him and everything he'd worked so hard to be cut deep.

She continued, "'I have had some time to reflect upon what I saw and have come to the following conclusion. We the people of the United States must do everything in our power to train and support Captain Monroe and the men and women like him who defend our nation so ably.'"

Tex lurched in his seat like an electric shock had just shot through it. A buzz erupted. It echoed off the chamber's vaulted ceiling and rattled loudly inside his skull. She *supported* what he'd done? Shock and elation warred for a position as foremost in his gut. Kimberly Stanton, antimilitary lobbyist extraordinaire, holder of his heart, had not turned on him after all?

Senator Norwood stared at Kimberly in surprise. "Am I to understand, after your harrowing ordeal, that you are completely reversing your position regarding the disbanding of military hit squads?"

"That's correct, sir."

Another buzz, even louder than before. The chairman rapped his gavel for quiet. "I must say, you've taken us by surprise, Miss Stanton. Perhaps a recess would be in order for my colleagues and me to review your new position papers."

There was a quick motion to that effect made and seconded by other committee members, and the hearing was adjourned.

And just like that, it was over. Tex sat in his seat, stunned. He wouldn't have guessed in a million years that Kimberly would support him and Charlie Squad like that. And then a need to see her, to talk to her and touch her—hell, to *thank* her—propelled him to his feet.

People swarmed all around him as he searched for her. Over the heads of the crowd pressing in on him, he saw an equally large throng mobbing Kimberly. He tried to push through the press of people, but got nowhere fast.

He vaguely registered Colonel Folly slapping him on the shoulder and murmuring his congratulations. His lawyer steered him toward the chamber doors. Away from Kimberly. But he wanted to talk to her! To thank her, if nothing else. Hell, to get her phone number. But the lawyer was politely insistent that Tex go outside and give interviews to the media. Good P.R. for the Air Force, and all that.

The press had latched on to the whole Tarzan and Jane nature of their ordeal and had been hounding him ever since the story hit the wires, trying to make some sort of hero out of him. He'd made one official statement that he was just doing his job and he'd dodged the microphones and cameras since then.

He and his lawyer reached the doors leading into the main corridor, and there the crowd abruptly stopped. The tall, double doors didn't open on cue. A congressional page explained apologetically that there would be a bit of a holdup because the camera crews outside weren't set up yet. Nobody had anticipated such a quick recess in this closed session, apparently.

Tex cooled his jets while the reporters were tracked down and the lights turned on. Kimberly must be looking forward to this press conference. She'd been plastered all over the news ever since they'd come home, and rumors were flying that she'd announce her own bid to run for Congress any day. Riding the wave of being a hero had launched her father's career; it would no doubt work for her, too.

A hand touched his arm and he spun around. He'd know that light touch anywhere.

"Kimberly." Dammit, his heart leapt into his throat like he was some awkward teenager. He nodded politely, vividly aware of the staring eyes and straining ears around them, as they met for the first time since their return to civilization.

"How's your leg?" she asked equally politely.

He looked deeply into her eyes. His feisty, smart, passionate Kimberly was still there beneath all the varnish. He could see it in her eyes. God, he'd missed her. "Leg's good as new. Your pressure bandage really did the trick."

She stared back, her emerald gaze brimming with words unsaid between them. "I'm glad."

Someone jostled through the crowd, somehow managing to push through the crush of avid spectators to this little reunion.

"There you are, Captain." A huge bear of a man held out his hand to him and boomed, "William Stanton. I wanted to thank you in person for bringing my daughter home to me." He leaned close and slapped Tex's shoulder, adding in an undertone pitched for Tex's ears alone, "And I mean that in more ways than one, son. I owe you an enormous debt."

Tex blinked, careful to betray nothing in his expression. He glanced over at Kimberly, who smiled fondly at her father. Had they made up? Were the rumors true that the elder Stanton was going to endorse his daughter's bid for his old seat in the House of Representatives? A hundred more questions leapt into his mind.

"Three minutes till camera!" someone shouted.

Tex grimaced. Kimberly might love the limelight, but he wanted nothing to do with it. In some ways, hiding from the press had been harder than avoiding the rebels in the jungle.

Kimberly leaned close and murmured, "You don't look too thrilled about going out there and facing the media."

He rolled his eyes and murmured back, "I'd rather face a firing squad."

"I know a back way out of here," she breathed. "Wanna make a break for it?"

Kimberly Stanton skip out on all the bright lights and publicity? "Are you sure?" he asked in surprise. "Your career…the coverage…"

She rolled her eyes in turn. "There's plenty more of that where it came from. Besides, it'll probably make even more headlines if we sneak out of here together. What say we blow this Popsicle stand?"

"You're on."

He followed her as she unobtrusively elbowed her way through the crowd. He rolled his eyes as she murmured something about going to the rest rooms to make sure their makeup was right for the cameras. *Their* makeup? He wouldn't be caught *dead* wearing *makeup*. God, he'd never live it down with the rest of the guys.

However, the inane excuse had the desired effect.

Everyone ignored them as they slipped to the back of the crowd waiting to leave the room.

"This way." She led him across the chamber and out a small door that led to a series of smaller caucus rooms.

"Are these the infamous back rooms of Congress where all the deals get made?" he asked as they whisked through the maze of doors and corridors.

She grinned over her shoulder. "The very same." She pushed open a door and they stepped outside onto a sidewalk. Alone.

Tex took his bearings quickly. "My car's right around the corner. Let's get out of here before anyone realizes we're gone."

"Lead the way, Tarzan."

He took her elbow and steered her across the street. "After you, Jane."

He helped her into the car and then slid behind the wheel. He breathed a sigh of relief as he pulled out into traffic. "Where to?"

She answered lightly, but he knew her well enough to hear the tension in her voice. "I seem to recall promising you the best seafood dinner on the East Coast if you'd clean a fish for me."

He glanced over at her. Why was she so wired? Worried about being seen with him, maybe? Would that be so bad for her image? Probably. If she ran for Congress, she'd be expected to date only East Coast blue bloods with last names that were household words. His jaw tightened and he replied casually, "I also recall promising you a greasy hamburger with all the trimmings. What's your preference?"

The moment stretched out, a microcosm of their two clashing worlds. A four-star restaurant versus a greasy spoon. It was a no-brainer which one she'd choose.

"I'd like a hamburger," she replied.

He about swerved into the curb and had to correct the car's course hastily. He hadn't seen that one coming.

He drove across town to Bud's Brew House, the darkest, roughest beer joint he knew. Might as well test Kimberly's resolve to go slumming. Not to mention Bud served up the best burgers this side of Jersey City.

Every biker in the place about threw their neck out of joint gawking at Kimberly when she walked in with him. He rested his hand lightly on the small of her back lest there be any question about whose woman she was. At the gesture, the regulars swiveled back to their beers. He'd busted up enough brawls here before for them to know he wasn't a man to tangle with.

Bud's was smoky and loud, and the vinyl seats in the booth were sticky. But Kimberly merely shed her suit coat, unbuttoned the top buttons of her blouse, and took out the clasp holding her hair up. The transformation was shocking as her golden hair cascaded down around her shoulders. She went from uptight politician to soft, sexy and all woman in the blink of an eye.

It almost hurt to look her, she was so beautiful. To think he'd ever dared to love her—who had he been kidding? He scowled into the mug of beer the waitress sloshed down in front of him.

An awkward silence fell between them after the waitress left with their orders for burgers with the works and fries. He cast about for a neutral topic of conversation and failed. He settled for, ''How's your dad doing?''

''Good. We had a long talk. He told me about some of the stuff he did in Vietnam. We talked about why it messed up his head so bad.''

Tex flinched. ''I'm sorry, Princess.''

She blinked in surprise. ''For what?''

''I gave you enough nasty memories to mess up your head for a good long time to come.''

She shrugged. ''I'll live. I talked to my dad about what happened in Gavarone, too. He helped me see that you didn't do anything that wasn't necessary.''

''You mean I didn't kill anyone I didn't have to,'' he

amended for her. "After all, I am a nearly unstoppable killing machine."

She frowned at her iced tea and fiddled with the lemon. Kimberly only fidgeted when she was nervous. He made her *nervous?* Damn. That was no way to win her back.

"It's an expression, Tex. A sound bite for the media. You're no more of a killer than I am."

His eyebrows shot up. "Correct me if I'm wrong, but didn't I single-handedly reduce the population of Gavarone by a measurable amount a couple weeks back? I'd say that qualifies me as a killer."

She gazed at him, unperturbed. "Are you planning on wallowing in guilt until you crack up like my father, or are you going to face reality? You did what you had to."

He leaned back in the booth, nonplussed. She really hadn't reversed political positions on the military for the sake of winning votes. She'd meant it! It was almost too good to believe. He asked skeptically, "You're defending what I did? Since when?"

"Since I talked to Colonel Folly about the full capabilities of the RITA rifle, and since I talked to the other guys on your team about what you guys do."

"You talked to the other guys in Charlie Squad?"

"Yes. I needed more information for my report to the Senate Arms Committee, and my lawyers wouldn't let me call you. So I asked them. They were very helpful. Nice guys."

"They're all nearly unstoppable killing machines, too, you know."

She laughed. "Yes, I know." Her gaze went serious and she leaned forward to grasp his cold hands in her warm ones. "I also know that you're a sane, decent, honorable man. You're no psychopathic ax murderer. And neither are the guys you work with."

She was for real, all right. His jaw sagged.

"When I saw that mock-up of the White House, something snapped inside me. I realized there *are* a few things out there worth dying for. Once that clicked in my mind, the rest fell into place pretty fast. I believe in what you do, Tex. I believe in *you.*''

He stared at her, not quite able to believe what he was hearing. "You're okay with what I do. With who and what I am.''

She nodded readily. No hesitation. No doubts. "Yes.''

She hadn't cut and run. The thought burned across his brain like a shooting star. She'd stood by him at that fork in the path in the jungle when she could've left. Again, during the big firefight when she could've slipped away in the chaos. And today, in front of *Congress,* for God's sake. His heart felt like it was actually getting bigger inside his chest as it expanded to embrace the reality of Kimberly's unswerving loyalty to him.

He jumped when a plate of hamburger and fries was thunked down on the table in front of him. He hadn't even heard the waitress coming.

"How about you, Tex? Are you okay with who I am?''

He stared at her in disbelief. "Of course!''

"Don't answer that so fast. I actually am considering running for my father's old seat in the House of Representatives.''

So. The rumors were true. What were the implications of that to a long-term romantic relationship between them? His heart, so light a moment ago, plummeted to the ground like a brick. "You'll make a great congresswoman," he said quietly. He felt like she'd just dragged a machete across his body and spilled his guts out onto the floor.

"I haven't decided whether or not I'm going to run, yet.''

He frowned. "Why not? It's exactly what you wanted. A chance to make a difference and be heard.''

Her gaze skittered away from his and she chewed absently. Whatever was holding her back from running for Congress must be huge. She'd just chowed down a greasy

French fry slathered in ketchup without a single word of complaint.

She continued to eat, oblivious to her food. She might as well have been popping termite grubs into her mouth for all the attention she was paying.

"What's up, darlin'?" he finally asked. "What's keeping you from running for Congress?"

She hesitated a long time and finally answered, "You."

A knife twisted in his gut, cutting his heart wide open. It felt like all his blood was draining out of him. Sonofabitch. Just when he'd started to believe in her…

He dragged a French fry through the pile of ketchup on his plate, drawing deep, slashing lines in it. He managed to grit out, "I gather I'm a skeleton you'd rather leave in your closet? I'll sign a legal release swearing never to say anything about it if that's what you want. I'd never stand in the way of your political career, Princess. And besides, what happened between us is in the past."

He risked a glance up and saw Kimberly's eyes fill with tears. Dammit. *Now* what was wrong? He'd given her what she wanted. Even if it was ripping his heart out.

Kimberly swiped at her cheeks, mad that she was giving away her feelings so blatantly. She closed her eyes against the searing pain cutting through her. He'd already moved on with his life. Like the straightforward, honest guy he was, he'd taken her at her word in that helicopter when she'd questioned the cost of their survival.

She'd been exhausted and scared out of her mind, and they'd just avoided dying by the narrowest of margins. Thinking about those last moments on the roof of that burning building still gave her the willies. She'd spoken out of fear in the helicopter. Babbled the first thing that came to her mind. And she'd driven Tex away for good with that one stupid question.

Yes, there'd been a cost to their escape. A high one. But it was a price that the United States government had been more than willing to pay to get the RITA rifle and its dangerous technology back. It hadn't been her fault or Tex's that all those rebels died. She'd finally seen that when she talked to her father about Vietnam.

Her dad wasn't responsible for being drafted and sent to Southeast Asia, where he'd dutifully carried out his orders. The men in charge, the men who gave the orders— the president, his cabinet, Congress—they were the ones responsible for what had gone on in Vietnam.

She and Tex had been tools in Gavarone, the warm bodies on the ground in the right place at the right time. Colonel Folly made it crystal clear in his talk with her that if she and Tex had failed or died trying to get the RITA rifle back, somebody else would have been sent in to take their place.

After witnessing the RITA rifle's deadly accuracy and the carnage it could wreak, she understood why the people in charge had sent Tex after it.

She was determined to become one of the people who gave the orders to the men and women like Tex. Level-headed people, who really knew the price of force, needed to be the ones with their fingers on the triggers of men like Tex and Charlie Squad. Hence, her run for Congress.

"Hey, you solving world hunger over there?" Tex's voice interrupted her thoughts.

"Uh, no. I was thinking about what you said."

He threw up his hands in mock surrender. "Honest. You don't have to kill me to ensure my silence. I can keep a secret." A flash of remembered passion glinted in his gaze, belying the casual tone of his voice. "I'll take the memory of our time together in Gavarone to my grave."

"Is that what you want?" she barely managed to whisper past the constriction in her throat. She'd so hoped there was a way she could have both her career and the man she loved. "To leave what happened between us in the past?"

"Hell, no, it's not what I want," he answered savagely.

His voice ripped into her, rending her flesh with its serrated edge.

Her gaze snapped to his. His eyes were as hard and brilliant as diamonds. "What *do* you want, Tex?" she choked out.

"I want you. All of you. To myself. Forever."

They were exactly the words she'd longed to hear for the past two, long, miserable weeks without him. Exactly the words she'd feared most.

Some of her inner conflict must have shown on her face, because Tex asked abruptly, "What the hell's going on in that purty li'l head of yours? Spit it out, darlin'."

She smiled reluctantly at his abruptly thick drawl. "Tex, my feelings for you haven't changed one bit since we laid on that burning roof together."

Fierce light leapt in his sapphire gaze, as bright and hot as the inferno around them had been that night.

She continued doggedly. "But I don't know how you'd feel about being married to a politician."

He shoved back abruptly in the booth. He stared at her for a long time, his expression completely unreadable. It took all her self-control not to fidget under his intense scrutiny.

Finally he drawled, "Are you *proposin'* to me, Princess?"

She blinked in surprise. "I suppose I am."

"You'd better be sure, darlin'. It ain't fittin' to lead a guy on about something as momentous as that."

Was she sure? She looked inside her heart and found nothing but jubilance at the prospect of a lifetime with him. A slow smile spread across her face. "Yes, I'm sure. I'm definitely proposing to you, Tex Monroe."

Still, he showed no reaction whatsoever. No hint at all of his thoughts on the subject. She rushed onward, saying her piece before she lost her nerve. "The thing is, I'd really like to run for Congress. I think I could win, and I think I'd be a good representative of the people. But I don't want to lose you, either. If you don't think you can deal with all the media badgering, I need to know now, before I accept any nominations.''

Tex leaned forward, his voice deadly serious. ''Are you telling me you'd give up running for Congress if I asked you to, so we could be together?''

She nodded, her heart in her throat.

His gaze bored into her, looking straight into her soul. ''I'll be damned,'' he breathed.

What did *that* mean? ''Tex, help me out here. Throw me a bone, a scrap, anything. Tell me what you're thinking!''

''Well,'' he drawled slowly, ''I'm thinking I'd better give you a bridle for a wedding present. Any woman with enough starch in her britches to propose to her man is going to need a little reining in, now and again.''

Her heart skipped a beat and then kicked into overdrive. ''Really?''

He moved so fast, she hardly saw him slip out of the booth and come around to her. She only knew she met him halfway and his arms were suddenly wrapped around her, hard and strong. And then his mouth was on hers, warm and possessive. Where he ended and she began, she stopped being able to tell. Their two loves swirled together and mingled into one, passionate and powerful enough to last a lifetime.

Eventually, the noise of a bar full of cheering bikers intruded upon her consciousness. Heat flooded her cheeks as Tex lifted his mouth away from hers.

Without releasing her, he nodded slowly. ''I'm thinking a hand-tooled leather bridle with some fancy silver trim would look just right on you.''

''If you ever even think about putting some leather contraption on me…''

The waitress, check in hand, threw up her hands. ''Whoa! Too much information! Don't need to be hearin' about your love life in here!''

Kimberly jumped. She hadn't heard the woman approach.

"Honey," the woman continued. "There's a whole slew of reporters outside. You want me to send out the boys to run 'em off?" The waitress hooked a thumb over her shoulder at the row of bikers at the bar.

Kimberly looked up at Tex. "It's your call."

He stared down at her gravely for a moment, and then a slow smile, the one she liked best, spread across his face. "How about if I be the one to announce our engagement since I didn't get to do the asking in the first place?"

She grinned. "Be my guest."

He flipped a bill at the waitress and told her to keep the change. While the woman blew a kiss at him, Tex took her elbow and steered her toward the exit.

"One more thing, darlin'. I'd like us to announce our engagement before you tell the press you're running for Congress. That way I'll be old news first and the press will leave me alone sooner."

"You catch on fast." She laughed.

His grin matched hers. "Have I told you today that I love you?"

"I don't think so," she answered, her heart so full it felt ready to burst right out of her chest.

"Well, I do." He dropped a quick kiss on the end of her nose.

"Glad to hear it," she murmured as they stepped outside and emerged into the rosy glow of the setting sun. Flashbulbs went off and cameras lights flared all around them.

Tex stiffened momentarily beside her and then the muscles in his arm gradually, forcibly, relaxed under her hand.

"Welcome to my war zone," she murmured to him.

He smiled at her for the cameras and said through his teeth, "If you can stand beside me and face a rebel army, I can stand beside you and face the press."

She smiled up at him, her heart shining in her eyes. "You're a brave man."

A reporter shouted out from the crowd, "Who's the guy with you, Miss Stanton?"

Tex's hand came to rest reassuringly over hers.

She answered proudly, "This is my hero. Tex Monroe."

* * * * *